# *The Moonlit Door*

ANNE MAYBURY, daughter of a poet, describes herself as 'very English'. She adores London and lives in a top floor flat in Knightsbridge.

She began her career working as a kind of 'girl friday' on a monthly magazine, later becoming a part-time journalist. Her first really successful book, *The Terracot*[illegible],
was published in the United [illegible]
went straight into th[illegible]
narrowly missed [illegible]
Since then [illegible]
of the [illegible]
has ha[illegible]
latest be[illegible]
now be [illegible] ...ges,
including [illegible] ..., Turkish,
Spanish, Fin[illegible] ... Swedish.

*Available in Fontana by the same author*

Jessamy Court

ANNE MAYBURY

# The Moonlit Door

*Collins*
FONTANA BOOKS

First published in Great Britain in 1967 by Hodder and Stoughton Ltd
First issued in Fontana Books 1977



Made and printed in Great Britain by
William Collins Sons & Co Ltd Glasgow

## CHAPTER ONE

I was six years old when my parents brought me to live in Issandre. Now, I am twenty-three, but the memory of that bewildering, momentous day has remained vivid in my mind.

I can still relive my inarticulate misery as I sat between my father, whose bulk spilled over the driving-seat, and my mother who was fair and plump and seldom ruffled. Staring through the windshield at the hot Provençal countryside, I was like a little imprisoned cat, alert and jumpy. I wanted only to escape back to the ugly, beloved house on Wandsworth Common.

In London, at the start of our long journey, with our luggage stowed away in the back of the car and the engine running, my father looked up at the house where I had been born. Then he turned to my mother. 'Well, Nan, we'll never see that place again!'

She said happily, 'Never!' and, sliding an arm round me, held me closer. 'You're going to love your new home, Rachel.'

'I'll hate it.'

They looked at each other and laughed in a secret, knowing way. I had no choice but to go where they took me; nobody asked me if I wanted to live in that place with the outlandish name – Issandre. I couldn't even pronounce it properly.

When three days later, after a night in Paris, we arrived, I was still sulky with unhappiness.

'Look, Rachel,' my mother said. 'You see that house? I told you I used to stay here for my school holidays when I was a little girl. Now it's to be your home. It doesn't have a number and a street name like our London house. It's just called the Villa Daphnis.'

The house was long and low and built of rough stone. It had an uneven rose-coloured roof and there was a vine growing over the veranda. When I was older, I learned the names of the trees that ringed it – black cypress, umbrella, olive, and a walnut tree which stood in the middle of an overgrown lawn. A profusion of flowers starred the weed-filled garden.

But there were no friendly buses roaring and rasping along the road; no children playing on a green stretch like Wandsworth Common; no houses huddled close. I hated the Villa Daphnis on sight.

My father stopped the car and pointed. 'Look behind you. You see those towers? That's a French castle, the Château Sonnengarde.'

I looked back obediently. I saw four stone piles, like huge copies of our grey china saltcellar, rising into the sky. Then I looked beyond the towers to a line of vast jagged rocks. 'There's another castle up there,' I said and pointed.

'Part of it was once, hundreds of years ago,' my mother said, 'but most of it is just rock, huge and very bare. The place is called Maladieu.'

'Oh,' I said, and burst into tears.

When I was older, I learned that my mother had inherited the Villa Daphnis from an aunt. In London, my father had worked in a newspaper office. After the success of his first book, a biography of Henry IV which he had sat up half the night for five months to write, he gave up his job and devoted himself to writing.

Then, when my unknown French aunt, Amalie, died, the house in Issandre was put up for sale. On the day the letter arrived at our London house from the estate agents in Avignon, making my mother an offer for the Villa, it was raining hard. There was also a high, bitter wind; the roof was leaking and my father was in a bad temper.

'Damn it.' He had screwed the letter my mother had passed to him into a ball and flung it across the room. 'We must be mad to think of selling the house. We'll live there.'

For eighteen months after we arrived, I went on hating my new home. I was lonely. The children of my own age whom I met at the day school I went to had unfamiliar names and spoke a strange language. They were friendly and inquisitive, but I was shy with them.

Then, on our second Christmas, Francis came to live with us.

He was three years older than I, a fair, friendly little boy, English and stockily built, with long blond eyelashes and pale blue eyes which in those days I envied, for he could see much farther than I. 'Seaman's eyes,' my father called them.

When he arrived, my mother said, 'Francis has just lost both his parents, so we have adopted him. Be kind to him, darling.'

I had lost a tooth and I was proud of the gap in the dead centre of my mouth. I grinned widely at Francis, and he grinned back. From that moment I decided I was going to like living at the Villa Daphnis.

A year after Francis joined our family Elise arrived. She was five at the time. A quiet Englishwoman in a tweed suit brought her, and she stood in our living-room, in a dress too long for her and holding a big, brown grown-up handbag, which she clutched like a prize. She had curly, mousy hair, blunt features and a mouth that, after those first forlorn days in our house, tilted up at the corners so that she always looked happy.

I was never told what happened to Elise's parents. Not that it was important. What *was* important was that we were as fortunate with Elise as with Francis.

When Lucia joined us, I was becoming resigned to the fact that every year another child was adopted into our family. 'Nan's Circus' my father called us.

Lucia was nearly seven, entirely French, and so lovely that for the first few days I just stared at her. There were red lights in her dark hair and her eyes were violet. She was exquisitely boned and she moved delicately, like a fawn, alert and graceful. She came to us from a poor home in Vals, but even as a child she had a poise that intrigued us. We were ready to love her, but she made no attempt to be loved. She was scornful of us and fought against learning English, which we spoke among ourselves.

Francis said once, 'It's not as if she were an affected little monster who wants to be "mother's pet." She just behaves as if she's a visitor to our house and is counting the days to going.'

And that was exactly it.

After Lucia, mother seemed to be satisfied with her family. The only newcomer in the next few years was Peppina, who scared me the first time I saw her because she was exactly like a witch. She was a peasant from the Carmargue with a genius for cooking, and she had come to help mother in the house.

She arrived with her clothes bundled into a huge basket, an outsize umbrella, and a beautiful old Nevers porcelain jar, which contained (so she said) an ancient remedy for gout.

She had crooked, blackened teeth, a neck like that of an under-fed hen, and small black eyes, and it was a long time before we children realized that she was on our side at times when we'd done something to infuriate Father, that she feared no one, and that she made the most wonderful sweets, which she kept in tall glass jars.

I was twenty when the news came of an earthquake in Agadir. A few weeks later five-year-old Nikki joined us. He was half-French, half-Algerian and had been rescued and brought to France – although none of us knew exactly how. Adopting him didn't seem an easy matter, but my mother fought like a tigress to have him, pulled strings, chased to Paris to argue with officialdom when she was in danger of being thwarted – and got him.

'Our first task,' she said, 'is to fatten him up.'

Nothing did that. Every bone seemed anxious to break through the tender, café-au-lait skin. His eyes were enormous, his wrists and ankles so thin that I was for ever afraid they would snap. His hands were delicate, but the soles of his feet were like leather because, until he came to us, he had never worn shoes.

His face was so grave, his smile so rare and enchanting that we all tried to spoil him – all except Lucia, who ignored him.

My father wrote three biographies during those first years at the Villa and all of them were enormously successful. He had built himself a studio at the end of the garden, behind the bougainvillaea. It was a splendid domed affair in white stone, and Francis called it 'Plato's Palace.'

Father was a gregarious man and needed the stimulus of people around him. So at the far end of the lawn, near the road, he built four guest huts. After that, our house became a mecca for established writers, would-be writers, and those fringe people who never achieve anything but who haunt the literary world.

I had always wanted to be a fashion artist and when I was old enough, I went to study in Paris. The design of clothes, of fabrics fascinated me and I had two wonderful years at the Sorbonne.

My mother's sudden death changed my life completely.

My father had always treated us rather like amusing encumbrances. Now, bereft of my mother, he decided that his children were important to him. We were a family; we must remain together. For the first time in his life, he became sentimental about us. He sent for me and I had to leave Paris and come home.

As soon as I arrived, half-loving to be back, half-hating having to leave my carefree, rather tatterdemalion Paris life, my father called a family conference. 'We must think of some sort of industry we can run from the house,' he said. 'Something that will keep the family together.'

Francis, who worked in an engineering firm in Issandre and hated it, asked what. There were plenty of things to choose from if we set our minds to think about it, Father said impatiently.

Such as?

Well, weaving?

I looked at Father's black brows, raised hopefully, and flung cold water on the idea. 'We weren't going to be arty and homespun for anyone.'

Then what?

In Paris, I had become friendly with a young man from the Sorbonne. One spring evening we went for a walk together, bought apples from a fruit barrow near the Fontaine Médicis and, leaning against a terracotta wall, ate them while we talked. It was there that I learned a little about the art of mosaics, which was his hobby.

Now, recalling our conversation, I said suddenly, 'Mosaics. We could make and sell mosaics.'

It was, I explained to the family, something we could all do. It would be an expensive industry and there wouldn't be little tourist novelties for a few francs. But it would be rich and rewarding if we really set our minds to it and concentrated on large pieces – panels, for instance, for concert halls and private houses; plaques; beautiful coffee-table tops. We might, I added, warming to my subject, one day graduate to commissions for churches or some new cathedral.

So we decided on mosaics.

At the eastern end of the garden near the guest huts, Father built a pottery with everything we would need – a huge kiln, shelves, storage places, and benches. There was a second room which was to be used as a showroom.

Francis, who was practical and good with his hands, would be in charge. I, the supposed art expert, would do the designing. The rest would work under us.

For months we studied Roman and Byzantine mosaics, made mistakes, cut our fingers, and got ourselves and our clothes into dreadful states with clay and cement and glass chips. When we thought we were efficient enough, we opened our doors three times a week to tourists. Creating mosaics, when every piece is hand-cut, some in stained glass, some in tessera, is a slow process and so, of necessity, expensive. We didn't expect much in the way of tourist sales, although we tried to cater to them. We were exultantly surprised. Coachloads visited us on their way to Arles and Maladieu and we began to pack and export to England and America.

Throughout the years we scarcely noticed the Château Sonnengarde. An olive tree, an avenue of cypresses, and a terrace of vines separated us. We seldom saw the old recluse, Comte Fabian d'Arachenne who lived there. When we did, he was seated, hunched and sour, in the back seat of his ancient Mercedes. I don't think he was even aware of our existence.

Lucia was the exception. While the rest of us forgot there was a great historic house almost on our doorstep, she would stand, biting her lip and staring at the towers.

One day Francis, impatient at her idleness in the pottery, exclaimed, 'If you're thinking of seeing inside that place, don't waste your time. Nobody's going to take you on a conducted tour.'

She gave him her curious, cold smile. 'I don't want a conducted tour. I can guess what the place is like. I was born in a château.'

'In Chenonceaux, perhaps,' said Francis dryly. 'With Catherine of Medici as your ancestor. All right, have your dreams.'

She turned on him, her eyes brilliant and scornful. 'One day I shall go to Sonnengarde, and it won't be a tourist but by special invitation.'

Less than a year later it was I, who had no dreams of grandeur, to whom fate offered a château and a title. The title was Paul d'Arachenne's; the château, Sonnengarde.

## CHAPTER TWO

I had been staying for a fortnight with Aunt Solange, my mother's stepsister, in Paris. She was a tall, plain woman whose husband, a shopowner, had left her a fortune.

While she lived, a trace of the old glamour of the *salon* remained, for her apartment near the Place de la Concorde was a gathering place for musicians. She herself was a talented amateur pianist.

Whenever I stayed with her, I met people whose names were famous in the music world – singers, violinists, cellists. They were all kind to me, but because I knew nothing about music, I was just 'Solange Fontvallé's little niece from the country.'

It was at one of these gatherings that my aunt brought a

young man to meet me. I had been standing alone near the terrace which overlooked the Place with the fountain and the colonnades. It was a view of Paris at its most beautiful.

'Rachel, this is Monsieur Paul d'Arachenne,' my aunt said. 'He has asked to meet you. His uncle is your neighbour at Issandre.'

'Oh, of course. Sonnengarde.' I looked up into a narrow face with a pointed chin and merry eyes.

Someone with a nearly unpronounceable Polish name was announced from the door. My aunt said, 'Oh, dear! And he's brought his impossible wife,' made a little gesture of dismay, and left us.

Paul asked, 'Are you a budding pianist? Or do you sing?'

'If I did, I'd clear this room of connoisseurs. I sing off key. I may as well tell you, so that you won't have to waste your time on me, I don't know Delius from Delibes.'

'That's fine. Nor do I. So let's get right away from those who do.'

He led me on to the long terrace. Among the potted shrubs there was a statue of Minerva. She seemed to be smiling at us.

'My mother is the musician of the family,' he said. 'But she's not well and she sent me to the party instead. I think she hoped a session here would reform me. It hasn't,' he added, and he drew me down on to one of the white-cushioned chairs. 'Tell me about yourself. I didn't catch your Christian name.'

'It's Rachel. Rachel Helston.'

'I like it,' he said. 'But I shall call you Mignon because you are little and dark.'

We were together the whole evening. We talked sometimes in English, sometimes in French, and he was the first of Aunt Solange's guests who didn't make me ashamed that I knew nothing about music.

I learned a lot about the d'Arachenne family that night. They had been merchant bankers for three generations. Paul's uncle and two of his cousins were directors. Paul himself was, he explained lightly, just an employee.

'My Uncle Artois is head. He's very rich, of course, but I always have a sneaking suspicion that he's a robber baron at heart and that he'd pirate ships if he could get away with it. He has a vast estate about fifty miles from Issandre. Do you know him?'

'Good heavens, no!'

Paul laughed and said cheerfully, 'I'm notorious in the family for not liking work and they take a poor view of me. But it doesn't matter. My mother holds too important a place on the board, since my father died, for them to protest too much about my idleness. And anyway, I'm the only son of an ageing woman and I'm spoiled, I'm indulged, and I like my own way in everything. Do you mind?'

'I? Why should I?'

'Because you're going to see a lot of me.'

'Am I?'

'Don't be silly,' he said and kissed me.

We met every day of my last week in Paris. We danced and dined at places that up to then had been just names to me.

I had never looked so hard and long in a bedroom mirror. I went to a hairdresser's and had a colour rinse, hoping to give a russet glow to my dark hair. It remained just dark. The assistant, however, cut it and coaxed it to lie smooth around my head with ends that bounced lightly. 'Your hair dances when you move your head,' Paul said.

At the cosmetic counter of the Galleries Lafayette a charming black-haired girl advised me to change the colour of my lipstick. 'This,' she said holding up a soft pink one, 'with your green eyes. How lucky you are, Mademoiselle.'

I knew she was flattering me, but I lapped it up.

All that week I swung between states of utter bliss and deep depression. I was in love with Paul and although he had been a charming companion, I didn't fool myself into believing that I had any lasting attraction for him.

Every day I found myself waiting for the catch in it all, for I came from a quiet country world which he had never known except superficially. I couldn't see Paul living simply, even on holiday. And I supposed, because I was different, I amused him.

It would have been easy to have let the fact that I would never see him again spoil my last night in Paris. But I sailed through it on champagne and Paul's infectious company.

We had been dining and dancing at a place he knew near Passy. It was two o'clock in the morning when we left and the moon was riding high above the Ile aux Cygnes.

Driving away from the restaurant, Paul turned left. I put a hand lightly on his arm. 'You're going the wrong way.'

He stopped the car just beyond a street lamp, kissed me, and said softly, 'I know where I'm going . . . where *we* are going. And it isn't home.'

'It is for me at two o'clock in the morning. I'm tired.'

'That's all right. So am I, we shall sleep together. I have it all planned.'

I held myself very tightly, trying to hide the mixed excitement and alarm. 'I'm sorry to spoil your plan but, as I've said, I'm going home.'

He gave a heavy sigh. 'When you talk like that you are a little bore. So, I don't listen.' He restarted the car. 'We go to Fontainebleau. I know a hotel there where the bedrooms have sky-blue silk hangings and crystal chandeliers.'

'I can quite believe it's very romantic. But please turn the car around.'

He just drove faster, so that the tall trees whizzed by like files of giants. I gripped the door handle. My own voice became stiff and pedantic as it always did when I was nervous and didn't know how to manage a situation. 'Short of throwing myself out of the car, which I've no intenion of doing, I can't stop you taking me to Fontainebleau.'

'No, my darling, you can't.'

'But it'll be an awful waste of a journey because I shan't share your bed. And I'm afraid you don't know everything about me. I'm very obstinate. When we get to the hotel – *if* we get there at all at the rate you're driving – I shall ask for a settee in the lobby if all the rest of the rooms are full. I'm sorry if that will make you look foolish, but there you are.'

The car slowed down, swerved to the side of the street, and stopped again. A street lamp shone on us. Paul took me by the shoulders and pulled me around to face him. 'If you think I'm going to ask you to marry me while we're sitting uncomfortably in a car – '

'You said . . . marry . . .'

'That's right. What do you think this past week has been about?' His fingers stroked my throat.

All I could do was to keep whispering his name.

He kissed me, his hand wandering over my body. 'I don't want to let you go, but I must. Let's hurry and get there.' Once more the car moved forward, away from Paris.

I said, shaken and reluctant, 'Paul, I can't spend the night with you. I'm not a prude but, darling, please understand.'

His answer was to accelerate.

'Paul, stop!'

I heard his low chuckle. 'Stop. Go. Stop. Go. We are behaving like traffic lights.'

My fingers closed conspicuously over the door handle.

Immediately Paul's mood changed. He said coldly, 'My dear, I have never in my life been accused of being a boor and you aren't going to make me one. Very well, we will go home.'

I leaned against him. 'If we love each other, it'll keep. There'll be thousands of days . . .'

'But the ones past never come back,' he said sadly.

I twisted my hands in my lap and felt a tightness around my heart. My own dismay shook me. As if I cared, either, for those damned thousands of days I talked so glibly about! Paul was right. There was only one time that concerned anyone and that was the present – the everlasting present. Today. Tonight. And I had thrown away its happiness.

Why? Plucking and pulling at the white beads of my evening bag, I asked myself whom I would be harming if I spent the night with Paul. Well, whom would I harm?

The shred of common sense left me after my intoxicating week gave me the answer. I risked hurting myself. It wasn't morality but my own instinct to prolong my happiness. A night in the blue-silk room at Fontainebleau would be for me the strengthening of a love affair which must last through all our lives. But for Paul? I had no idea how deep his feeling for me was and I was afraid to take the risk of this night being the beginning and the end. It didn't occur to me then to wonder what my aunt might have said about it all had I telephoned her from Fontainebleau.

I jumped when Paul spoke to me. 'And now, Mademoiselle Helston? What happens?'

I looked ahead of me at the steady stream of light made by the car's headlamps and did not answer.

'I'll tell you.' He answered his own question. 'We kiss on your doorstep and that will be a dreary anticlimax. Well, you chose it. When are we supposed to meet again?'

'Do *I* have to say?'

He felt in an inside pocket, took out a slim gold case and tossed it into my lap. 'Light me a cigarette, Mignon.'

As I lit it, he said, 'I suppose you think I'll be racing down to Sonnengarde to stay with my dried-up toad of an uncle in order to see you. Well, I won't. But you'll come to Paris again; to me. That's a prophecy.'

'I won't be able to with a houseful of people to look after.'

He shot me a glance and his face broke into a smile. 'I'll win, you know. I always do. I'll have you in the end.'

'Of course.' I laid an arm lightly on his shoulder.

He put his head sideways and rubbed his cheek lightly

against my hand. 'Fontainebleau?' he whispered.

'Go home,' I said, and moved to the far end of the seat.

We drove in silence for a few miles. Then he said, 'I'll make a pact with you. You return to Issandre and for a month we won't contact each other; we'll neither write nor telephone. At the end of that time I'll call you from Paris and you'll leave your pedestrian household and come to me.'

I didn't answer him.

When we stood outside my aunt's apartment, he kissed me again. 'In four weeks' time I shall telephone you.' He tilted my face and his eyes were burning and over-bright. 'I want you so much,' he said. His hand touched my breast. Then he turned abruptly and walked away from me back to the car.

I was fitting the key into the lock, my hand as unsteady as my heart, when I heard him behind me. He curled my fingers round something heavy. 'These were for you tonight at Fontainebleau,' he said. 'And don't return them or I'll just throw them into the Seine.'

I was holding a small rawhide suitcase. 'But Paul . . .' I was talking to the night air. He was gone.

Upstairs in my room, with the door closed and the lights on, I opened the little case. Inside was a nightdress of sea-green chiffon, severely cut and without lace. There were slippers of the same-coloured silk – a little too small for me – and a carved ivory hairbrush and comb. There were toilet things in a green bag and a Maltese lace handkerchief.

I shut the case and went to bed. I hardly expected to sleep, and I didn't. I kept thinking of the room with the blue hangings. I lay with my lips against the pillow, saying into it, 'Paul . . . Paul . . .'

A month seemed a world away.

## CHAPTER THREE

Every day, all day and half the night, the tables of the Café Chinois in Issandre's main square were filled with people. Everything was talked over, from politics to the yield of the vines.

Francis often broke off work about half-past twelve and drove to the café from an aperitif with his friends before lunch. Two weeks after I returned from Paris, Francis was late for lunch. We were already seated at the table on the vine-covered veranda when he arrived.

I was serving herb omelette and Father was holding forth to a patiently listening table on the question of his next book. Richard Cœur de Lion interested him. Or perhaps he might try his hand at writing a book about a woman – a French courtesan, for instance. He looked up as Francis came out on to the veranda. 'You're late.'

'Sorry Father. Old Fabian d'Arachenne died last night and Issandre can't stop speculating on what happens next at the Château.'

I spilled some omelette on the table, mopped it up, and thought excitedly: Paul will come down for the funeral. Paul will be here in Issandre and we will meet before the month is up, and then, oh then Issandre will have something more to talk about....

I scooped the last of the omelette on to my plate. 'I suppose he had another stroke,' I said.

'Another?' Francis took me up on the word. 'How did you know he had any previous ones? So far as Issandre is concerned he could have had a dozen and no one would have been any the wiser.'

I had spoken without thinking. Of course Paul had told me. I went to the veranda door saying over my shoulder, 'I must have heard it somewhere.'

It could have been my imagination, but they all seemed to be looking at me with too much interest.

I felt my face flush. 'For heaven's sake, you know how news runs round this place. The Château servants drink in the market square like anyone else.' My voice was over loud. 'I'll get Peppina to make your omelette now,' I said to Francis and escaped.

When I came back to the table, they were still talking about it. I sat down and broke the omelette on my plate. My heart was still turning over and over with part excitement, part fear. I was as afraid of my luck as an inveterate gambler who never wins.

'For heaven's sake, Rachel, watch Nikki,' my father exploded. 'He'll have his plate in his lap in a minute.'

Nikki looked at him with grave eyes. 'But, Papa, I can't reach my food on the table.'

'Then sit up closer.'

I helped him with his chair.

Lucia gave him a bored look. 'I suppose dropping the plate

in his lap is one degree better than eating with his fingers like he did when he first came to us.'

'But I don't ever do that now, do I, Rachel?'

'Of course you don't, darling.' I gave Lucia a furious look.

Father, who hated not knowing his neighbours, said, 'Perhaps the Château will liven up a bit now. This nephew could be married and bring a family to live there.'

My face began to burn in the maddening way it did when I was off guard. Of course, I should have told the family about Paul. But ever since I was small I'd had a superstition that something lovely, talked about before it became a fact, would never happen. I wanted to keep Paul to myself until he was by my side while I told the news to my startled family.

The day after old Fabian's funeral, I had to collect our weekly supply of peaches and grapes from Monsieur Camé. My way lay past the Château and as it was only a short journey, I never took the car.

It was a hot morning. In front of me, far into the sky, rose the jagged pinnacles of Maladieu. I remembered what my mother had told me about the place. Back in the Middle Ages, a duke whose family had been wiped out in old battles, had cut a fortress-palace out of the rocks. Feasting and strange rites had taken place there; perhaps even old gods had been worshipped. The palace had a glamorous and evil reputation. Wars and weather had crumbled it so that it was now a shell. But its legends remained and, from the place I walked, it was impossible to see where the man-made crenelations ended and the natural rock began.

The road past the olive grove was deserted, but then as the locals said, the Helstons were a mad family and only the papa took a siesta. However, a car came racing towards me. When I saw the rich polished red of the enormously long bonnet, I felt suddenly dizzy with joy. Without thinking twice I ran into the road waving, my heart thudding up in my throat so that my voice croaked as I cried out, 'Paul.'

The car pulled up with a rasp of brakes. The familiar dark head shot out of the window. 'What are you doing? Do you want to be run over? . . . *Rachel!*'

As he climbed out of the car, I ran to him and held out both my hands. 'Darling – this is wonderful.' I searched his face. He looked older, harassed. Then he smiled and his features became young again. 'Mignon.'

It was like music to hear that name. I lifted my face to be kissed. His lips brushed my temple.

'It was to be a month,' I said happily. 'But let's forget the pact. You're here . . .'

He ran a hand over his hair. 'I should have telephoned you when I arrived yesterday, but there has been such chaos. Mother has inherited Sonnengarde and she always planned to live here when Uncle Fabian died. Getting her settled is posing quite a problem. She expects the whole place to be geared to her way of living in a day. Rooms altered, servants' duties changed around – '

I watched his face and brought the words out with a rush. 'Are you going to live here, too?'

'I suppose so. Nothing is settled yet. Lawyers and uncles and cousins are swarming all over the place.' He looked down at me and smiled again. 'But the real question is our meeting, isn't it? Perhaps tomorrow?'

'Oh, Paul, yes, tomorrow. Where?'

'Somewhere quiet. I want to be alone with you.'

I looked upwards. 'Maladieu?'

'Fine. Maladieu it is. In the Hall of the Seigneurs.' His eyes deepened and darkened as they moved slowly over me. 'You are so lovely, Mignon,' he said.

'Tomorrow . . .'

'At eight o'clock.'

As he got back into the car, I began to walk on. I felt as light as air and later when I was walking home with the weight of six pounds of grapes and peaches, I felt no different. In some way the waiting until tomorrow was worth it for all the hours of excited anticipation it gave me.

That afternoon, a close friend of my father's arrived to stay a few weeks with us. His name was George Bannock and back in England he had worked on the same newspaper as my father.

I had known George all my life. He had been a godfather at my christening. He was a broad-shouldered, sandy-haired man with a red face, caused, so he always insisted, not so much by high living as the fact that he lacked a layer of skin. He and my father talked, got into political arguments, drank cognac by the bucket and got on perfectly. He so often came to stay with us that the patch of lawn under the walnut tree where he was most frequently to be found, was called 'George's lay-by.'

He usually came alone, but this time he brought with him a young English musician, Dominick Rond. We had never met him before, but Elise, who was the musical one of the family, told us what she knew about him. Dominick started his career by studying the cello and had taken all the prizes and scholarships possible until, at a music Academy in Italy, he had decided to change his career and become a conductor. He was still in his thirties, but already most continents knew him.

Elise told us, 'All the critics say that when he's older and has had more experience, he'll be among the great musicians of the century.'

Dominick had been in Paris as guest conductor for an English orchestra giving a series of concerts there. He was, George explained in a letter, badly in need of a holiday. And Father, who was casual about his invitations, merely wrote back, 'Bring him down with you.'

Since George knew even less about music than I did, I wondered how those two had ever got to know each other. Dominick was a complete contrast to George. He was tall and very slim. He reminded me of a young monk, with his pale aesthetic face, his controlled movements, and the curious haunting gravity of his eyes.

I put them in guest huts in the grounds and when I left them to unpack, I joined the others in the pottery.

'If I didn't know that he was used to people and crowds,' I told Elise, 'I'd have said he was very shy.'

'Oh, he's going through a bad time and it probably makes him wary and uncertain as to whether the people he's talking to know about it or not. He has a wife and they don't get on, though I believe she's rich and gorgeous and very musical. Aunt Solange told me about them when I was in Paris.'

Francis was cutting glass mosaics for one of the Signs-of-the-Zodiac panels he and Elise were doing for a new villa at Arles. 'So George brought Dominick down here to escape from her?'

'Probably. His wife is the daughter of Russell Dart, the composer.'

Lucia was staring out of the window. 'The Comtesse d'Arachenne has come to live at Sonnengarde,' she said dreamily. 'Monsieur Cambé told me. And since she can never bear to be parted from Paul, her son, I suppose he'll live there, too.'

I looked across the room at her. Aunt Solange had once said, 'Lucia can have any man she chooses. She has the fatal quality that no one can explain.'

Something inside me set like steel at the memory. Lucia could have every other man in sight, but she wasn't going to take Paul from me. And then the battle glow left me and I felt a little afraid. What weapon did I have with which to fight for Paul if, as had happened in the past, a man who had been attracted to me came to the Villa and met the girl whom they called my sister?

Well, I had one weapon, a desperate win-or-lose way. Paul would be my lover and, virgin though I was, I would make it a lovely and unforgettable experience for him.

The next day was sultry and there was a faint khaki smear over the blue of the sky. We knew the sign so well. Thunder was in the air. The storms, when they came to our corner of Provence, were always violent. I think the jagged peaks of the naked rocks of Maladieu broke the clouds and hurled their fury into the valley.

After dinner my father took George and Dominick to his studio where Peppina served coffee and cognac. I called Elise and asked her to see that Nikki went to bed. 'I'm going out.'

When she asked where, I said, 'I'll tell you when I get back.'

'You're holding out on me!'

I laughed into her pretty, curious face. 'Yes, I am.'

Nikki sat on the stairs, knees hunched. 'You'll come and say good night to me, Rachel, won't you?'

'It all depends what time I get back. I may be very late.' (I would be. Maladieu had many secret places and I wanted Paul badly. Love? I was rash and hungry for him.)

I kissed Nikki. 'Be good.'

'I won't go to sleep till you come back.'

'That's silly. If you don't, you'll have dark circles under your eyes in the morning.'

'Why?'

I looked at Elise and laughed. 'You take over,' I said.

She was glancing up at the sky. 'It's going to rain. Lucia has grabbed the big car and Francis has taken the runabout.'

'Oh, damn! Then I'll have to walk.'

The storm was already murmuring over the hills. I ran to the cupboard under the stairs, pulled out an old hooded mackintosh, and flung it round my shoulders.

Lightning danced round the high peaks; thunder rolled, mocked, and echoed. But the rain kept off. Not that I cared. I'd go to Paul looking like a drowned rabbit and no amount of rain-soaking would give me pneumonia tonight.

I was a quick walker, but I knew I would be late. I should have staked my claim earlier on one of the cars. I did wonder, just before I reached the gate, whether I should go back and ring Paul and ask him to pick me up. But I decided against it and walked on. To justify my own shyness, I argued with myself that he had probably already left and anyway I was too much a stranger, as yet, to call a bereaved house.

After I had been walking for a quarter of an hour, the rain began. By the time I reached the steep turning that led upward between the cliffs to Maladieu, it became a torrent.

I clutched the mackintosh hood over my head and began to run. The cliff sides closed in on me and the lightning dazzled my eyes. My feet were sodden and it would be another five minutes before I reached the ruins that crested the mountain of rocks.

On either side, cut into the cliff faces, were little tourist shops, closed and shuttered now with their owners back in Issandre. There was also the Hostelrie Sainte Bérénice which had long ceased putting people up for the night and where tourists now stopped only for coffee and tea and ices. The old man who had owned it had died and his cousin, whom we didn't yet know, had taken it over. I remember Francis saying, 'He'll have to spend quite a bit of money on improvements. The place as it stands is just a tattered remnant.'

The Hostelrie was up on the right. I passed it, rambling and pitch-black, outlined for a moment in lurid light. There was a bend in the road. I turned it and saw a car. It stood, nose thrust into the rock.

Another car was drawn on to the opposite side of the road, which was so narrow that the two cars made it impossible for another to pass between them.

Lightning lit up the scene and I saw that the second car also had its nose pointed into the cliff face. There was a silver model of a unicorn on the bonnet. It had the face of a man and its tall pointed horn gleamed in the few seconds of dazzling primrose light. Then it was dark again.

'Don't stand there doing nothing,' said a man's voice.

I swung around and saw that the first car was not just parked close to the rock – it was jammed into it. The bonnet was flattened by the unresisting stone; mudguard on the driving side crumpled like dirty silver paper. The car was long and expensive and dark red.

A man was bending over someone lying on the ground.

'Oh, God!'

I must have cried aloud, for the man straightened and turned. He was a stranger, but his voice rasped at me. 'Yes, there's been an accident. Go and get help.'

I was staring at what remained of the bonnet of the red car. Then, dreading to look yet forced to do so, I read the number plate.

'That car . . . I know . . . that car . . .'

He flashed his torch and I put my hand across my eyes, but not quickly enough.

I saw the man lying on the ground. The sound I made came dully, through layers of sudden pain. I stumbled forward.

The man's arm held me back. 'Whoever he is, he's dead now. Do what I tell you. There's some sort of house down there.' His powerful torch raked the road. 'Go and telephone the police.'

The convulsive violence of the storm shook the crenelations of Maladieu. I couldn't stop the hypnotic pull of my eyes towards the man on the rain-soaked ground. There was a rug over him, but I could see part of the dark battered head; I saw a hand outstretched. The vicious lightning lit up the carved lapis lazuli in the ring he wore.

'Paul . . . Paul . . .'

I leaned against the rocks, my hands pressed against the sodden stone. I couldn't even shut my eyes. It was as if my lids were stuck.

I had to get help. Help. The word hung hollowly, like the sound in a sea-shell.

'Paul.'

'Hey, don't do that. I've enough here without your fainting.' The man held me as I swayed.

'I'm all right. I must ring . . . for a . . . doctor . . .'

'I'm a doctor,' he said. 'Go and get the police. This car must be towed away and the accident reported. I'll see that he . . .' He glanced down and pulled the rug so that it covered the whole head of the man who had been Paul. 'I'll cope with this.'

I shook with wild unreason. ' "Cope with this"? Can't you be more human? Why be so sure he's dead? He can't be. I'm sure he can't be.'

The stranger swore sharply. '*Sacre Dieu*, must you be so stupid? Do you think I don't know a dead man when I see one? Do what I tell you. Rouse someone in that house.'

I made a tremendous effort to speak. 'All right. But please don't take him away. You mustn't move him till the police – or the ambulance – arrive. Besides, I . . . I want to go with him. I know him. I know . . .' Muddled, half blinded by grief that seemed both unreal and yet too real, I began to run down the road.

The rain had practically ceased, but the lightning still ripped the sky above Maladieu. Sainte Bérénice was shuttered against the storm like a dead house in a dead place. I hammered on the door with my fist, pressed the bell, and leaned against the rickety iron stand that, during the day, displayed post-cards of the ruins and the rocks.

I heard the clang of bolts. The door opened and there was a light in the hall behind a man with a shock of blue-black hair and a huge stomach. He looked me up and down with bright, narrowed eyes. 'Mademoiselle?'

'Monsieur, there has been an accident. May I . . . use your . . . telephone?'

'An accident here? Come in. Come in. What has happened?'

'A car has crashed into the side of the rocks. A man is . . .'

'Injured? Dead?'

'A motorist has stopped – to help. He says – he says – the man – is – dead.' I looked wildly round for the telephone. He pointed to a corner. 'It is there, Mademoiselle.'

I ran to it, asked for the police and reported the accident in a series of sharp, staccato words. I can't have made myself very clear, for the man at the other end became impatient. 'But you have not said where you're calling from . . .'

'Here,' said the hotelier. 'Let me,' and took the receiver from me and gave precise instructions. Then he turned to me. 'Your name, Mademoiselle?'

I gave it backward like some filing in an official form. 'Helston. Rachel.'

He turned to the telephone. 'She is very shocked. If you will come . . .'

I think the line went dead, for he replaced the receiver with a shrug and turned to me. 'You see, I try to spare you. I do not give your name.'

'I don't care whether you give it or not,' I cried. 'Just come and see what you can do.'

We went to the door together and he said, 'When I saw you pass, I thought you were asking for trouble. It was sheer madness driving like that and you fighting for the wheel.'

'I don't know what you're talking about. I've only just arrived.'

'Have you, indeed? Well, you'd better stick to that story – hadn't you? – or you'll be in trouble.'

I stared into his small red eyes. I wasn't hearing properly. I was stupid with shock. I said again, 'I don't know what you're talking about.'

'You – in that car. I know. I saw. I was taking in a chair that had been left out in the storm and the hall light shone on you as the car zigzagged up the road. It had to pass quite close since the street is so narrow. Street, my eye!' he exploded. 'Alley's more the word, and a Godforsaken place it is too, at night. "A legacy," they said when the old man died. "Aren't you lucky, Gaston Bigorne? You'll make a fortune there with tourists." ' He swore loudly.

*'I wasn't in that car,'* I said across his vituperative words, 'No one was – '

He shot around, his face thrust at me. 'Ah! And how do you know *that* unless you were here?'

I said wildly, 'If there'd been anyone else, they'd have been injured, too. It – it was a terrible smash. Or, if by some – miracle they weren't hurt, they'd have – have stayed, wouldn't they?'

'But you didn't, did you?' He touched my arm as we ran up the street, ducking our heads against the rain. 'You didn't stay. Were you scared? You may well be, for the police will find your fingerprints on the wheel.'

'They won't.' I could have explained; have said, 'I came up here to meet Paul d'Arachenne.' But I had enough sense left to keep quiet. I didn't like this man, nor did I trust him.

'*Mon Dieu!* Oh, *mon Dieu!*'

We had come to the accident scene. The man cried, 'The car. What a wreck! Smashed bonnet; smashed lamps. But you spoke of a dead man, Mademoiselle. Where is he?'

My heart was in my throat. I put my hand to my neck to stop the throbbing.

The second car, the stranger, Paul, were all gone.

The man rubbed his chin. 'What the devil's been going on?'

All I could do was to murmur, 'They've gone. They've gone,' as though I were telling a blind man.

Monsieur Bigorne went on, 'An ambulance would take half an hour to reach here. I suppose this motorist who stopped thought he'd save time and take the man to hospital himself. Though if he were dead . . . Oh, well, then moving him wouldn't matter. I suppose his injuries – '

'Please . . . please . . . stop.'

'I forgot. You're in this.' He reached out a podgy hand and touched me. His fingers were hot and sensuous, feeling the flesh on my arms. 'You mean to say you have no cuts, no bruises even? Well, what did you do? Throw yourself out?' He pulled the hood of my mackintosh over my hair. 'That's how I saw you in the car, with this over your head.' His fingers touched my face. 'Such a predicament for a pretty girl!'

I wrenched his hand away. He must have sensed my terror, for he said more kindly, 'So, a lover's quarrel ends in an accident and death. Well, it has happened many times. You'd better go before the police get here. I'll be kind to you, Mademoiselle, and keep you out of this terrible thing.' He pawed my arm again. 'But you will come and see me, eh? One of these days, you will come to Gaston and –'

'Tell the police what you like. Say what you like. It doesn't matter to me. I wasn't with Paul –'

'*Paul*? Ah, so now we have proof, have we not, that you were? This man Paul . . .' He gave an ugly chuckle. 'Well, he is dead. It is very sad for you, but it is over. And you are young and charming, *ma petite*, you will come and see Gaston Bigorne? You will come soon and . . .'

I felt sick. I stumbled away from him. He called after me. 'When the police arrive, I will tell them that this man you call Paul was alone in the car. I will swear –'

'Swear the truth!' I shouted back.

I don't know whether he heard me, for my voice cracked and broke. Ahead of me was the steep, downhill road. I went uncertainly over the rough stone from Maladieu, with the passing storm echoing over the dark valley. There was all the way to walk home and I had little strength.

A woman in Paul's car? But of course there had been no one.

*Paul is dead.*

The ragged clouds parted and the moon rode high above the groves of trees in the valley. I moved mechanically putting one foot before the other, not keeping a straight path for more than six paces at a time. Like someone drunk.

*Paul is dead.*

Where had the strange man taken him? There was no hospital in Issandre. To Arles, then? To Avignon?

I escaped from Maladieu and wove my way along the valley, past fields and the olive grove. A car hooted at me and the driver glared. I found that I had been walking in the middle of the road.

The Villa Daphnis was lit up as if for a party. The lights that streamed towards me like life lines were the impetus I needed for that last two hundred yards.

## CHAPTER FOUR

No one saw me enter the house. I crept to my room. Pale moonlight lit it and without switching on the lamp, I stripped off my soaked clothes, felt for a towel and dried myself. Then I lay flat on my bed.

The storm had not cleared the air and my skin was clammy. I rolled over on my face and closed my eyes. It was not easy to think coherently, but I had to make the effort.

Had Paul skidded on the wet road? Had some woman passenger to whom he had given a lift, become difficult? Who was she, anyway, to be wandering in that wild, isolated place?

And who was I to ask such a question? At no time in its history had Maladieu stopped being a meeting place for lovers. The toppled stones made resting places; the vast walls hid them from view and muffled the sounds of their whisperings.

I tossed and turned on my bed, exhausted but fretting for some activity that would stop this terrible chaos of my thoughts. There had to be something I could do, something practical that would break the blind fog that enveloped me. If I could find a car, I could make a tour of the hospitals. Arles . . . Avignon. Or I could telephone.

Telephone!

I sprang out of bed, switched on the light and dragged on some clothes. I paused at my door and waited, listening, clinging to my frantic need for secrecy.

The hall was empty. I crept into the small back room, full of the family's schoolbooks and paperback novels, which we grandly called the library. The telephone stood on an old scratched desk. I searched for the number of the nearest hospitals, made a note of them, and dialed Avignon first.

Someone, obviously in a hurry, answered me. Yes. Yes. Monsieur d'Arachenne had been brought in by a doctor who had come upon the scene of the accident. There was nothing they could do for him. He must have hit his head when the car crashed into the rocks and died instantly. The voice paused, softened, became less harassed. 'Is it one of the family who is calling?'

'No. A . . . a friend. They . . . the family . . . have been told?'

'Monsieur Artois d'Arachenne has called and identified his nephew. It is distressing news, Madame? . . . Mademoiselle? But we have an emergency here, so if you will forgive me . . .'

'Of course. Thank you.' I don't know if she heard; my voice was barely audible even to myself.

Someone was crossing the living-room floor. I sped down the hall to my room and crossed to the window.

Moonlight lay on the towers of Sonnengarde. I seemed to hear Paul's laughing voice: 'I'm the only son of an ageing woman, and I'm spoiled.'

Those who suffered loss had a common need – the longing to share their grief with someone who felt as they did. Somewhere in that great grey mass of medieval stone that was Sonnengarde was an old woman whose son lay dead.

Paul's mother and I . . . My restlessness vanished.

I didn't stop to consider the wisdom of what I was about to do. It was something beyond common sense. It belonged to humanity and need and the terrible loneliness of loss. I was going to see the Comtesse d'Arachenne.

Elise was in the front hall, calling out that if Lucia was too lazy to go and find her little cat, she'd go and search. Then her sweet, clear voice began calling, 'Cléry, Cléry.'

To avoid her I went out the back way, through the empty kitchen. The roads were almost dry again in the heat of the night. Clouds played round the moon so that it was silver-clear one minute, luminous the next, then pitch-black.

As I reached the tall gates of the Château, I began to run. If I hadn't speeded, I would have turned back. The high dark trees met over my head and every shadow seemed to move a little. There were tufts of grass on the unkempt drive which caught my toes, so that I kept having to save myself from falling.

I went up the steps, pulled the heavy bell, and heard it reverberate through the house. There was still time to run. I turned on the top step and, poised for flight, heard the door open.

A bald, enormously tall man looked down at me.

I dispensed with preamble. 'I am Rachel Helston. The Comtesse d'Arachenne doesn't know me, but I – I know her son. You have heard – ?'

The man had the exaggerated dignity of an over-trained servant. 'The Comtesse can see no one. I have instructions that the house is to be closed to strangers. There has been a tragedy.'

'But that is why –'

The door was shut in my face.

It was my fault. I should never have come. Had I been less shocked, I should have stopped to reason that loving Paul did not give me the right to intrude. I was a stranger to his mother.

I walked slowly away, not knowing where I was going. Only when I felt the long wet grass whipping around my ankles did I realize that I had left the drive and was walking across the Château lawns. I wasn't troubled by the fact that I was trespassing. No one would care whether I was here or not. On a night such as this they would be enclosed with their own tragedy.

My foot hit something hard. A fleeting moment of moonlight lit it up. It was an old dried-up stone foundation with weeds growing in the basin. If it hadn't been there, I'd have sunk down on the sodden grass, my energy spent. I sat down on the wide stone rim.

Gardens as old as Sonnengarde are outside time. Tonight, I fitted perfectly into the place, for I was no one, belonging to no time. My body and my mind were in limbo. I closed my eyes.

If I could talk to someone, I might feel human again, feel normal pain. But I was afraid of my own family. They would be sympathetic; they would promise not to talk to anyone about it. But because they were all, with the exception of Lucia, extrovert, one of them might unwittingly let my secret out merely by a word, a glance even. Under their indolence, the Issandrians were quick, alert people. They would seize on the word, the glance, and work its meaning out among themselves. Then the story would be all over the town. So little happened that was exciting that my link with Paul and the Château Sonnengarde and the tragedy at Maladieu would be a highlight for months to come. Every time I went into Issandre, I would be looked at curiously, covertly, and the whole dreadful thing would be resurrected for me. I couldn't stand that.

But the need to tell just one person gnawed at me. My

father was the obvious one and the one most likely to avert gossip. But although Father was clever, successful, and very gregarious, he lacked the art of getting close to people. We lived side by side, friendly enough, but we never touched in understanding. It wasn't easy to talk to him about things like hopes and feelings and despairs.

Now, sitting in the dark, timeless garden, I felt more alone than ever before in my life. The crack of a twig in that intense quiet had the impact of a pistol shot. I started and turned my head.

A man stepped between the trees. 'Don't,' he said. 'Please, don't.'

I put my hands to my face and realized that I had been crying. I must have been sobbing aloud, for at that moment there was no moonlight, so he could not have seen my face.

He came nearer. 'I'm sorry. It was probably unfair of me to tell you to stop. People say that it does you good to cry it out, whatever it is.'

He was just a black shadow with a low, rather crisp voice. I realized that I was trespassing and that he could tell me to go. I'd no idea who he was – one of the family, a friend.

He sat down beside me. 'As I said, don't let me stop you. Do you want a handkerchief?' Without waiting for a reply, he gave me his. 'I wonder how many men down the ages have lent women handkerchiefs to cry into?' He said it kindly, hoping perhaps that by being casual, he'd ease my embarrassment.

I took the handkerchief and sat screwing the crisp linen into a ball. I was beyond even the common courtesy of thanking him. The tears were running salt down to my lips.

The man just sat by my side, neither moving nor looking at me. It didn't occur to me at the time that he might be a prowler and have no more right to be here than I. All the same, his nearness made me feel awkward and presently I moved a little farther along the fountain's rim.

Whoever he was, he had eyes like a cat, for although the moon was hidden, he saw my movement. 'Feeling better?'

'Yes, thank you.' I put my hands on the stone on either side of me and started to rise. 'I must go.'

'I know you're trespassing,' he said, 'but don't worry. No one's coming to turn you out, so you can relax.' He put out a hand and touched my hair, smoothing it very gently back from my forehead. 'That's fine. Now you've finished crying, you can tell me about it.'

I wiped my face with his handkerchief, blew my nose, gulped twice, and said, 'You're a stranger here, aren't you? You even speak French with an accent.'

'I'm English.'

I broke into English and asked without any real interest, 'A visitor?'

'Yes. My name is Lambert. Max Lambert. But it won't mean anything to you.'

'If you're a stranger, you're probably trespassing like I am. Or . . . are you staying at the Château?'

'I am.'

Here was the link I longed for; here was someone who must have known Paul. I said, 'Then you know – what – what happened tonight.'

I sensed an immediate tension. Nothing had stirred. The trees were quite still, as exhausted by the shock of the storm as I was by the shock of death. But something was suddenly wrong.

His voice came with an unexpected harshness. 'Your name?'

'Rachel Helston. But you – '

The violence of his next movement checked my words. He sprang to his feet, and said in low fury. 'So that's it! I might have known. God in heaven, I should have known!'

Even his anger couldn't arouse me. 'Known what?' I asked wearily.

'That you weren't crying from grief. You're scared, aren't you? Scared to death someone will find out what really happened up at Maladieu. That's why you're crying.'

As he swung around on me, the moon came out brilliantly and lit his face, a gaunt face with a high-bridged nose. I couldn't see his eyes, yet their stare hurt me.

I opened my mouth twice before a sound came. 'Just what do you mean . . . about Maladieu?'

'You should know. You were there.'

He wasn't the man who had found Paul. That one had been shorter, stockier and unmistakably French.

I said, 'If you know that, then you – '

'Oh, I was there, too. But you were in too much of a fury to see me.'

Stabs of anger shot across my despair. I hadn't known I had so much energy left. 'Why in heaven's name didn't you come and help? That's what we needed – help.'

We were both standing now and the next cloud had not yet hidden the moon. We were bathed in strong white light.

'Well? Why didn't you?'

He made me wait for his answer. 'Because when I passed the second time it was too late. They had taken Paul away.'

The night sky became black again. I looked at the man. The cloud had turned him into a dark statue, but though he stood motionless, I could feel his anger blazing at me.

'I was the man who passed you when you were fighting with Paul for control of the car. What were you trying to do? Kill yourself as well as him? I was the man who hooted a warning at you as I went up the hill. Remember me now?'

'How can I when I never saw you?'

'Because you were too absorbed in your quarrel. You caused that ccident, didn't you? Or no, I suppose it's no use asking you that because you'll only deny it.'

'I wasn't there. I came later and I'm not lying. *I'm not lying.* I . . .' Breath I had been holding came out with a harsh, rasping sound. I choked a little and the rest of the words were caught back.

'That's better,' said the man. 'For a moment I thought you were going to have hysterics.'

'Not in front of you. If it would give you any satisfaction –'

'Satisfaction? Good God!'

'Then why won't you believe me? Or don't you want to?'

'I want to believe only the truth. You're a stranger, but Paul was my friend. And if you were responsible for that accident and then ran away and left him to die –'

'Is that what you *want* to believe? Is this the way shock has taken you? Blame anyone – what does it matter, so long as you can find what you think is a satisfactory explanation for it all? You've got to have a whipping boy, is that it? Oh, go!'

He said coldly, 'If anyone goes, surely it should be you. You're the trespasser here. But before you do, you may as well know how I came to be out on that road tonight. At this stage it's no use telling half a story.'

'And I doubt if it's any use telling the whole of it, either.' I said bleakly.

'But I'm going to all the same. I'll tell you what I saw and then perhaps you'll stop protesting that you weren't there.'

'But I –'

He cut me short. 'I was on my way up to Maladieu to watch the storm from the Isis Tower when I saw you and Paul in his car. You wore a dark coat and there was something over your hair. I think all hell must have been let loose between you because the car was weaving from one side of the street to the other. I thought at the time that you must both have been drunk. All I could do was to sound my horn as a warning as I passed. I stayed in the Tower some time watching the storm. When I came down again, I saw Paul's car jammed into the rock. There was no sign of anyone, so I knocked up the hotelier at Sainte Bérénice. He told me that a man had been injured – or killed – he wasn't certain. All he knew for sure was that a young woman had knocked on his door and asked if she could telephone the police. She was in 'a state' he said, and he described you: a small girl wearing something dark over her hair. He said you ran away. So you see, Miss Helston, there were two of us who saw you up there.'

It was like conducting one's own defence without being able to think of the salient point that would break the prosecutor's argument.

'The fact that I knocked on the door of the Hostelrie for help doesn't prove that I was in Paul's car.'

'Oh, come! Don't tell me there were two women with him up at Maladieu in the middle of a violent storm. That would be too much.'

'You want it to be too much,' I cried.

'Good night, Miss Helston.' He turned abruptly and walked away.

Trembling and sobbing I shouted after him, *'I've told you the truth.'*

He didn't turn around.

I sank on to the wet grass, my fingers clinging to the stone rim of the fountain. 'I've told you the truth,' I whispered to no one, for I was alone.

## CHAPTER FIVE

'Tsch, tsch, Rachel! What have you done to yourself?' Peppina was coming out of the kitchen. She peered at me. 'What is wrong?'

I pushed my hair back. 'I'm all right.'

She glanced at my torn nylons, my stained dress, my dripping hair. 'You are *not* all right. You have fallen?'

I let the question go unanswered, passed her, and went down the hall.

'So!' She called after me. 'You do not tell Peppina. You do not trust her any more.'

I knew she was thinking I'd had a tussle with a lover and was burning with curiosity to know who he was. Though I tried to pacify her by smiling, I was certain the result was a grimace. The whole thing was like a dreadful secret locked up inside me. Or not quite a secret, for a stranger had ripped it from me, turned it into an accusation, and flung it back at me.

'Nikki has been crying for you.' Peppina clung to a lower banister, her wizened face gazing at me.

'I said good night to him before I went out.'

'He thinks he heard you come in some time ago. I told him you hadn't, but he didn't believe me.'

'I'll look in on him now.' I edged towards my room.

'He thought he had done something wrong and you were angry with him.' Her reproof followed me along the passage. 'He cries like a little waif, so quietly, as if he has no hope. I tell him we all love him, but he still does not look happy. *We* do not matter, Rachel. Only you. Mother of God, bless him.' Her tone implied: *And forgive you for causing his tears.*

I knew Peppina was being unreasonable and was blaming me without cause because she was cross with me. Something was wrong and I hadn't confided in her. We were her world and she would listen at keyholes if she thought there was something she should know.

She watched me all the way to my room. I heard her little snorting 'Humph!' as I closed the door.

I went to the dressing-table mirror and did the best I could with my face. But powder didn't hide the brown shadows under my eyes, nor did a comb help very much with my wet hair.

It wasn't going to be easy hiding my mood from Nikki. He was acutely sensitive, watching faces for lights and shades of feeling. I tried to fill my mind with Nikki to stop the horror that nagged at me. When would he ever get over his fear of angering us? He still behaved like a little boy told to be on his best behaviour at a party. If ever a natural boyishness made him naughty, he would shake with terror at being reprimanded as if the fear and poverty of Agadir hung over him like a menace. So, I made the best of myself before I went to his room. I even put on a little scent.

Nikki was awake and turned quickly to me as I opened the door.

'Peppina said you weren't cross with me.' His delicate hands clutched the blue sheet that I had embroidered for him with animals. 'But you didn't come to say good night.'

'Darling.' I gathered him close. 'You know perfectly well I'm not cross with you. I – I had to go out hurriedly. I said good night before I went. And I've only just come home.'

He strained away from me. 'Why are you looking like that?'

'Like what?'

'Like people look when they've been crying.'

I pulled his head against me, laughed softly and said, 'If you'd been out in that terrible storm, you wouldn't have come home looking as if you'd stepped out of a bandbox.'

'What's a bandbox?'

'I'll tell you in the morning.'

'No, now.' He nestled against me again. 'You smell nice. What's a bandbox?'

I laid him down on the pillows and kissed him. 'I'll buy you one for Christmas, full of chocolates and tied with red ribbon.'

'You promise?'

'Of course.'

'And everything is all right?'

'Yes, darling,' I said. 'Everything's all right.'

I stood looking at him and wondered how life was going to toughen him without hurting him too much in the process. He was not unintelligent, but I supposed the fact that he was young for his age was a kind of subconscious defence against a hard realism he could not cope with. It was I who must help him cope. I thought bitterly that I was pretty badly equipped for the task.

I left Nikki and went downstairs. Peppina was in the living-room setting a tray on the coffee table.

'For you,' she said. 'Coffee and Armagnac. There's nothing like it for consoling you after a quarrel.'

'But I haven't quarrelled . . .' I began. Then I gave up, sat down, and said, 'Thank you.'

'Tomorrow you make it up. Yes?'

I ignored the question. 'Is everyone out?' I poured hot, strong coffee into the cup.

'Monsieur George and Monsieur Dominick have taken Elise and Lucia into Issandre. Lucia wore her ruby dress. She looked so beautiful. But perhaps,' she added hopefully, 'the young Monsieur Dominick will like Elise the best. That would be good.'

'The young Monsieur Dominick,' I said firmly, 'is married. Where is my father?'

At that moment I heard his footsteps on the tiled floor of the hall. When he entered the room, I knew that I had to tell him about tonight. He sat down in a chair opposite me. 'I'll have some of that coffee.'

Peppina went scuttling on slippered feet for another cup and saucer.

I said, 'Father, I must talk to you.'

He dominated a room. Not only because of his physical bulk, the vividness of his colouring – black hair, black brows, deep blue eyes – but also because of his positive, uncompromising personality. Unfortunately, there was one thing he shrank from and that was what he obviously feared I was now going to indulge in. He hated heart searchings. He twisted and turned in his chair, felt for a cigarette, and made a business of lighting it.

Peppina returned and poured out his coffee. She despised men. At the same time she waited on them like an old black slave. Francis said that she had a love-hate relationship with his sex.

I sat very still watching, not fidgeting at all. When Peppina had gone, I said, 'Something terrible has happened, Father. I don't know what to do – but then, I don't see that there is anything I *can* do, now.'

He wouldn't look at me, but pretended to be absorbed in the strap of his espadrille. 'Well? What is it?'

'It's about the accident tonight.'

'What accident?'

'I thought the whole town would know it by now,' I said, and told him briefly that I had seen a crashed car and a man killed.

He said matter-of-factly, 'So you saw an accident. I suppose it was pretty horrible. But it's past and you'd better put it out of your mind. For goodness sake don't get neurotic about it. It has nothing to do with you.'

'It has. It has.' I took a gulp of Armagnac and, staring into the glass, explained, 'The man was Paul d'Arachenne. I met him in Paris when I was staying with Aunt Solange. We – we had a date tonight up at Maladieu.' I watched his eyebrows twitch, as they always did when he was alarmed. 'We were going to be married,' I said.

He sat up straight in his chair. 'Well I'm damned! And you didn't tell me.'

'Father, listen, please. We had only known each other a week. We wanted to be quite sure. So we kept quiet about it

– until we *were* sure, I mean. Tonight . . .' I couldn't go on. The picture came back – the steep, narrow road ravaged by lightning; the wrecked car; Paul's hand with the signet ring on it, Paul's face turned into the sodden ground . . .

My father coped with the emotional moment by drinking his coffee, then lumbering across the room to find an ash tray.

I clenched my hands on the chair arms, fought my sick reaction to the picture in my mind, and wished I hadn't had the impulse to tell him.

'Paul is dead,' I said. 'I keep saying it, but I don't really believe it. I can't. I – '

'Hey, don't go to pieces.'

'I won't. Only – Father, there's something else – I've got to tell you . . .'

His eyebrows twitched again. I could read his thoughts: Rachel spent a week with her lover in Paris and now she's in trouble. That a daughter of mine should be such a little fool! But, since she has been, why the devil doesn't she tell some woman friend? Why saddle me . . .?

So I began to explain, to put his mind at rest on that point. I told him that the 'something else' was the fact that two people had said they saw me quarrelling with Paul in a car at Maladieu.

I hated smoking, but I took a cigarette from the alabaster box and lit it.

Father sat squinting at his cigarette while mine burned slowly between my fingers. It was stupid to be so self-conscious with him that I talked hesitantly, telling him facts in brief, jerky sentences, shy of emotion in front of him. When I stopped talking, I heard the thunder again. The storm was returning. I lay back in the chair.

My father wandered on to the veranda. He'd heard my story and he had nothing to say, so, characteristically, he was escaping. I might have known he couldn't help me and was incapable of even trying.

I wronged him. He came back, sat down opposite me again, and said, 'Well, you tell me you weren't the girl in the car, so what are you worrying about? Forget it. The hotelier up at Maladieu had probably been drinking to ease his boredom and in his befuddled state, one girl looked just like another. Always remember, Rachel, to keep silent when you're involved in something unpleasant and no purpose is served by talking. Never plunge voluntarily into trouble. If you do, you stir up a hornet's nest. Nothing is truer than that silence is golden.'

He looked pleased with himself over his bit of philosophizing. 'I suppose that man Lambert is staying at the Château. He probably had as big a shock as you to learn that a friend was dead. People react oddly in times of shock, you know. So, keep quiet and try to forget it all as soon as you can.' He picked up my brandy glass and drained it. 'And don't go drinking a lot of that stuff – you know you haven't got a good head for liquor.'

To my surprise I found that his matter-of-factness was the salutary reaction I needed. I said in a calmer voice, 'I don't understand any of it. If there was someone with Paul in the car, who was she? And why were they quarrelling? He was on his way to meet *me*.'

'And some other girl was jealous and got there first. How old are you? Twenty-two? Twenty-three, of course. Well, then you're old enough to stop being naïve.' He got up again, pulled me to my feet, and marched me to the window. 'Look at them' – his arm swept the moonlit scene – 'The towers of Sonnengarde. Don't you *know* who the d'Archennes are?'

'Of course I do – they're the banking family.'

'In which money marries money. Money, Rachel, not moonshine and champagne, dictates their *affaires du coeur*. So you had a good time in Paris.' He peered down at me. 'How far did it go?'

Father was realistic about sex, so I said without embarrassment, 'Not that far!'

'Well, thank heaven for your good sense.'

'It wasn't like that at all; it wasn't – flippant. Paul asked me to marry him. Men don't say that to a girl unless they mean it.'

He thrust his fingers through his hair. 'Well, I don't know! You come home from Paris and you say nothing to anyone. How do you expect me to see the affair as serious?'

'I told you, we were going to have a month's separation from each other.'

'In other words, you weren't that sure of him.' He thumped my shoulder in a clumsy effort at reassurance. 'And because you weren't, it'll be easier to get over.'

'But I was – ' I began. Then I stopped. It was never any use trying to make people believe what they didn't want to. And, anyway, how convincing had my argument sounded?

Father was saying, 'Unless the police come questioning you, you can stop worrying about being implicated in this affair at Maladieu. If they do come, I'll be around to testify that my daughter is not a liar. Now, I'm going down to the pottery to see how they're getting on with those Zodiac panels. Are you coming with me?'

I shook my head, insisting, unconvinced, 'Do you really think the police won't come questioning . . .?'

He said with a touch of kindly impatience. 'I've told you not to worry. All you have to tell them, if they do, is that the accident happened before you arrived on the scene. If there's an autopsy, then the man who took young d'Arachenne away will have to appear. But I've a feeling it will be recorded as a skid on a wet and damned dangerous road.' He beamed at me. 'Now, do what I tell you and keep quiet about it. Put some music on, read a book, watch television. Do something. But don't sit here brooding, there's a good girl.'

He tossed ash from the cigarette. It missed the tray and fell on to the carpet. I watched him step on one tiny burning pin-point. Then he left me.

I sat where I was, hunched in my chair.

How relieved he must be that I hadn't burst into tears or thrown a hysterical fit. Poor Father. I knew he loved me in his way, but not only did he dread to be embarrassed, he didn't want to consider the possibility that one day I might marry.

I could understand how he saw the Paris affair. Had Elise been in my place, I'd probably have seen it that way, too. Being a biographer, he should know that truth was often as fantastic as a fairy-tale and melodrama an everyday thing.

I sat with my meandering thoughts and had no idea of the time when George and Dominick walked in. If I were going to take my father's advice, this was the moment to make the effort. I looked up as they entered the room, fixed a bright smile on my face, and said, 'Oh, hullo. Where's Elise?'

George said, 'She and Lucia met some friends at the Chinois. The night was young for them. But we came home.'

I said in surprise, 'It's the first time I've known you to come back early from Issandre.'

'I'm getting old.' He grinned at me and looked at Dominick. 'I suppose you're going to talk half the night.'

'I'd like to stay for a while.'

'Well, don't look so apologetic about it,' George said briskly. 'I've been coming here for years. I know the drill. Providing you drink with your host before lunch and after dinner, and keep out of his way when he's working, you can do as you like. That's the beauty of this place. That,' he added with a comic leer at me, 'and the charm of Les Girls. Lucia, as you've seen, is the beauty; Elise is a sweet little sentimentalist. But give me Rachel. She's a honey. Good night.'

To my amazement I found myself smiling. 'Do you want anything,' I asked Dominick when George had left us. 'Coffee? Cognac? They're always on tap for Father and his guests.'

'I want nothing but this,' he said and leaned his ashen-fair head against the dark green cushion. 'This peace.'

The silence was easy. He was one of those rare people with whom one didn't have to make conversation.

It was I who broke the silence. 'I'm afraid our piano isn't a terribly good one. But it's there if ever you'd like to use it.'

'Thank you, but I want to forget pianos and orchestras and music scores,' he said. 'I'm here to escape and lick my wounds.' He gave me a quick, uncertain glance. It was a signal for my interest and my sympathy.

I said, 'We're an easy going family. I think you'll be happy here. I hope so.' I glanced at the clock. It was too early for bed, but I wanted my room, my own company. I made a slight movement to rise.

'It's amazing. I've been here such a short time,' Dominick said, 'but already everything seems easier. I begin to feel I can cope with life again.'

He expected me to say something. 'I'm glad.' I rose, picked up a cushion that had fallen to the floor, and plumped it up.

'You see,' said Dominick, 'I've left my wife.'

So now he felt he could cope with life again! *I* couldn't. I wanted to clap my hands over my ears and run before the confidences began. I knew the signs too well. He wanted to lay a burden by talking. But I was the last person to help him.

Clèry came into the room on silent, padded feet, curling herself into a ball, and closed her blue eyes. Sometimes I thought she was the only thing Lucia loved.

I bent to scoop her up and take her to her basket in the kitchen on my way to bed. Then I paused, rubbing her sleek back. She let out a yowl of delight. I felt suddenly mean about Dominick. He didn't know of my tragedy and his own was burning him up. I could at least listen.

I said gently, 'I'm sorry,' and wondered, since it was some seconds after he had spoken, if he realized I was referring to his break with his wife.

It was the signal he wanted. The story came flowing out of him as if every word had been on the other side of flood gates. 'The terrible thing about a broken marriage,' he said, 'is that it takes only one to break it. In my case, I'm the one.' He gave me a slow, curiously sweet smile. 'I don't want to be a bore, but as I'm staying here I think it only fair that you should know the set-up.'

I said unhappily, 'You don't need . . . really, you don't need to explain things.'

'I'd like to – that is, if you don't mind. You see, all our friends – Irene's and mine – know about it and they're biased. You would have an outsider's eye.' He paused and felt in his pocket for a cigarette. I pushed the bóx on the coffee table across to him. He said, 'Thank you, I only smoke my own brand – Turkish.'

Simultaneously with the snap of the lighter I thought I heard a sound outside. Francis or Elise and Lucia coming back? Elise, I thought, would be the one for Dominick to talk to. She had little experience of life, but she was a wonderful listener. And that was what he wanted.

The noise, however, was nothing more than a tiny gust of wind stirring the trees. The storm had changed its course and had not returned.

'When a marriage fails, the sensible thing is to break up,' Dominick said. 'That's what I want. But Irene won't hear of it.'

'Perhaps she thinks that it can still work.'

A cloud of smoke from his cigarette veiled his face. 'People tell me how lucky I am to have a beautiful and clever wife. But outsiders never understand, do they?'

I made no comment; I don't think he even needed one.

'My mother died three years ago,' he said, 'and I've never got over it. We were very close and she understood me perfectly. All the time she was alive I wanted no one else. She died very suddenly and the emptiness was terrible. It's still terrible. Not even my marriage filled the gap. I suppose nothing could – it was that kind of relationship.'

My shock had been terrible, too, and I was not out of it yet. I suppose that was why something about the way he talked drained my sympathy. I lifted my eyes and saw him watching me, waiting for me to say something.

At other times I would have been gentle. But I couldn't muster gentleness now. I said, 'You mean you loved your mother more than you loved your wife.' After the words were out, I thought in dismay how offensive they sounded. I hadn't meant to be cruel.

Before I could think of something to soften what seemed like an accusation, Dominick said without resentment, 'That's quite true. I did. I know now that I should never have married Irene. I should have looked for a woman like my mother.

Irene is the exact opposite.'

He had roused me from my shocked apathy. I wanted to tell him that he would never find his ideal because wives don't behave like mothers to their husbands. Not unless they were much older women; women with 'all passion spent' and only tenderness and good housekeeping and mother love to give. I felt a touch of pity for Irene, with an impossible role to fill.

Dominick said, 'And so, you see, it's no use trying to keep our marriage together. She'll break me with her demands and then my career will suffer. That mustn't happen. Now that my mother is dead, it's the only complete thing I have – my music, I mean.'

I hadn't meant to sigh. It gave him the wrong impression. 'I'm sorry,' he said quickly. 'I've talked too much about myself. It must have been your father's excellent after-dinner brandy making me expansive. Or your own wonderful restfulness.'

Restfulness! I shook my head impatiently.

Dominick smiled. 'It's true, you know. You have that quality; my mother's quality of listening.'

'That's where you're so wrong,' I said sharply. 'I'm not being restful. I'm just exhausted. Oh, not by you. Please don't misunderstand.'

'Having guests like George and myself gives you too much work.'

'Good heavens, I'm used to it. And I'm strong.' I should have left it at that, but I didn't. I rushed on. 'The shock of your mother's death is some years old. A shock – a . . . a tragedy – happened to me only a few hours ago.'

There was a moment's silence in the room.

'Tragedy?'

I leaned my arms on the mantel shelf and stared up at a lovely abstract mosaic plaque in beige and white and green. 'Someone I loved was killed in a car accident tonight.'

I had stunned him. He sat for a moment staring at me. Then he sprang to his feet. 'And you let me go on and on talking about myself? Why didn't you scream at me, hit me to make me stop? Oh, Rachel, what can I say?'

'Nothing. Nothing, please. Only I thought you ought to know why I seemed so unresponsive.'

'But you weren't.' He paced the room. 'I heard down in the town that someone had been killed tonight at a place called Maladieu. Is that – ?'

'I don't want to talk about it.'

He stood looking at me, inarticulate, distressed.

'And I don't want you to discuss it with anyone,' I went on. 'Do you hear? My father knows, but no one else. I can explain it all to you now, but I'd be grateful if you'd just keep what I've told you to yourself.'

'Of course. Saying I'm sorry sounds pretty poor sympathy, doesn't it? But I don't know what else to say.' He waited, watching me. 'Do you want me to go?'

Quite suddenly, I didn't. 'Stay if you like. Talk to me. Tell me about your music.'

I don't know how long we sat there, but as Dominick talked, I found I was actually taking an interest in what he was saying. I suppose, in a way, it was therapeutic – a complete stranger's life story forcing me away from myself.

Presently he spoke again about his mother. From the way he talked she had seemed to be always there, at concerts, at social functions – like a bride and a wife, I thought, cherishing him, watching, encouraging, and by those subtle methods of smothering love, becoming indispensable.

Again, looking at him across the sleeping Clèry, I could see Dominick in monk's clothes; his fair hair shining, his eyes of a clear, innocent grey. An aesthetic face. Certainly there was fire in his voice when he talked of music. I wondered whether there was equal fire when he touched his wife.

## CHAPTER SIX

'Of course,' George was saying, 'I'm not surprised to hear of that crash. Maladieu is a death trap for young heathens in fast cars. The road's too damned narrow and twisting and the gradient in itself is a gift to suicides.' He was spreading cherry jam in huge chunks on a golden-brown croissant.

Elise said, 'But it's the first accident there I've ever heard of. It isn't really dangerous, is it, Father?'

He was busy slitting open an envelope with his agent's address on the flap. 'Young d'Arachenne was driving a Ferrari. I don't know if he knew the road – he certainly has never been at the Château since I've lived here.'

I had a feeling that he had even forgotten what I had told him last night. He was bent over the letter, looking more pleased at every close-typed line.

'Well,' Francis observed, 'there's something to be said for being poor. You can't afford Ferraris that need expert hands.'

They went on talking, but I made an effort and shut my ears. I tried to fill my mind with impressions. *This is my family; this is where I must go on making my life*. I looked around the table. Yellow china patterned by the light and shade seeping through the vine that hung over the veranda roof; seven people sitting buttering croissants, reaching for cherry jam. The light danced on their bright hair; their gay, casual clothes. An aura of vitality quivered like a current round them. I'd seen five of them like this for so many hundreds of days, yet I'd never observed them so clearly as now when, paradoxically, they seemed a little unreal. Like characters in a play, they sat talking about a man who would never appear on their stage.

'. . . and he was an only son.'

Lucia said, 'Aunt Solange knew his mother. Did you meet him when you were in Paris, Elise?'

'A few times. But he had some ravishing beauty in tow and never looked my way.'

Lucia turned her brilliant eyes on me. 'You?'

I pretended to be busy helping Nikki spread jam. 'Uh-huh,' I said, which could have meant 'Yes' or 'No' or could have been complete indifference.

Francis had opened a newspaper. 'Well! Well! The accident has already made headline news in our local. Now I wonder –'

I heard myself shout, 'Stop it!'

Their eyes turned my way. I took a gulp of scalding coffee.

Lucia laughed. 'Since when have you been squeamish about violent death with breakfast? Or are you different from most people who love crime in their morning papers? And we *won't* stop talking about it. I met Paul when I stayed with Aunt Solange in Paris. Good-looking, rich, spoiled. Do you know, I once did an old trite film act on him and slapped his face? It did him good.' She laughed again.

Dominick had given me one swift glance and then looked away. He said with a clumsy effort at changing the conversation, 'Can someone tell me why the English can't make croissants like these? It's only in France . . .'

I was out of earshot. I was carrying the coffee pot to the kitchen to be refilled.

It was inconceivable that the morning was like any others, but it was. When I had finished my jobs about the house, I went down to the pottery.

Nikki squatted on the floor gathering broken chips of mosaic and putting them into labelled pots – carmine in carmine, jade in jade.

Lucia was sitting at her bench finishing the sign Aquarius for the Zodiac plaque. Sunlight slanting through the window behind her shone on to the soft golds and greens of the design. Francis was at the kiln, piling tesserae on to trays for baking. Elise had jabbed a sharp corner of a mosaic piece into her finger and was sucking it. The charming antique turquoise ring Francis had given her last Christmas glowed as blue as the sky. Elise and Francis were very close, their sunny, uncomplicated characters fitting perfectly.

I sat down at my bench and picked up the clippers. The two fish of my Pisces mosaic were grey and shell-pink and they had silver spines. The sea undulated round them, green and tipped with creamy white. I had been rather pleased with it. Now, it was as if a stranger had worked on it.

Francis looked at the wall clock. 'It's just struck nine. I'm going to start baking. Don't anyone open the kiln door. Do you hear?' he looked hard at Nikki.

I said quickly, 'You know he never does.'

Lucia laughed. 'Rachel's little ewe lamb – *black* lamb!'

I turned on her angrily. 'Don't say that.'

The telephone bell rang and stopped what threatened to be a near quarrel. Francis, who was nearest, answered it.

I watched his broad, fair-skinned face break into a delighted grin as he listened. 'Why, of course, Monsieur.' He glanced up at the clock. 'In half an hour? Yes, I'll be there and I'll bring some designs along. . . . As you wish, of course. We can do this work either in stained glass or in tesserae. We have supplies of both . . . No, Monsieur. I appreciate your time is limited. I won't keep you waiting. I'll leave now.' He replaced the receiver and turned to us. 'An order for two panels for the pavilion of the new bathing *plage* down on the river. I have to go right away to talk it over with the architect. That means I can't go to the sale this morning.' He looked at me. 'You'll have to go, Rachel.'

'What sale?'

'At the old monastery, of course. You hadn't forgotten that we were going to bid for those stained-glass windows? They're broken and no one's going to want them. We could probably get them for a song.'

I had forgotten. I sat quite still, cutters in one hand, a tessera in the other. Francis was feeding the last of the clay strips into the kiln.

The old monastery was at the far edge of the d'Arachenne estate. It was a ruin except for the Monk's Hall which had been locked and bolted ever since I could remember. As children we had often wanted to go inside, for there were rumours in Issandre of treasures there, of golden candlesticks and a crucifix studded with precious stones and lovely old paintings. But I suspected that the legend had grown with the centuries.

A few months ago old Fabian d'Arachenne had decided to sell the contents of the Monk's Hall and agents for dealers from as far away as Paris had come to the preview. They had left in their great cars and no one knew what they had found in the locked-up ruins. If there were fantastic treasures there, they kept it to themselves. The stained-glass windows were high up in the walls and time and storms had broken them. As windows they were useless, but we could use as much stained glass as we could get.

Before Paul – before tragedy had stuck me, I would have been as thrilled as anyone to have gone into that Hall and made my bid for the glass. Now, I shrank from it.

I said clearly and very firmly, 'Elise can go. You can tell her the limit you're prepared to offer for the glass. You don't need me as well, and I'm busy.'

Elise was tidying a bench. 'I won't go alone.'

'Why on earth not?'

'I can't bargain.'

'There won't be any bargaining for the glass.' I said. 'Lucia can go with you.'

'I have a hair appointment this morning.' She looked at me and her eyes narrowed. 'But I suppose I could put it off.'

Francis shut the kiln door. 'Rachel knows more about this side of the business than any of you. You'll go,' he said to me. 'And take Elise, since you seem to want moral support.'

'But I said – ' Lucy began.

Francis cut her short. 'If you must shy off work this morning, go and get your hair done.' He strode to the door. 'And for the Lord's sake, do as I tell you, all of you. Either I'm in charge here or I'm not. Rachel, you'll get that glass for us. The sale starts at eleven o'clock. Now I'm off to see the architect.'

Through the open door I watched him pause to pull down the green sun blinds which made canopies over the big windows. The bright morning light turned his gingerish hair to the colour of marigolds. He always stood like a sea captain on a pitching ship, legs apart, and his square, stocky figure never looked its best in shorts. His easy going manner always stiffened as soon as he stepped into the pottery, but then, three sisters and a small boy could not have been the easiest people in the world to control.

Lucia was saying, 'I don't suppose there's anything to see, anyway, in that dreary old Monk's Hall. All that talk of treasure is probably just town gossip. People wouldn't leave valuable things in that dingy place.'

I said, 'I'm surprised they're having the sale so soon after what's happened.'

Elise sat with her chin on her hand, her face dreamy and a little sad. 'But sales often take place just after people die, don't they? It's rather pathetic really, isn't it, the way treasured things get sold, or treated as junk?'

Lucia said irritably, 'Oh, don't be so sentimental. In this case it was old Fabian himself who planned the sale before he died. Anyway, the ruined monastery is quite far from the house, so I doubt if the Comtesse knows much about it.'

The Comtesse. Paul's mother. Of course she wouldn't come near the place during the sale. But what of the man, Lambert?

'There's a gate on the far side of the estate,' Elise was saying. 'I suppose they'll use that. They won't come up the main avenue and past the house, so the sale can go on without anyone up at the Château knowing anything about it.'

I left them still talking and went to my room to change into something a bit more formal than the sun dresses we wore for working. Then I put our business cheque-book in my handbag, got the car out, and called Elise.

As she had said, the gate that led to the monastery was at the far side of the estate. We drove in a great half circle to get there. At least a dozen cars were already parked outside and I saw how ivy, which had overgrown the studded wooden door, had been torn down and hung in festoons on either side of it.

Men in town clothes were walking past the broken colonnades of the cloisters and through a door to the left.

'Come *on*,' Elise said. 'We can look round the ruins afterwards.'

I didn't move. 'You go.'

'But I *can't*. I know nothing about the prices of stained glass.

Rachel, what's the matter with you?'

I urged myself forward, and we went together into the gloom of the hall. The place was lit by lamps and before I even noticed what was on display, I looked for Max Lambert. So far as I could see, he wasn't there.

Elise whispered, 'Isn't it disappointing? No jewelled cross, no gold candlesticks.'

But there were three huge paintings which, judging from the men crowded round them with torches, were old masters. There was a splendid chair with lions' faces on the arms, some intricate carvings, four ancient refectory tables, and a cross, not of gold, but of what looked like ebony and ivory. I made a guess that the men had come because of the pictures. If even one of those paintings was a Rembrandt or a Tintoretto, it would have been worth their while.

I looked up at the stained-glass windows. It was difficult to see them clearly with the ivy sprawling over them, but, cracked and broken as they were, they had all the beauty of jewel colours.

At the far end of the hall was a small door. I don't know when it opened, but I was aware of light streaming in. I was also aware of a hush among the murmur of men's voices.

Two women stood just inside the door. One was middle-aged, thin, and black-haired. The other was older, smaller, and her hair looked like snow.

Then my heart gave a lurch. Max Lambert walked behind them. With the light at their backs, I couldn't see his face very clearly, but I knew that he had seen me.

I felt myself go hot and cold. Quickly, I turned away from him to the older woman. I knew I was looking at Paul's mother, the Comtesse d'Arachenne.

Her voice cut across the low murmurings. 'And who gave you permission for this . . . outrage?'

The auctioneer, who was standing by a vast painting of a dark Madonna with palm leaves above her head, said, 'It was arranged some time ago, Madame. Comte Fabian allowed these gentlemen to examine the paintings last month.'

'The Comte Fabian is dead. This is my property.'

'But, Madame, the arrangement for the sale was not countermanded by you, so we presumed that you wished it to go ahead today as planned.'

'You presume too much. I do not wish to sell. And now you'll please leave.'

'But these men have come a long way. The paintings are

masterpieces. It is criminal that they should be left hanging in a damp, disused hall. They are already showing signs of deterioration. If I dare to say – '

'You may not. Now . . . I have ordered you to go.'

I heard the murmurs of protest around me. These men were experts, they were also hard-headed townsmen. They had no fear of an old patrician woman nor of her orders.

'You have a fortune here, Madame,' one said, 'but in another few years you will have nothing. Those canvases will split and rot – '

'I would rather they did that than get into the hands of commerce,' she said.

Someone behind me murmured, 'And where the hell does she think her fortune came from if not from commerce?'

The auctioneer, however, had begun hustling everyone off the premises.

Elise whispered, 'We'd better go, too. She won't part with anything, not even a scrap of that glass.'

I took no notice of her hand on my arm. My movement towards the Comtesse was quite involuntary. I felt as if I were in a dream as I let the men push past me. I must have been within six feet of Paul's mother, when she seemed to see Elise and me for the first time.

'Why do you not go?'

'Of course, Madame,' Elise said. 'Only, you see, we didn't come to bid for the pictures, only for the stained glass. It is so badly broken that it doesn't keep out the weather. If we might buy it from you and then proper windows were put in here, they would protect the pictures . . . I mean . . .' Her courage had failed her.

'Who are these young women?'

'One is Miss Helston from the Villa Daphnis.'

I heard a sharp indrawn breath. I began to say, 'We are both – '

I was interrupted. 'Which one? . . . Which one . . .?' she murmured, looking at us, first one, then the other.

Max Lambert stood directly in front of me. I waited tensely for the Comtesse to speak. With the light from the open doorway behind her, she could see my face far more clearly than I could see hers. I took a step forward.

She turned with an amazing swiftness and with her hand on the arm of the younger woman walked out through the door.

I started forward. Max held me back. 'I shouldn't if I were you,' he said.

'But I must talk to her.'

'Haven't you done enough damage?' he said and strode to the door, went through it, and closed it in my face.

I heard Elise say, 'What on earth was all that about? What damage have we done? All I did was to ask about the stained glass. How did that man know our name? And what did the Comtesse mean by "which one"?'

I didn't answer her. I almost ran across the hall, my steps too noisy, breaking the stillness that had now fallen on the place. Outside the auctioneer was surrounded by men protesting that such prizes were to be left to rot and moulder in an ancient hall.

'Let's get home.' I climbed into the car.

Elise shot a longing look back at the cluster of men at the gate. 'You don't think that perhaps the Comtesse will change her mind?'

I started the engine, slid the car in gear, and edged out of the queue. 'Did she look to you like someone who changed her mind?'

'N-no.'

'We've lost the glass and that's that.'

But it wasn't the lovely crimson and sapphire glass which held my mind as we went home, it was the way Max Lambert had stopped me following the Comtesse. I had no proof, of course, but I had a feeling that she had expected me to follow her out, perhaps to go to the house. I was quite certain she wanted to know the girl her son had loved. And Max Lambert had seen to it that we didn't meet.

## CHAPTER SEVEN

Francis had been disappointed that we couldn't have the stained glass from the Monk's Hall. But two mornings later he was offered a supply from an old villa in Carcassonne which was being demolished. He had just finished bargaining on the telephone with the demolition people when the bell rang again.

'That's probably Avignon to ask about their panel.' He

listened, then said, 'I'll call her,' and held the receiver out to me.

I perched on the window sill and heard the line crackle. Then a voice asked, 'Miss Helston?'

'Yes.'

'Miss *Rachel* Helston?'

'Speaking.'

'I am telephoning for the Comtesse d'Arachenne. She wishes you to call on her at ten o'clock this morning.'

I was given no opportunity to question or to refuse the elaborately formal command. The man rang off.

Elise said, 'That was brief and to the point.'

'It was.' I knew that they were waiting for me to tell them who the caller was. I said nothing. But I was suddenly in a state of confusion. I longed, hoped, yet dreaded, to meet Paul's mother.

It was a quarter to ten by the clock on the wall. I left the pottery and went to change. I was still tense. Paul's mother. My friend? My enemy? The fact that she had summoned me gave me comfort. Paul must have told her about me, after all, and because of our shared grief she wanted to meet me.

I remembered how, in the Monk's Hall, she had looked from Elise to me, murmuring, 'Which one? Which one?' And now we were to meet and talk together. And Max Lambert could do nothing about it this time.

The mistral was blowing. It was my companion as I walked past the olive grove and turned into the long elm avenue that led to Sonnengarde.

It was not the tall servant who awaited me at the front door, but Lambert. He stood framed in the ancient stone, watching me approach. Of course he wasn't waiting for me. He was probably going out, but I wished he'd just leave the door open and go. At the sight of him I was apprehensive again; his steady gaze made me nervous.

'Good morning, Miss Helston.'

'Good morning.' I walked up the steps and added defiantly, 'This time I'm not trespassing. The Comtesse sent for me.'

'I know.'

He stood aside and I entered the house. I was in a lofty vaulted hall, shadowed and sombre, hung with tapestries. A huge fireplace was flanked by two bronzes of a man and a woman. Somewhere a dog barked and was silenced. I remembered that Paul told me his mother owned a saluki, 'So beautiful and so stupid!'

Max Lambert followed me into the house and closed the door. 'You're a few minutes early.'

I pretended to be absorbed in a tapestry of fawns and shepherdesses. 'Have you told the Comtesse your version of what happened at Maladieu?'

He said quickly as if my question had startled him, 'Did you think I wouldn't?'

'Why should I care, since you're so wrong about it?' I swung around and faced him with more apparent courage than I felt. 'Well, have you – told her, I mean?'

'You want me to tell you so that you'll be prepared?'

'I don't give a damn. I spoke the truth so there's nothing to be prepared for.'

'You have courage,' he said, 'or audacity.'

I suspected that every pointed thing he said to me had a purpose – probably to upset me, to needle me into a retort that would give me away. Thank heaven I was not guilty, or he would have trapped me ten times over, for I was no good at the swift answer, the apt phrase.

Max's eyes were steady, but I refused to let mine flicker. I had to stand up to this man, to make at least an outward show of courage. I knew that he was too strong for me and I did not trust him.

Yet, I managed to pull myself together before nerves overwhelmed me. It was the Comtesse's opinion of me that was important. I turned on my heel, affecting dignity. But when you are small and a man so tall, it is difficult to look superior. The little woman has to resort to subtlety, and I was not a subtle person. 'Can't you see,' I said shakenly, 'this isn't the time for anger?'

'What do you want? My hand in friendship?'

Again the deliberate needling. I wheeled around and faced him again. 'Don't you know that anger is infectious? I don't want to catch it – not because I care any longer what you think, but because I've enough to feel without adding anger. Can't you understand? But you don't want to, do you?'

'You're right,' he said savagely. 'I don't want to understand. But God help me, I can't help it.'

'You mean you can't help believing some circumstantial evidence against me? You wouldn't make a very good lawyer, Mr Lambert.'

'I *am* a lawyer.'

I couldn't take my eyes off him as he turned away from me. There was a certain grace about his movements, pride in the angle of his head. I thought bitterly: Appearances? Oh, heaven, how appearances fool one! If I'd met him casually, at a party, I'd have said he was kind and quiet and just.

I sat down on a cushionless seat under a tapestry. When I leaned back, the elaborate carving of the chair dug into my spine. I said, 'It is perfectly safe to leave me here, Mr Lambert. I shan't steal anything. I'm not a thief as well.'

He walked away without another word.

I had no idea how long I remained in the high, magnificent hall. I stayed as I was, quiet and uncomfortable on the carved chair until the servant who had shut me out on the dreadful night of Paul's death appeared silently from the arched shadows.

'If you will come with me, Mademoiselle . . .'

I rose and followed the man. The room into which I walked was as dim as the hall. I had an impression, however, of the same splendour, although there was not light enough to see anything clearly.

Madame la Comtesse stood by one of the shuttered windows.

'Leave us, Morven.'

The door closed so quietly that I didn't hear the latch click. I was alone with Paul's mother.

'Mademoiselle?'

'I am Rachel Helston.'

'We met when you had the impertinence to come to the Monk's Hall.'

'We were all misled over that, Madame. I apologize.'

I did not know how much she could see of me, but she gave me a long look. Then she moved to a carved desk, flicking an envelope across the leather surface with a gesture which suggested that it pained her to touch it.

'Read that.' Her tone and her manner were peremptory.

I walked over to the desk and picked up the envelope. I had to tilt it towards the slits of light slanting through one of the shutters to see that it was addressed to me.

Someone had opened it.

My hand shook as I took out the sheet of embossed notepaper:

Ma petite,

How shall I begin? Here in this moment when I am wanting you so badly? Or in that other mood when the idea of marriage terrifies me? Because that is the truth. I do not want to be tied to a wife.

To tell you this in a letter is cowardice, but I never pretended to be brave. You have every right to be hurt and angry, yet I think you are also forgiving. Perhaps you will forgive me.

Paul.

My first wild thought was: *How do I know Paul wrote this? I've never seen his handwriting. In Paris we were so often together that he never needed to write. This is a fake.*

'This is a fake,' I heard myself say.

'If you think that, then you are very foolish. Such a thing could be so easily proved. I can show you Paul's handwriting on a document. Do you wish me to do so?' Her hand went towards a drawer of the desk.

The room was silent. Not even a clock ticked. Outside the tall, darkened windows no bird sang. There was so much I wanted to say to Paul's mother, but the atmosphere in the room was so close to hatred that it numbed me.

Mechanically I folded the letter and put it back in the envelope. The silence became impossible. I had to do something; say something – and there was nothing to say.

Oh, but there was. It came to me in a flash. 'But Paul didn't send this letter. So . . .?'

'If you think he changed his mind and merely forgot to tear it up, I must disillusion you. That it was not delivered was my servant, Morven's, fault. Paul gave it to him on the morning of the day he died. But in all the agitation of moving into the château, Morven put it in his pocket and forgot it.' She came closer to me. Hands clasped over the great jewel that hung at her waist by a golden chain, she said slowly, 'Perhaps if that letter had been delivered, my son would be alive today.'

'I – I don't understand.'

'Oh, I think you do. *Perfectly.*'

Her tone with its cold insolence stung me. 'Perhaps, Madame, you will tell me what I am supposed to understand.'

'That knowing nothing of the letter, you went to Maladieu to meet him. I can only think that so far as my son was concerned, he hoped you were so besotted that you would take a chance on his being there and go in spite of what he had written. That you would – er – compromise. Now do you understand?'

'I do.' My voice was clear and sharp, though my limbs

trembled. 'You believe he went to Maladieu, hoping that I would agree to sleep with him – to have anything rather than nothing.'

'So you went there. You forced yourself into his car and, in your rage that he had no intention of marrying you, you quarrelled with him. You seized the wheel of the car and drove it into the wall – '

' – and managed not to get even a scratch myself?'

She had an answer even for that. 'Oh, but you knew what you were going to do. You were prepared. My brother-in-law, Artois, has examined the car, which was towed to a garage in Issandre. He tells me that the passenger side was quite undamaged.'

I opened my lips twice before any sound came. The third time I managed to say, 'I've told you the truth. It's you who are telling me lies . . .' I took a step back and my leg touched a chair. I sank into it because I was shaking all over.

'I did not ask you to be seated, Mademoiselle.'

I shot up as though she had struck me.

'For some reason' – she looked me up and down with deliberate scepticism – 'I suppose you attracted Paul. Perhaps you are very clever and you know how to play with a man's desires – although to look at you, I would not have thought you capable of such subtlety. God forgive you for choosing my son for your ambitions!'

I should have had more pride than to stay and listen to her insults. But something about her hypnotized me. Or perhaps it was a deep-down pity for her and a mad, wild hope that I might find some words that would pierce her hatred of me and make her understand.

'You suggest I was clever?' I said. 'Is one ever clever when one loves?'

She ignored the question. 'On the other hand, perhaps you did have an affair with Paul; and perhaps you hoped to blackmail him.'

The pity I felt stopped the furious wounding protest I was on the point of hurling at her. Instead, I said, appalled, 'You really do credit me with being an opportunist, don't you, Madame? It's a pity you are such a bad judge of character.'

She was implacable. Her head with its white coil of hair was lifted; her fingers played again with the crimson jewel on the black dress. 'Did you have an affair with my son in Paris?'

'If you mean did I go to bed with him . . .'

'It is a revolting expression, but yes, that is what I mean.'

'Then I didn't.'

'Ah! Then as I say, you were clever. You kept his interest and your own – er – mystery. That is how you hoped to hold him.' Her voice quickened; her breathing became heavy. 'You saw yourself, after my death, as the new Comtesse d'Arachenne, didn't you? *Didn't* you, Mademoiselle? Go on, admit it. There are just the two of us here. You may as well indulge yourself in a little honesty.'

I managed to hold on to my self-control only by gripping the carved top of the desk. I had to try to understand. Facing me was a distraught and ailing woman, half out of her mind with grief.

I tried to speak quietly. 'I have had a very democratic upbringing, Madame. I have no interest in titles. The whole thing was far more simple. I loved Paul.'

'Love and hate – the reverse side of the same coin.' She turned her head away, and I could see her profile with its angular, almost masculine lines. Was this the mother of my gay, irresponsible Paul?

I leaned against the table, my heart thudding, and prayed that she would dismiss me or, if not, that I would have the strength in my legs to walk across that vast stretch of floor to the door.

I said, wanting these to be my last words before I steadied my shaking knees and left her, 'Please believe me, Madame. Paul and I did not quarrel up at Maladieu. We did not meet there. He was – he was dead when I arrived.'

'I do not believe you.'

To be predeterminedly disbelieved is something against which there is no defence. Neither words nor actions were of any use. So, somehow, I must escape. Standing there in the moment's hideous silence, I steeled my limbs. Then I pushed myself away from the desk. The room was enormous and the door too distant. I seemed to walk and walk and, as in a nightmare escape was as far away as ever.

I heard the rustle of silk behind me. A shutter swung back and the room was filled with light. I looked over my shoulder, but I didn't stop making for the door. Something on the desk, long like a dagger, sparkled with crimson and sapphire light.

'Mademoiselle.'

I paused and waited.

'You have wasted so much time in protests. I gave you a chance to admit your guilt. As you did not, I will tell you that I know you were with Paul at Maladieu.' Her lips barely moved. 'A man – a complete stranger – told us so.'

'Who?'

'The innkeeper at the Hostelrie Sainte Bérénice told my brother-in-law that he had seen you with Paul in the car. He also said you came later in a shocked state to telephone for help.'

'I did go to him for help. And he can tell the police that when they question him.'

'Oh, they've questioned him already. But he hasn't involved you. In fact, Mademoiselle, he told the Inspector that he saw no one in the car when my son drove past the Hostelrie.'

The light blazing through the window shone full on me. It was like a spotlight they throw on criminals in films. It hurt my eyes, but I tried not to shut them. Instead, I fixed her with a dazzled stare. 'But I understood you to say that he told your brother-in-law he saw me in the car?'

'That is correct.'

'Then why did he tell the police a different story?'

She didn't answer; she had no need to. I said, unbelievingly, 'You forced him to, didn't you? *Didn't* you? Why? Surely not – '

'To save you? That's the last thing I'll do.' Her lips were so tight drawn that her mouth was a pencil line. 'I persuaded Gaston Bigorne to deny he saw you in the car because I have no intention of allowing any scandal to be attached to my dead son's name. We are not an ordinary family, Mademoiselle. We have a great name, a great tradition and, because of our business, a reputation to keep. For myself, I would rather be dead than disgraced. That is why you have got off lightly – *with the police*.'

'Then I shall go to them and tell them the truth.'

'I do not think you will, Mademoiselle. On the one hand, you will risk a charge of manslaughter against you. On the other, if they believe M. Bigorne (and I would do all I could to see that they did), you would be accused of fabricating a story, obstructing the law in order to gain notoriety. A girl who had a sordid affair and wanted the whole world to know.'

'There was nothing in my relationship with Paul that I wouldn't have the whole world knowing.'

'Ah!' In the vivid morning light she appeared much older than her voice, which had been clear and firm, had made her seem. Her face was crisscrossed with fine lines; her skin thin as tissue paper. Only her hands and her eyes were strong. I watched her walk across the room to the window and back again to face me. 'Perhaps you have an idea that a newspaper will buy the story of your intrigue with the son of a great house. I believe there are certain papers that pay well for such stories. But you will never have that opportunity. I have great influence, Mademoiselle. Try to make money out of this and I shall break you.'

I said, 'You appal me, Madame!'

'I would rather I shamed you.'

I said, 'If you were given proof that I was not there when the car crashed, then perhaps it would be you who would be shamed, Madame.'

'And where do you imagine you could get such proof?'

'The man who took Paul to hospital. It's possible he knew I'd only just come on to the scene. If I could find him – '

'And even if he could prove to be an ally, which I doubt, how do you think you will find him? He even left the hospital before he could be asked for his name.'

'If he did that, then the police will be looking for him.'

'I think not. There are so many tourists and businessmen in a hurry. It appears to be a clear-cut case of a skid causing the accident – '

'And – and that's what they say?'

'Of course. No, Mademoiselle, you will not find your stranger. It is probably as well, for he might not be your ally. He, too, might have seen you in the car and have been a witness to the accident. It is bitter justice, Mademoiselle, that you do not find him. But for Paul's sake, the story police will accept is that the car skidded on the wet road. Only you and I know differently.'

'If there was someone with Paul, then find her, Madame. *Find her*, since you are bent on punishment.'

'I have found her.'

I felt that if I spoke another word to this small, cold woman, I would choke.

I turned and looked at the door. Somehow, this time, I had to reach it. My feet moved soundlessly over the carpet, my hands fumbled with the gilt handle.

I was nearly safe; nearly . . .

'Be assured, Mademoiselle Helston, that you are not escaping as easily as it would seem. I shall find a way to punish you. And I shall see to it that it will be far more bitter and will hurt you more deeply than any physical violence.'

I gripped the handle of the half-open door, dragged it wide, and stepped into the dark, vaulted hall.

Her voice followed me. 'And I do not make idle threats.'

I looked straight ahead of me as if I hadn't heard. The manservant, Morven, was in the hall. Without looking at me, he walked to the huge double doors and opened them with a mannered flourish. I went like a sleepwalker into the sunlight.

## CHAPTER EIGHT

The hot, scented air; the play of light and shade on the trees; the sense of space worked a miracle.

I had had an ugly interview with a woman crazed by loss. Because I was shocked and nervous in her presence, she had intimidated me. Now, I could see the meeting with the Comtesse d'Arachenne in its true perspective. If I were her age, how would I react if I lost my only son in an accident? Would I be reasonable? Wouldn't I hit back at life?

How could she possibly harm me? Since she was at pains to keep secret the fact that Paul and I had known each other, she had destroyed the weapon with which she might have fought me: '. . . I shall find a way to punish you . . . it will be far more bitter and will hurt you more deeply than any physical violence.' She had used power and harshness in her voice as a shield to hide her own weakness. Since our lives crossed nowhere and we were not likely to meet again, she was in no position to hurt me.

The heat of the morning made me turn for shade into the olive grove. There, the real shock of the morning hit me: Paul had never really loved me.

Had I received his letter, I would not have gone to Maladieu; not have experienced the dreadful shock of seeing him lying dead; not have been accused of his death. The man called Morven had been, all unwittingly, the cause of my ordeal this morning.

Yet the reason for it went further back, to the time when I had refused to sleep with Paul. The swift instinct that had made me reject Fontainebleau on that last night had been correct. Had I gone, that would have been the end of the matter. Paul had talked of marriage in order to get me to that room with the blue silk hangings. Like the spoiled charmer he was, he wanted frantically and immediately what he could not have.

I faced the stark truth and it increased my own pain. I'd known all along what he was like. He had never deceived me. 'I'm spoiled,' he had said. 'Indulged. Idle. I like my own way and I'll get it by fair means or foul.'

I believed now that, had we not met by accident outside the Château, I would never have seen him again. But, in my love-blind artlessness, I had forced him to stop. And, perhaps, afraid that I might call on him at the Château, he agreed to meet me in the Hall of the Seigneurs.

If he did not know that the letter, written probably in panic that I might trap him into marriage, had not reached me, why had he gone to Maladieu? Had he just taken a chance that I'd be there, hoping that I might compromise and agree to sleep with him and perhaps, then, be paid off? The blood rushed to my face at the cheap climax.

My father had been right, of course. If I told him of the existence of Paul's last letter, I knew what he would say, 'Well, there you are! You're only one of thousands it has happened to.'

I came out of the olive grove and stood for a moment in the sharp sunlight. Immediately to my left, the jagged crenelations of Maladieu rose to the sky. The sun's heat pricked my forehead; I felt the hot stones burn through my sandals. But I didn't move.

Up there, in the narrow winding street that led to the ruined rock-castle, was the Hostelrie. I remembered the old man who had owned it until a few months ago. Monsieur Jacques had known us as children. He would not have mistaken the girl in the car for me.

I had never met the new owner before last night and quite frankly I never wanted to see him again. But I intended to. I had questions to ask him. And immediately. For if I waited and thought about it, I would not have the courage to face that bold, sly man.

As I went towards the house, I saw Elise wheeling the coffee trolley across the garden. I avoided her, ran around to the back door and told Peppina that if anyone wanted me, I would be out for a while. She asked me what she should prepare for lunch.

'Oh, *ratatouille*,' I said. 'Monsieur George always wants it when he comes. If you haven't eggplants, Elise will go into town for some.'

The cars were missing from the garage. I guessed that Father, having just delivered a new book, was giving himself a holiday and had gone to meet his cronies at the Café Chinois. Someone had also taken the runabout. So I would have to walk.

I was lucky. Monsieur Cambé, who managed the vineyards, was coming up the hill. He sat like a fat Buddha on the cart he insisted on using instead of the new car he had bought recently. He loved horses and his pony was a thoroughbred. The cart had red-painted wheels, gay as a gypsy caravan. Issandre said that Monsieur Cambé was eccentric.

He stopped when he saw me. 'Ah, Mademoiselle Helston! Can I take you somewhere?'

'If you are passing Maladieu – '

'I am. I am going to Espine to put in an order for a new vat.' He reached down and helped me up to the seat next to him. 'You are going to Maladieu? That was a terrible thing that happened there the other night.'

I didn't want to talk about it. I asked carefully, 'Did the storm do much damage to the vines?'

'A little. But not too badly. They are sturdy, my vines. But up at Maladieu – '

'I hear that a tree fell across the main road to Arles.'

'Ah, yes, and a car hit it. But no one was hurt. Not like the dreadful thing that happened up there.' He looked towards the grey peaks.

All the way, as we clopped along, I chatted to keep him off the subject of the accident. Also, I knew he was longing to know why I was going there this morning. Only tourists visited the place, with guides to tell them its dark, troubled history. Or lovers who had their own reasons for wanting to meet in secret.

At the narrow opening to Maladieu, I got down, thanked Monsieur Cambé, and started to walk. It was unbelievably hot and the high, jagged rocks closed in on me.

Gaston Bigorne was sitting on a bench in the shade of a nettle tree. The day's tourists had not yet arrived and he was alone in the garden.

He sprang to his feet when he saw me. 'Ah, Mademoiselle.'

I avoided the hand he held out.

He gave me his sly smile. 'Be seated, please. Next to me. Here, this bench is comfortable and in the shade. I will fetch you an aperitif. A dry Martini? A Dubonnet? You have only to name it. It is my great pleasure, Mademoiselle, that you came.'

I avoided the bench, pulled one of the little iron chairs from a table, and sat on it, facing him. 'I don't want an aperitif, thank you. I just want you to take a good look at me.' I met his eyes coldly. '*Look at me*, Monsieur. Do you honestly believe that I was the girl you saw in Monsieur d'Arachenne's car?'

He made a finicky little gesture of distaste. 'But, Mademoiselle, on such a lovely morning, do we have to talk of tragedy?'

'Yes, we do. You say you believe it was I – '

'I do not say anything more. It is over. It is finished.' He sat on the bench, hunched like a huge bear, and his eyes went slowly over me. 'We forget it. We talk about you. You have come here – '

'I have come to find out why you told Monsieur Artois d'Arachenne that it was I you saw in the car. Yet you gave the police a different story. You said you did not see anyone.'

'To protect you, Mademoiselle. Of course, to protect you.'

'And you've just thought *that* one out!'

'I haven't. I swear – '

'Don't then.'

'But I can't be certain, you understand? I can't be certain it was you.'

'If the people at the Château had asked you to swear that it was I you saw, then you would,' I retorted. 'How much did they pay you to say what they wanted you to say?'

Outraged pride swept across his face. I was no longer someone with whom he might pass the boring hours of the morning until the tourists came. He no longer looked at my legs, but at my face – and what he saw he didn't like. I hadn't intended him to.

He drew himself up, pulled his stomach in, and said, 'I think, Mademoiselle, we have nothing further to say to each other. The tragic incident is not my concern and it is closed. Good morning.' He bowed.

I got up and took a few steps from him. 'True,' I said. 'We have nothing more to say to each other. When lies are told, we reach an *impasse*.'

I walked out of the garden, past the ugly iron tables and the tattered yellow umbrellas and the postcard stands. The grass I walked on was like dry green matted hair. Even the sign sticking out from the wall, 'Hostelrie Sainte Bérénice: Café; Citron; Glacés et Chocolat,' badly needed paint. . . . How much *had* the Comtesse paid Gaston Bigorne to swear he had never seen me?

I glanced down the street to the few cave shops that were

already open and awaiting the trailing tourists from the motor coaches. Then I turned my head and saw Max Lambert. He was sitting on a rocky ledge and I felt sure he was waiting for me. In the sunlight, his hair looked a dark beech-leaf colour; and the contours of his face, etched against the rock, were harsh and haggard.

A silly, hilarious little quotation sprang to my mind. 'And the Devil came too . . .' It didn't amuse me. In fact, I shuddered.

The man stood in my path, holding out his hand. For a moment, I imagined he was offering a greeting. But the idea was as unlikely as his waving a green olive branch at me would have been.

I could have turned and run. I didn't. I waited until he came within two feet of me. Then I saw that his hand was closed into a fist.

He opened it slowly. Something spilled out, spreading over his fingers. 'Take it.' He dropped it over my wrists.

It was a mantilla of lovely hand-made lace. I stood for too long, looking down at it.

Max whipped it from me, his eyes resting coldly on my face. 'Well?'

'Some tourist must have lost it,' I said. 'Leave it in one of the shops in case she comes back for it.'

'No, not a tourist.'

'What do you mean?'

'It's yours, isn't it?'

'I've never seen it before in my life.'

'Oh, come. You were wearing it when you were in the car. But when I saw you later your head was bare.'

I said sharply, 'When did you think you saw me again?'

'You don't intend to be trapped by words, do you?' he said dryly. 'I don't *think* I saw you. I know. I was on my way back to the Château. I saw a girl running towards the house by the olive grove. I was going to stop and give her a lift because she was stumbling as if she were exhausted, but she turned in at the gate. I didn't connect you at the time with the accident at Maladieu. You were bare-headed. I remember the moon shining on your hair. You lost this' – he ran the mantilla lightly through his fingers – 'in your haste to escape, didn't you? I found it the following morning, lying near where the crash occurred.'

'I wore a mackintosh that night,' I said, 'and it had a hood. I can show it to you.'

'You could show me any mackintosh and swear that it was the one you wore that night. But it wouldn't be proof.'

'And you can't prove that this piece of lace is mine.'

'No, I can't.'

'Any woman going out in that storm would have worn something over her head. But if you want to believe it was I, then there is nothing I can do.' The charming thing in his hand could have been bought by anyone in Paris, or Orleans, or even Issandre. He was using it to confuse me, to make me think his discovery more important than it was.

I leaned against the burning rock. It didn't matter what Max Lambert thought. I didn't care if he hated me for the rest of his life. He didn't belong to Issandre. One day soon he would go away and I would never have to see him or think of him again.

'You've had a wasted journey, haven't you?' he said. 'Gaston Bigorne has been suitably silenced. Whether I approve or not is not the question. The fact remains, you are lucky.'

To strike this man would be stupid, melodramatic and futile. Yet I had to clench my hand to stop it reaching out to that dark, accusing face. 'You want to make me so mad that I'll lose my head and say something that will incriminate me. That's it, isn't it?'

'Perhaps.'

'You even admit it.'

'I need the truth, Miss Helston.'

A kind of impotent rage took hold of me. I forgot where I was; I lost sight of the little cave shops from which anyone might be watching us. Blazing, I faced Max Lambert.

'Must I say it all again? *Must* I? All right, I will. Perhaps it takes a long time for the truth to register with you.'

Max leaned lightly against the sunburned rock. 'Well?'

'According to you, I was the girl in the car because Paul was your friend and you want someone to be blamed for his death. I don't quite see the logic of that, but perhaps you're one of those people who want everything explained, neatly tied up, and it doesn't matter whether it's the truth or not. Is that the lawyer in you? Are some lawyers like that? Explain away anyhow, so long as you have an explanation. I suppose that's vanity. If so, then heaven help anyone facing you in a court of law. You'd find the angels guilty if there were no one else. All right! Suspect me if that's the way you want it. Why should I care?' I stopped for breath.

Max Lambert turned his head and looked about him. I had

expected him to defend himself and his profession. He did neither, and that angered me even more.

'I suppose you'll be leaving Issandre soon. Well, you can take the truth with you – or leave it. *The truth*, Mr Lambert.' Suddenly aware that I was shouting and that I must be audible to every cave shopkeeper hiding behind his display stand of postcards, I lowered my voice. 'The truth is that I loved Paul. Whatever he did to me, I would never have tried to harm him. If I had been there when the accident occurred, I would not have run away and left a man lying injured on the ground. I wouldn't have done that to my worst enemy. Not even – to you. And now if you don't believe me, I – I – '

The last words were shaken out of me, for Max had seized my wrists and pulled me towards him. 'Believe you? I wish to God I could!'

The heightening mistral whipped my hair across my face. Max pushed it back, holding it against my head. I felt his hand against my temple, hot and dry and heavy. He didn't take his eyes from mine.

My heart seemed to rise and beat in my throat. A sensation so powerful that it shook me, swept over me. I said to myself: *This is fear. It's a new sensation for you; that's why you don't recognize it.*

I jerked my head away. 'It doesn't matter any longer what anyone thinks of me.' My voice sank to a whisper. 'Paul is dead. Damn you. Damn you for making that harder!'

'Do you think you're the only one who cared for him? What about his mother? And what about me?'

'Well, what about you?'

He said in a flat, unsentimental voice, 'I loved him, too. Our families had been friends for a generation; he was like my younger brother. So, you see, you aren't the only one who mourns him.'

'But you aren't being accused of causing his death. *I* am. I'm the one who is supposed to have hated him when he no longer wanted to marry me. You know that part, don't you – about the letter he wrote to me that I never received?'

He nodded.

I cried, 'So what do you call it, you and the Comtesse d'Arachenne, manslaughter? Or – or murder?'

He answered me in a gentler voice, 'Heaven knows, I don't believe you meant to kill him. You couldn't – '

'Then why are you hounding me? For that's what it is, isn't it? You follow me here – '

'I didn't. I came, like you, to see Gaston Bigorne.'

'Why?'

'You ask a lot of questions.'

'And so do you. But like a prosecuting council, you expect all the answers. I'm to have none.'

I was getting nowhere. I felt so low that I had no more heart for talking, for trying to make this implacable man believe me. I turned away.

I heard Max Lambert say, 'I wish I knew . . .'

I'd almost forgotten who had spoken last and what had been said. 'You wish you knew what?'

'What you know,' he said.

The road downhill was steep. I walked away from Lambert, going carelessly, kicking up the rough stones. One or two of the cave shopkeepers knew me and greeted me and I suppose I threw them a greeting back.

To know that one is innocent is never enough. To the Comtesse, to Max Lambert, I had lied to save myself a court enquiry; perhaps a charge of manslaughter. But that had been before I had learned that there was no question of the d'Arachenne family permitting such publicity. According to them I was lying for a different reason now – because I feared them. Everything was against me. Paul's letter; my presence at Maladieu; even the fact that I had put the hood of my mackintosh over my head for protection from the rain.

If there hadn't been a storm, the girl in Paul's car would probably have been bare-headed and her face would have been clearer. No one would have mistaken her for me. If there hadn't been a storm the road would not have been dangerous and Paul would not have skidded into the cliff face. . . . Skidded?

I would never know now and I would go through the rest of my life aware that two people believed in my guilt.

I was a good walker and the thirty-minute downhill journey from Maladieu would normally have been nothing to me. This morning, however, I arrived home with a feeling that I had taken part in a marathon.

Nikki was in the garden. 'Catch!'

I caught the red ball he threw at me.

'Papa is angry with me,' he said.

'Oh, Nikki, what have you done?' It was all so normal that the other might have been a dream.

Nikki came up to me, took the ball, and bounced it. 'I only went and sat in the car and pretend to drive.'

'And you touched things?'

'We-ll.' He gave me a sideways glance.

'You know you mustn't.'

'Papa said next time you all go on a picnic, I've got to stay behind with Peppina.'

'Well, then, darling, I'm afraid you must. You've been told about playing with the car, haven't you?'

'But you won't let me not go to the picnic, will you? *Will* you, Rachel?'

'If Father says –'

His mouth began to turn down at the corners. 'But you can *make* him let me go. You can, can't you, Rachel?'

I had taken the place of my mother in his world. I could do anything; I could perform miracles. I said briskly, 'Well, there's no talk of a picnic for some weeks, anyway. This is the busy season in the pottery. Come and let's see if Peppina has made any ice cream.'

His hand crept into mine. Swiftly I bent down and pulled him towards me.

## CHAPTER NINE

It was my father who, coming home after a morning session at the Café Chinois, told me that there would be no inquest on Paul.

'The Commissaire decided against it. He says it is obviously a straightforward case of a car skidding in a storm, but he does censure whoever the man was who took young d'Arachenne to hospital. It's usual to leave one's name, and he just slipped off. There's to be no autopsy, either,' he added.

I sat, fitting pieces of silver tessarae into the spine of the fish in my Pisces design.

We were alone in the pottery. Father touched my shoulder. 'You heard what I said?'

'Yes.'

'So, you must now try and put the whole thing out of your mind. It was distressing, but it's over.'

The door behind us opened and Elise came in. Father walked away, whistling loudly. His attempts at secrecy were sometimes a little heavily laid on.

What most disturbed me was that I was unable to answer

strong and recurring questions. What difference did it make that Paul had written me that letter? What did I feel most strongly? Like a ghost, the thought, the questions haunted me. But I was in far too emotional a state to know the answer yet. . . . And who was the girl in the car?

Perhaps these questions would never be answered. In any case, the haunting had to be conquered. I tried to do that during the next few days by flinging myself into every task, every chore, with all my abundant energy. I wanted to tire myself out.

One morning I saw my father go down the drive. My first thought was: Has he looked at himself in the long bathroom mirror and decided that he's developing a paunch and needs exercise? It was such an unusual sight to see him striding towards the gate that I just stood staring. He had never before gone more than a hundred yards on his own two feet. It was a joke among us that, if he hadn't thought he would have looked ridiculous, he would have bought himself a scooter to take him to and from the studio.

Half an hour later he returned.

A fresh supply of silicone polish which we used for the mosaics had arrived and I was taking it across to the pottery.

I called to Father that we were just going to have coffee. 'Come and join us.'

'I've just had some of the finest coffee I've ever tasted. And I drank it out of a priceless old Minton cup' – he loved dramatic effects and his smile was broad and triumphant – 'with the Comtesse d'Arachenne,' he said.

'You've been to the Château?'

'I have. I was sent for. The Comtesse has a proposition; one that couldn't suit me better. She wants me to write a history of the d'Arachenne family.'

The news hit me in the pit of my stomach. 'But she *can't* . . . after what's happened. She wouldn't suggest such a thing. Father, I don't believe . . .' Words failed me.

The smile froze on my father's face. 'She was quite serious about it. And I've every intention of accepting the commission,' he said stiffly. 'She's offering big money.'

The sense of foreboding did not come quietly. It leaped at me. 'Father, don't. Please don't take on this work. Say you're too busy. Say you're not interested. Say you're tired at the moment – after all, you've only just finished a book.'

His eyes had a way of darkening when he was angry. 'How

do you think we're going to live if I turn down commitments? And come to that, why should I?'

As if it were the complete answer I said, 'Paul.'

'Just because you had some affair in Paris with her son is not, to me, a reason for my refusing the Comtesse's commission. Don't be silly, Rachel.'

I had to try and make him understand. 'There's something I haven't told you. I didn't want to talk about it to anyone – it's too horrible. But now you'll have to know and then you'll see that I'm not being unreasonable.' I went on to tell him how the Comtesse had sent for me and the things she said. 'She believes I caused Paul's death. She wants to punish me. She said so.'

He began picking leaves off the honeysuckle bush. To him, I was behaving like a boring child. His understanding of people, which could be so wide and generous, narrowed when he and his own welfare were involved. 'And how in the name of goodness do you think my writing the history of the d'Arachenne family can punish you?'

'I – I don't know.'

'Of course you don't; nor do I. That outburst of hers was the wild talk of an overwrought woman. Her son had just been killed and she took it out on the person she could hurt most – you. It's the kind of thing some people do in blind grief. But she's over it now. I can tell you that this morning she was an extremely poised and intelligent woman. She even talked calmly about Paul. He was the last of the direct line of d'Arachennes, she said. The others, the uncles and cousins and nephews were, as she put it, mere side branches of the great tree. That is why this is the moment to write their history – from beginning to end.'

He fidgeted, obviously wanting to get away. 'It was a bad experience for you. I know that. But it's over. The verdict, as I told you, was that Paul's car skidded on a wet road. There was no autopsy; the funeral is over and the matter closed. Don't worry.' He took comfort from my silence and smiled at me. 'You don't have to feel squeamish about meeting the Comtesse. She won't be coming over here. I shall go there occasionally to study the portraits and perhaps have one or two of them photographed for the book. Otherwise Max Lambert, who'll be staying at the Château for a time, will bring the material over. There's a mass of it, so I'll need it by degrees – letters, manuscripts, photographs, drawings. The family goes back to the thirteenth century.'

I should have known it was never any use arguing with Father. I said in a faint, hopeless voice, 'You *won't* understand, will you?'

'My dear girl, I understood people and their motives and their ways long before you were born. Paul d'Arachenne never intended to marry you, you know.'

I said quickly, because I didn't want to talk about Paul, 'Why did the Comtesse choose you and not a French historian to write this book?'

I'd touched a raw spot in his pride. He said offendedly, 'It seems, from that remark, that outsiders rate my work more highly than my family.'

'I didn't mean it that way. You know I didn't.'

He lifted his huge shoulders in a shrug. 'Dominick has been asking where you are. I left him being questioned by Nikki about what he conducted. Nikki probably thinks he drives a train or something. That child has the mind of a four-year-old.'

'He'll grow up suddenly,' I said. 'He's alert enough.'

'Well, you'd better go and rescue our guest.'

'Father, be kind to Nikki.'

He looked at me in utter amazement. 'Good God, what do you think I am, an ogre?'

'Of course not. But he's afraid of you. You remember Mother said he must have had a terrible time when he was very little and that it might take years to erase fear.'

'All I'm doing is to try to make a real boy of him. Why the hell doesn't he want to ride and swim and why is he always near the bottom of his class at school?'

'Be patient with him. I've a feeling there's great talent in Nikki somewhere.'

'I'd like to see it.'

'You will.'

'Well, for the moment your job is to go and stop him worrying Dominick.'

'He likes talking to Nikki. He told me so.' I picked up the carton of silicone from the seat where I'd dumped it. 'I'll take this to the pottery first,' I said. 'They're waiting for it.'

I didn't want to rescue Dominick. Much as I liked him, he was beginning to get under my feet in the house. At first I'd welcomed his constant companionship because it stopped me from brooding in my own company. But the family had begun to notice and to call him, with typical family unimaginativeness, 'Rachel's Shadow.'

I was caught, however. Dominick was coming towards me.

'You're not going to be busy all the morning, are you?'

'Probably. Why?'

'George has gone up to the vineyards. He says when he comes here he always spends a few hours poking around the vaults and indulging in some wine tasting. I have the use of his car for the morning, so I thought perhaps we could go for a run somewhere.' His eyes lifted, looking away east. 'I believe there are some interesting ruins among those cliffs.'

*Oh, no, not Maladieu.*

He must have seen the shadow cross my face, for he said quickly, 'You can take me anywhere you'd like to go. I'll be perfectly happy wherever it is.'

'You'd have enjoyed going round the wine vaults with George. It's burgundy country round here and they make you drink the wine out of silver goblets – they tell you it's the right way to taste red wine.'

He nodded acknowledgment of what I was saying, but he wasn't interested.

I said, 'All right, later we'll go for a run. I'll take you to a place I call my valley – about twelve o'clock.'

I knew as I went on towards the pottery that he was in a restless, emotional state and that George was too robust for him. Dominick wanted quiet. At the same time he was scared of being left alone with his thoughts. For the moment we were two of a kind, Dominick and I, wrapped in the cocoons of our intimate problems.

I stayed some time in the pottery to mix the pigments for the new dyes. Francis wanted a particularly rich purple such as was found in old stained-glass windows.

I'd no idea how much later it was when I stopped mixing and glanced out of the window. Max Lambert was crossing the lawn. He carried a bulging brief case. I remembered that my father had said that he would bring the material over. He'd wasted no time. I wondered if he was hating coming to our house as much as I hated seeing him here. Then why had he come? Was it that, as the old Comtesse's guest, he found it difficult to refuse to do what she asked him?

I saw Nikki run up to Max and touch the briefcase. He had an insatiable curiosity about little things. By my side, Lucia said, 'That, I suppose, is the man they call Max Lambert.'

'Yes.'

She stood, hugging herself, and her voice became dreamy. 'They say if you want a thing badly enough, you get it.'

I turned to look at her lovely, withdrawn little face. 'What do you want?'

'To get inside the Château, of course.'

'If you're hoping for neighbourliness, then you're going to be disappointed.'

She gave me a brilliant look. 'Do you think so?' She dropped the mosaic cutters on to the table with a clatter and walked to the door.

I watched her through the window. She had the fluid, gliding walk that characterizes many Eastern women; her head was beautifully set on her neck. She joined Max who was still talking to Nikki.

The little boy's face was tilted back as he looked up at the tall man. Nikki's eyes were screwed up in a way he had when he was trying to think of a word. I saw Max turn his head towards Lucia.

The sun was on her russet hair and her hand went out gracefully, expressively, to stress something she was saying.

Behind me, Francis exclaimed, 'Lucia knows we want these Zodiac signs finished today. Why can't she stick to her job?'

It was Elise who said, entirely without malice, 'She's bored here, Francis. You must let her meet people and talk to them. *We're* content, but she isn't. She's different.'

'She likes to play at work, you mean,' he said crossly.

I went on watching her. She shooed Nikki away. Max Lambert said something and she laughed. Then they walked together across the lawn and through the cluster of trees to my father's studio.

Lucia didn't return to the pottery for some time. When she did, she said, 'Max is staying quite a while at the Château. I can't think why, and he was quite cagey about it when I tried to find out what the attraction was. I shouldn't think it's much fun to have an old woman for a companion. I told him if he's ever bored in the evenings to come over here. Father invited him too.' She sat down at her bench and picked up the cutters. She had made her point and she didn't bother to talk any more.

Surely Lucia's elusive 'approach and retreat' manner, which men found so intriguing, wouldn't draw Max Lambert more closely into our home life. He couldn't be so insensitive or so cruel. The bare possibility alarmed me and I spilled some of the precious pigment on to the bench.

Nightmare pictures chased each other through my mind as I scooped up the powder. Max walking to and from our house;

talking to Elise and Francis and Lucia; even sitting at our table. A small, silly thought crept in. Of course, I could always poison the rice.

'Look out!' Francis's shout made me jump. 'That dye's expensive and you're spilling it. Oh, Lord, first Lucia and now you! Can't you keep your minds on your job?'

I had never felt less like laughing in my life, yet I wanted to giggle and say, 'I was just wondering how I could poison Max Lambert.'

If anything could prove to me that I was still in a state of shock, this did. I turned away from the table. 'Oh, *you* do it!' I said to Francis. 'I'm going in to see about lunch.'

'If the lot of you continue to come and go like this, I'll have to ask Father if I can get local labour,' he called after me crossly. 'It'll be a chore to train them, and it'll cut down our profits, but it would be better than a bunch of half-hearted amateurs.'

I shut the pottery door and felt guilty as I went towards the house. Francis worked hard, but so did I, as a rule. Now that orders for mosaic panels for house decoration were pouring in and the tourists who visited us twice a week bought tiles and teapot stands and things that would pack easily into their suitcases, we badly needed extra workers. I'd ask Father about it.

I had reached the place where the path divided, one going to the house, the other to the studio. There was a thick bush at the corner.

Two people came towards me simultaneously from different directions. Max, his brief case no longer bulging and Nikki, running to me, calling, 'Rachel. Rachel, Peppina's got a thing with peaches and ice cream and nuts for lunch. Oh' – he turned and saw Max – 'hullo.' Then he added politely as we had taught him to, 'This is my sister.'

Max looked at me. 'I know.'

'I've got two other sisters and a brother, but Rachel loves me best.'

Max asked, without interest, 'Does she? Well, that's nice for you.'

His cool scrutiny made me feel awkward. In the green dress, cut for comfort rather than smartness, I felt like someone going out to milk the goat. I walked past him as if he were invisible.

From the house came the sound of music. My mother's baby grand, so seldom used, stood on the far side of the living-room. Dominick was playing it.

I had always thought that when musicians found a piano or a violin, they lost sense of time and place and people. As soon as I passed the window, however, Dominick stopped playing, got up, and came on to the veranda. His playing, then, was merely a way of waiting for me.

'Are you ready for that run in the car?' he asked.

'Yes, but I'd better drive because I know the way.'

I took Dominick to the Val de Lys. It was a dip in the hills by a waterfall. I hadn't wanted to come, but gradually, as we left Issandre, my spirits lifted. We got out by a small twisting path too narrow for the car to go down. It meandered between trees and honeysuckle bushes, falling steeply so that we had to grab at branches in order not to slip.

At the end of the path the valley came into view. The waterfall danced and splashed into a swift-running stream. Little purple iris and a scattering of Madonna lilies coloured the rich green of fern and grass.

I threw myself down and laid my face on my arms. Blades of grass stroked my cheeks. For a long time we were silent. Only the water sang about us. I felt a slow peace stealing over me. I could have lain in the dappled sun and shade for ever, feeling outside emotion, outside bitterness and loss of disillusion. I was as young and strong and pagan as a naiad. Unhaunted at last.

'I am in love with you.'

I stirred and twisted my head on my arms so that I was no longer facing Dominick. 'Are you?'

The miracle was over. The weight of being human and full of conflict returned. It was Dominick's fault.

'Rachel, did you hear?' He leaned over me and turned my face towards him. 'I said, "I am in love with you." I'll tell you how the whole thing grew, wonderfully, day by day.'

'I'd rather you didn't.' I moved away from him, sat up, and clasped my hands round my knees. 'Talking about it isn't going to make either of us very happy.'

'Perhaps you could leave it to me to try.'

I made a bunch of myself so that he couldn't do anything like taking me in his arms. If I *had* to listen, I'd hear him out this way, chin on my knees, staring down at the deep green grass.

'First, it was just feeling that here was someone I could t-
to. Then, a mutual sympathy, for we had both lost so-

we loved. Gradually, as I saw the way you coped with everything in the house, I began to admire you, too. Now I know that something else is added – the feeling of a wonderful peace when I'm with you. Irene never made me feel that way. It's so rare – I've only known two really restful people.'

Your mother being the first, I thought, and watched an insect climbing a blade of grass. Aloud, I said, 'What you call my 'being restful' is really that I'm drained. I don't know which crisis is worse – yours that is still going on, or mine that ended suddenly at Maladieu.'

'But, darling, you've said it. Yours *did* end. You've no alternative but to make your life again. I've got a decision to make. Or rather,' he added, 'I have to force Irene to see my point of view; that it's over between us.'

I turned and laid my fingers on his arm. It was an unconsidered gesture which I immediately regretted, for Dominick misunderstood. He seized my hand and pulled me towards him so that I lost my balance and fell against him.

He kissed my cheek. Then he buried his face in my hair. 'Rachel . . .'

Paul had done that only a few weeks ago. Against the background of the singing waterfall I could hear, not Dominick's voice but Paul's saying, 'When will you let me make love to you?' Then, murmuring into my hair, 'Mignon, Mignon . . .' Nobody would ever call me that again.

Dominick was talking and I hadn't been listening. But then, whatever it was he had been saying, I didn't want to have to answer. I said in a clear and matter-of-fact voice, 'If we don't get back, you'll be complaining that we don't feed you properly.'

'I'll be content to starve if . . .'

He waited for me to ask 'If what?' I asked nothing.

'If,' he continued as though I'd spoken, 'you loved me.'

'It's a good thing I don't, isn't it? You have a wife.'

'If I went back to her, I'd end by hating her. And then heaven help us both. It was bad enough before I left. The rows – '

I should have insisted on returning to the car. It would have been safer. Yet I was still not quite certain what had really broken their marriage, and when you see a lot of someone, you start being interested in their lives.

'You must have loved Irene when you married her.'

'I've begun to wonder if I did. She is beautiful and her father is influential in the music world. She's tremendously knowledgable herself about music and enthusiastic about my career. I suppose those are the things that attracted me to her because I'm ambitious.'

'Did your mother like Irene?'

'She never knew her. We met later. It was the dreadful emptiness I felt after my mother died that really made me decide to marry. I needed so badly to find again what I'd lost; what my mother and I had.'

'How did you imagine it could possibly be the same?' I said almost angrily, defending Irene. 'One was a mother, the other a wife.'

He ran a hand over his fair hair. 'I suppose, without Irene, it would have taken me longer to get where I am. She and her father have helped me so much. But the price has been high. Dear God, it's been high!'

I think I was still angry with him for destroying my peace in this place. Or perhaps it was that I didn't want him to love me, and tried to sound hard. I said crossly, 'You're like a small boy who takes all the Christmas presents, but doesn't want to give any in return.'

'You're being unfair because you don't understand.'

'Or perhaps I understand too well.'

We sat in an uncomfortable silence. I watched the sun speckling the water.

When he spoke again, his voice was bitter and sad. 'You've got to know me, Rachel. Don't move.' He put out a hand to stop me from getting to my feet and leaned his head back against a tree. 'You see, I married a woman who believes that passion is the answer to all problems. "Make it up in bed." It sickened me.' He sucked in his breath. 'So I took to sleeping in one of the spare rooms and locking my door. I suppose you find that ironical.'

'Why should I?'

'It's usually the woman who tires of sex. So I'd be a hell of a nice husband for the average woman, wouldn't I? *Wouldn't I?*'

I said unhappily, 'I can't judge.'

'Well, you must have heard your married friends talk. Women get awfully bored with men's constant demands.'

He fell back on the grass, shading his eyes from the glints of sunlight through the trees. I still sat upright, clutching my knees. I wondered what his mother had been like. Whatever it was, it was all Dominick wanted.

'But there's one thing I suppose no woman can understand,' he said.

'What's that?'

'How a man feels about a broken marriage. The sense of failure . . .'

'I suppose the woman feels that way, too.'

'Irene accused me of putting all my energy into my music and having none left for her . . . for our life together.'

'And it sounds as if that's just what you did.'

'I don't know. All I *do* know is that neither of us can live for long in this no man's land between marriage and divorce. One of us has to make the real break. Irene won't. So I've got to prove to her that I can't go back and live with her. And there's only one way of doing that.'

'One – way – ?'

'There must be someone else in my life.'

The ant climbing the grass had reached the top and the blade bent right over with its weight.

'That's the only solution,' Dominick said. 'If Irene knew there was no possibility of a reconciliation – '

I said carefully, 'That's your problem to work out.'

'While she thinks there's no one else, I suppose she hopes I'll go back. Once she knows that there is . . .' His hand touched mine. 'Rachel, doesn't everyone want to belong to a particular person, to share a home with them? Don't you?'

'Yes.'

'Then . . .' His fingers tightened over mine. 'Can't you understand? I've met you – '

I slid my hand from under his. 'There's one thing you seem to be overlooking. I'm sorry,' I added inadequately, 'but you see, I don't love you.'

I got to my feet. A tiny grey-green thing that had been sunning itself slid, scared, across a warm rock by my side. I watched it. 'I'm hungry, if you aren't. And we can't eat lizards for lunch.'

# CHAPTER TEN

'First,' said my father to Max Lambert, 'there's the design. Rachel took an art course at the Sorbonne – she had some wild idea when she was seventeen, of being a dress designer. The whole of this' – my father waved an arm and knocked over a stack of brushes; he signalled impatiently to Nikki to pick them up – 'the whole of this was Rachel's idea and she became our chief designer.'

We sat there, Lucia and Elise and Francis and I self-consciously cutting tesserae while father acted as guide to Lambert. I kept my head down, feeling quivers along my spine as the two passed behind my chair.

Lucia said, 'Rachel *was* our chief designer until she and Francis entered designs for a big competition and Francis won it. Wasn't that marvellous of him?' She cast a laughing glance across the room at me. 'So I suppose you could call *him* our chief designer now.'

I said casually, 'I came nowhere in the competition.'

'Poor Rachel!' Lucia moved to the window and was outlined in light. 'It was quite a shock for her when Francis, who had no training, snapped up the prize. Secretly, she was really mad at being passed over.'

I felt my face flame. 'That's not true and you know it. It was wonderful for the business that Francis won. It meant publicity and lots of orders.'

Lucia was unperturbed. 'And now he has more or less taken over the designing.' She reached for a yellow tessera, snipped it, broke it in the wrong place, and threw it into the basket by her side.

Father said, 'Where's Nikki?'

'He has just gone out. He's probably playing somewhere.'

'He should be here. There's plenty he can do.'

I said, 'Let him be. It's his school holidays.'

I went on working feverishly, bent over the little silver piece I was cutting into a triangle, bitterly aware that nothing was escaping Max, who was standing behind me.

For the past few days he had been coming every morning to help my father sort the mass of material about the d'Arachenne family. And each time he came and went from the studio, pausing in the garden when someone came and spoke to him, I tore myself to pieces inside willing him to go.

What pleasure was he deriving from being here? Surely it must be painful for him, since Paul was his friend, to have this constant reminder of the tragedy at Maladieu? Surely any other man would avoid our house and the risk of meeting me? Then could it be that he derived a bitter satisfaction from the fact that he was hurting me by coming? And now he was being shown round the pottery, drawn closer into our lives.

Sitting at the bench, I didn't once raise my head. Father was taking much too long, explaining every piece of equipment. I was relieved when they moved into the next room where the mosaics were displayed for sale.

I heard them talking, heard Max asking questions like some polite, interested tourist. Father was showing him Francis's winning design, which would be on display until the municipal building in Avignon, the architects of which had sponsored the competition, was finished and the place on the wall ready to receive the panel.

'. . . his idea . . . taken from an old Persian tapestry,' I heard my father say. 'Fine, isn't it, that study of an Arab horse? Odd, you know, that Francis, who's had no artistic training, has managed to get that splendid sense of movement and the feeling that horse and rider are one. He intended to study engineering. But he likes working with his hands. With the house to run, Rachel doesn't have much time to spend here, so more and more of the designing falls on Francis. We'll have to get local labour to help us if we go on expanding like this – though the Lord knows where it's coming from. The young people of Issandre go to Lyons or Bordeaux or Paris.'

It was becoming impossible for me to sit there listening. I got up and went into the sunshine. Nikki ran up to me. 'Will you play with me?'

I took his hands. 'Look at them, you little grub!'

'You'd be dirty,' he said solemnly, 'if Francis had asked you to pick up all those mosaic bits from the floor.'

'Come in and wash. That cement dust is better down the drain than on your hands. And then we'll see how Pennina's getting on with the lunch.'

I stayed in the kitchen for quite a long time helping with the salad. When I went to the door much later to find Nikki and take him shopping with me in Issandre, I heard Max's voice raised, calling to someone. 'Come along down.'

Lucia answered from her window above the door. 'I can't. I'm not seeable. I'm changing my dress. What do you want?'

'Must I shout it?'

'You don't *have* to shout. Just make it a Romeo and Juliet act – you know, the soft words but without the moonlight.'

'By all means. I want to ask you if you'll come to dinner with me tonight.'

There was a moment's pause. Then: 'You mean – at the Château?'

'No, in Avignon at the Hotel de Manoir. Say I pick you up at seven o'clock?'

'I'll try to be punctual, but I've no idea of time.'

'I have infinite patience,' said Max Lambert.

I stood watching him walk away down the drive. So I had been wrong. Max had not come here in order to mete out a bitter kind of punishment to me. He came, like so many men, because of Lucia.

I waited until he was out of sight, then I called Nikki and went to fetch the car. As I backed out of the garage, he came running and fumbled with the door handle. I opened it for him and he scrambled in.

I edged the car out into the drive. Nikki cried, 'Ooh! You nearly ran over him.'

I braked and looked in the driving-mirror.

Max came round to my side of the car. 'I'm sorry. I was in your way. I came back for my brief case. I must have laid it down somewhere in the pottery.'

'I'll get it,' Nikki said and climbed out of the car.

Max remained beside me.

Go! *Go!* GO!

My willing had no effect.

'Do you know that your nearside lamp is a bit bashed in?' he asked.

'Yes, thank you. Father had an altercation with a lorry.' (Please, *please* go!)

I tapped my fingers on the steering-wheel, staring ahead of me. Someone would really have to stop the spread of those marigolds, lovely as they were, or they'd choke everything in the garden.

Since Max seemed to have no intention of leaving my side I had to break the silence. 'I suppose Father now has all the material he needs for the book?'

'Oh, not nearly.' He looked down at me, his voice polite, his eyes implacable. 'These things take a long time. The d'Arachenne family played a big part in French history from the thirteenth century on. Seven hundred years of living have to go into that book.'

Did he know he was distressing me by standing there and was he doing it deliberately? All right! If he intended to stay, I was going to find out what I could.

I said tersely, 'You seem to be having a long holiday.'

'Oh, I'm not entirely on holiday. I have things to do here.'

I wasn't going to fall into the trap of asking what things. The possible answer had flashed in my mind *To prove your guilt beyond any manner of doubt, Miss Helston.*

Not that he would be so blatant – now that he was a visitor to our house. He wouldn't risk deliberate offence. Did he wonder how much the family knew? Or did he assume that, like most guilty people I kept my secret and told them nothing? It was puzzling and unnerving. But it would end; he would go away and never come back.

I said, 'You live in London?'

'Yes.'

'And – and you work there?'

'In Lincoln's Inn.'

I said coldly, 'Of course, I remember. You're a lawyer.' Then beneath my breath, the words came out. 'The Devil's Advocate.'

I didn't think Max could possibly have heard. But he did. 'You could call me that.' He walked away.

Nikki raced up to him, gave him the brief case and climbed into the car. 'Can I have a mixed ice cream when we get to Issandre?'

'We'll both have one,' I said and started the engine.

We passed Max in the drive. I stepped sharply on the accelerator; Nikki leaned out of the window, waving.

'Oh!' He sat back in his seat. 'He didn't even *look* at us, Rachel.'

Nikki loved shopping. He was very small for his age and his chin usually just reached the counter. Monsieur Briac, the grocer, was his favourite shopkeeper.

I drew into the kerb and switched off the engine. Nikki turned to me, grinned, and licked his lips.

'All right,' I said. 'Ice cream first.'

We always had mixed ice cream and played a game of who could make the neater job of separating the colours, mint green from strawberry pink; chocolate from vanilla.

When we'd finished, I gave him the basket, some money, and a list of things to buy. 'You can get all these at Monsieur Briac's. And when you've finished, come straight back to the car. No crossing roads. Promise?'

He promised.

I bought some eclairs and a layer cake, which Peppina always pierced at the bottom, pouring in a mixture of real orange juice and sugar making it rich and luscious. Then I went into the shop next door for the little round golden cheeses with slender blue veins that were a specialty of Issandre. All these things took time, so that I expected to see Nikki kicking his heels in the car when I returned. He wasn't there.

From the grocer's shop I heard high, angry voices. Nikki's shrill, frightened protest came to me clearly as I went in. 'I didn't! I *didn't* take anything. I – –' As Monsieur Briac's glance lifted and saw me, Nikki swung round. 'Rachel, I didn't!'

There were about eight people in the shop. I said to them, 'Perhaps someone will tell me what this is about.'

I had known Monsieur Briac ever since I had come to Issandre seventeen years ago. He was small, black-eyed and energetic, kindly enough but giving no quarter with anyone who mistook his benign manner for softness. He was looking stern enough now. 'It's difficult for me to tell you, Mademoiselle. But this boy has stolen from my shop.'

'I don't believe it.'

'Mademoiselle, I do not lie. I show you. Look.' He held up a slab of chocolate and a packet of macaroons. 'They were there,' he rapped the counter where little piles of goods lay displayed, 'and he took them and hid them in his basket.'

I looked slowly round at the inquisitive faces and burst out laughing. 'But this is absurd! Nikki never stole anything in his life.'

A sententious voice said, 'There's always a beginning to delinquency.'

'Nikki.' I turned him around to face me. 'Were these things found in your basket?'

'Yes, but I didn't put them there.'

I turned to Monsieur Briac. 'If he says so . . .'

'Then he's not telling the truth. He was seen taking them.'

'Who saw him?'

The faces making a semicircle round us stared blankly back at me.

'Well, who?'

'It was a customer I have not seen before. He had been buying some tea and rice. He was turning to leave the shop when he saw the boy's hand slide the things off the counter.'

I said, 'But he's not here now. He accused and then left! Well, I can't see that that's very conclusive. The things could have been swept into the basket by Nikki's elbow, or – ' I broke off aware of the weakness of my argument. Then, angred by the silent, watching faces, I went on, 'It's monstrous to accuse a child and then walk out and let him be judged by people who didn't see what happened.'

'But that's just it, Mademoiselle,' Monsieur Briac kept wiping his hands on his apron. 'He didn't want to accuse. That is why he left. He said all he wanted was for me to know about it and reprimand him. No more. He said, "It may be a first offence. Perhaps all the boy needs is to be frightened out of doing such a thing again!" '

'It would surely have been better to have asked the man to wait and speak to me about it. You knew my car was parked just outside the shop. You saw me.'

'I told him that, and he said 'No. *You* are the shopkeeper. *There* is the evidence of theft. Now you deal with it.'

Nikki began to cry very quietly. I put an arm around his shoulders. The bones were so small, so slender. I crouched down and lifted his face and looked into his streaming eyes. 'Nikki, please. You know that I'll try to understand. *Did* you steal those things?'

'No. No. *No*.' He wrenched himself out of my grasp and ran towards the door of the shop.

A man stopped him and held him. I saw his eyes, greedy and excited; I saw his fingers gripping the child with a strength he would use on a man. Nikki writhed with pain.

As I darted forward, a woman cried, 'Give him a good sound thrashing.'

'I'll do it myself,' said the man. 'With pleasure.'

I was like a tigress. 'Don't you dare touch him!'

The man let go. I saw his eyes swerve to the telephone. 'Then I'll call the police.'

'No, not that,' Monsieur Briac said firmly. 'I know this young lady – I have known her for many years. It is enough that I have spoken to her about it – and of course, I'll speak to her father.'

'Father.' My heart beat up in my throat. 'Oh, no! You've told me, that's enough. Please, not Father.'

'But of course. That is necessary.'

I held Nikki close to me. It was useless to protest. The people of Issandre still considered the head of the family as paramount.

I was frightened for Nikki. Father would not be lenient. I said quietly, 'If you think you must do so, Monsieur Briac, then of course there is nothing I can say.'

With a silent group of people watching me, I paid for the things Nikki had bought, took his hand and walked out of the shop. They made a way for me, all of them silent until I reached the door. Then: 'Tan the hide off that Arab delinquent,' shouted the man with the greedy eyes.

There were other words flashing in and out of my mind as we went to the car. Father saying, when mother first begged to have Nikki: 'A child from the Moroccan gutters? Good God, Nan, have you any idea what sins he can have inherited?' Sins . . . such as stealing?

All the way home Nikki sat hiccuping, a habit he had when he was nervous and upset. For the first time in his life, he wasn't enjoying his car ride. Between hiccups, his muffled, plaintive voice protested. 'But I didn't want any chocolate. There's lots at home. And I don't *like* macaroons.'

From the two cars that passed, the drivers recognized me and waved. I lifted my hand both times in mechanical acknowledgement. I was busy going back over the years Nikki had been with us. Not once had he done a small mean thing. He had never raided the sweet jars without permission nor had he taken anything that didn't belong to him in the house. On the other hand, as the hateful woman in the shop had said, 'There's always a beginning to delinquency.'

And in between these two thoughts, tearing me apart, was the realization that I loved him very, very deeply.

He was asking, 'Will Papa send me back to Agadir?'

'Of course not. You belong with us.'

'I don't. I'm different, aren't I, Rachel? That's what the man in the shop said.'

I slowed the car and, with my eyes still on the road, I slid one arm around him. 'Stop saying silly things. You're no different from any of the rest of us and you'll never be sent away. Not from me. I'll look after you until you're old enough to make your own life.'

'Is that a *promise?*'

He doubted most things until that magic word was used. It was his 'Open Sesame' to security. Promises meant a thing would really happen, come flood and high water.

'Yes,' I said. 'It's a promise.'

I took my arm from around him and stepped on the accelerator. I knew I'd been rash. From now on, whatever Nikki turned out to be, I was committed.

That, however, was my long-term responsibility. I could shelve it for the time being. There was something nearer which I dreaded – and that was my father's anger.

When we turned into the drive, I saw him standing outside the house, legs apart, black head bent like an angry eagle. I thought what a terrifying sight he must be for an already overwrought child. He didn't take his eyes from Nikki as we approached, and he followed us into the house.

In the hall his hand came down on the boy's neck. He swung him around. 'Well?'

I said quickly, 'I suppose Monsieur Briac has called you and told you what happened this morning? Quite frankly I don't believe it. I think what happened was –'

'I'm not interested in what you think.' He pushed Nikki into the living-room with one hand, held me back with the other and closed the door. At the first sound of Nikki's cries, I fled. Father believed in corporal punishment.

In the kitchen, Peppina was preparing a salad dressing. She gave me her narrow, quizzical look. 'What is the matter with Nikki?'

When I had told her, she slapped down the vinegar bottle. 'So! So! Well, perhaps he did steal. When I was small, I stole, too. You know why? Because I was hungry. And when you are hungry you steal, and after that, it takes a long time, *a long time*' – with her fist she hammered in accompaniment – 'to learn not to steal.' The last words were flung over her shoulder at me as she marched out of the kitchen.

Alarmed, I followed her into the hall. 'Peppina, please. Don't go in there!'

She ignored me. The living-room door opened and slammed. I heard Nikki cry out. I heard Peppina's voice which, when raised, sounded like something between a scraped saucepan and a corn crake. We had often heard it when she was in a temper with a tradesman and had laughed. I wasn't laughing now. I was leaning close to the door, holding my breath and listening.

'You do that again and I leave. You hear? I leave your house. And your stomach says to you, "No, Peppina must not leave." You like my *Coquilles St Jacques*; my *rouget en papillote*. Well, so, if you like them, you do not touch Nikki again.'

'Get out of here!'

'Come, *mon gars*, we go together, eh?'

'You damned, interfering old hag!'

I scarcely had time to spring away before the door opened. Peppina beamed at me, showing her two solitary front teeth. With her arm around Nikki she went muttering back to the kitchen. Father had seen me in the hall. 'Rachel, come here.'

He lit a cheroot, poured himself an Armagnac and said, 'That woman is growing more impossible every day. We could, of course, sack her.'

'No, we can't. Not if you want me to put in the hours I do in the pottery.'

'Elise could help in the house.'

'*And* keep the pottery clean *and* your studio? Of course,' I added caustically, 'so far as the garden's concerned, we could rip up everything and Francis could concrete the two acres. And we could shut up your studio and you could work in your bedroom. We could think of other ways, too, to save work.'

He gave me a long malevolent look and I felt a bit like a carping wife. But I intended to fight for Peppina. She cared for us – even Father – in her love-hate way.

'About Nikki,' said Father. 'I think I scared the life out of him. First I walloped him, then I told him that just one more escapade like that and out he goes – and I don't give a damn where. I warned your mother when she wanted to adopt him the risk we were taking. It seems I was right. The thieving little – '

I spun around on him, the blood rushing to my face. 'I know what you're going to say. And don't! Whether you approved or not, you adopted Nikki, he's your child.'

A shadow cast by the sun moved between us. I looked over my shoulder and saw Max. 'I'm sorry,' he said to my father. 'I went to the studio and you weren't there. I've brought some old books which I found in the library. I think they'll be useful. Am I intruding?'

'Not in the least. You probably know what we're talking about. It'll be all over the town by now.'

'Father – '

He ignored me. 'I seem to have adopted a little thief. That's what you get for taking strange children into your home.'

'You're quite wrong, I – '

'And also,' he continued, glowering at me, 'my daughter is behaving like a thwarted spinster. I suppose women have to have something to expend their love on. If they can't dote on their own child, then it's someone else's, or a cat or a dog.'

'You can leave me out of this,' I stormed at him, 'and think of Nikki. If you can't have some sort of loyalty towards him, who can he expect it from? You're judging him on the evidence of someone who didn't even stay to accuse him to my face! *I* don't believe Nikki stole anything in his life. Do you hear?' I lashed out with my hand. An ash tray crashed to the floor. 'Leave him alone. If you think he should be punished, then you've punished him already. Now let it be.'

Max picked up the ash tray and set it on the table.

My father was standing, legs apart. The cheroot burned between his thick, steady fingers. 'I refuse to discuss anything with a hysterical woman. You'd better shut yourself in your room and get over it in private.'

'I'm not hysterical. I'm just furiously angry. There happens to be quite a difference.' I made for the door and slammed it behind me.

In my bedroom, I sat on the chair by my bureau. The shutters were not drawn over the windows and I stared out at Clèry crouched like the sphinx on the veranda.

When I was calm, I faced the fact that my anger had not been directed at my father for his lack of understanding of Nikki. I'd had my say over that. My last outburst of fury was because I had been treated like a child in front of Max Lambert.

I crept to the window. The pointed towers of Sonnengarde were like four black teeth in a witch's face grinning at me.

## CHAPTER ELEVEN

Every now and then as I went from room to room dusting, tidying, I would stop and listen to music.

Dominick, who was never far from my side, would sit for hours playing our piano and gradually I learned the names of the pieces of music. Chopin and Delius. The only one I recognized without being prompted was Beethoven's Moonlight Sonata.

In the beginning when I heard him playing, I would say, 'You said you wanted to forget music and scores and orchestras.'

And more than once he answered, 'Playing like this, knowing that you're somewhere listening, is a relaxation.'

At first, I wondered why Lucia was not more interested in Dominick. He was brilliant, he was extremely good-looking, and one day he would be famous. She herself gave me the clue one morning when we were together in the hall.

Dominick was at the piano, playing a piece with a lot of little light arpeggios. Lucia was arranging flowers in a tall white vase. I said, to start a conversation because she was never an easy person to be silent with, 'Dominick's a charming guest.'

'But so safe. So dully *safe*!' she said.

'I suppose a piano to him is like a casino to a gambler.'

She gave her small, insinuating smile. 'And an adoring listener an even greater attraction.'

'I'm not adoring,' I said crossly, 'and as for listening, how can I help it?'

The music disturbed me – not because it wasn't lovely to listen to even on our old piano, but because it accentuated the fact that I was becoming Dominick's absorbing interest. He wanted only to be somewhere where I was – and he didn't care who knew it.

He had been with us ten days when the invitation came through his agents for him to conduct the last of a series of concerts given by the Sevigny Orchestra, in place of Carlos Foix who had been taken ill. The last concert of the tour was to be in Avignon. He received the telephone calls from Paris with protests that he was on holiday; that he wanted to forget all about professional engagements. Didn't they realize he needed a rest? He'd been under a strain and . . .

In the end, however, persuasion wore him down. He agreed to conduct the orchestra at the big new hall.

He had to leave at once for rehearsals, but before he went he made us all promise to come to the concert. Father protested that he didn't know a violin from a viola.

Dominick laughed. 'Nor does George, but he has two hands to applaud with, and I need all the encouragement I can get.'

There were five of us – my father and Francis, Lucia and Elise and I, sitting in centre-back seats watching the orchestra straggle in and tune up.

I wondered how the rehearsals had gone. Even I knew Foix's name as a conductor and the Sevigny Orchestra by its high reputation. I wondered what these veteran violinists and oboists thought of the slender, reticent man, young enough to be the son of most of them.

I was apprehensive for Dominick's sake, fidgety and not very happy since, with my limited knowledge of music, I wouldn't know whether he controlled them well and interpreted the music correctly or not.

On the day before the concert I had received a letter from him from Avignon. In it he had asked me to come around and see him during the intermission. 'I have to know that you're there,' he wrote. 'Please, Rachel, don't fail me.'

Father sat on my left, complaining that there wasn't enough room for his long legs. I looked at my programme: Holst's 'Planets' – Delius's 'Walk in the Paradise Garden', Sibelius's 'The Swan of Tuonela'.

The tuning-up was over; the oboe stopped its long-drawn, testing 'A'; the murmurs in the audience died down. Dominick appeared, walked purposefully on to the rostrum, acknowledged the applause briefly, picked up his baton, and brought it down on the opening bars of 'The Planets'.

I listened and was amazed. He was no longer the withdrawn, self-conscious young man with what Francis called 'the lean and hungry look'. He had grown in stature. In life, part of him had remained still lost in adolescence. Here, on the rostrum, he knew what he wanted and where he was going. He was, in manner and command, the young maestro.

I remembered what he had told me in the dell by the waterfall. 'All my energies are given to music.' I knew now what he meant. There were men who were shadows in life, who became substance only in their work. Dominick was one.

When the music stopped and the dimmed lights brightened for the interval, Elise, who understood music, said, 'He knows his scores and he's sensitive to his orchestra. Did you notice, he didn't cue the wood-winds? He trusted them as veteran musicians to know when to come in.'

I watched him acknowledge the applause, turn and indicate the orchestra. A roar of approval followed him as he walked away. It was like looking at someone I'd never met before.

And this man was dangerous; this was the kind of thing that trapped women. Sometimes, in a man's ordinariness, you caught a glimpse of greatness and it stirred unexpected emotions. You forgot that the important thing was the man in everyday life, the one who could never stir and excite.

We had a great many friends in Avignon and when we all trooped out to the bar, we were surrounded. It was easy, in the crush, for me to escape. By asking various ushers, I found my way eventually to Dominick's dressing-room. I paused and hoped I had given him time to change his shirt and collar.

When I knocked, Dominick himself opened the door.

'Come along in.' He was laughing and completely at ease. 'I've changed and am dry round the ears and, I hope, immaculate.' He shut the door and put his arms round me. 'Well, Rachel?'

'It *is* . . . *wonderfully* well!' I said warmly. 'You only had to listen to that storm of applause.'

'I don't think I've ever conducted better. And that's odd, since the orchestra is a strange one to me.'

'It isn't odd, it's greatness,' I said, not quite knowing what I meant yet wanting to please him.

He put his lips to my hair. 'Do you know what my last thought was before I picked up my baton? I thought: Rachel is out there. That's why I must do better than I've ever done before. That's love, darling, to go out and give a performance for one woman.'

'You go out,' I said, 'to perform for everyone. *That's* the way to success.'

I don't think he heard me. His eyes had an introspective look. 'In the beginning, at my first concerts, it was the knowledge that my mother was somewhere in the audience that gave me the impetus to do my best. I had that same feeling just now about you.'

'And when Irene was out there listening?'

Exasperation flicked across his face. 'Why bring her into the conversation?'

'Because she's closer than anyone in your life.'

'Not any more.'

I walked to the dressing-mirror and stared at myself. I did this deliberately to break the disturbing new image of Dominick. I wanted him back as he had been at the Villa, 'Rachel's Shadow', because that was the man I was safe from. Not that I was afraid of loving him, but I feared some rebound emotion towards the new commanding Dominick Rond I'd seen on the rostrum.

I touched my hair, smoothed the folds of emerald chiffon over my hips, and fingered the thin gold necklace set with garnets, making little nervous gestures, not knowing what to do or what to say now that I was here, and, indeed, wondering why I had let myself be persuaded to come.

Dominick's reflection was behind me. He drew me back against him and I didn't pull away. We smiled at each other in the mirror. It was in that moment that I believed I really understood what Dominick needed and, for that matter, all that I needed from him. An emotion without stress; affection without a quickening of the blood. A passionless contact.

Nobody knocked on the door, but I saw it open. I leaned away from his arms. I was too late.

'Good evening, my darling.'

Dominick's arms dropped from me as if they had been shot down. We both swung round.

The woman wore a black lace dress that had the stamp of a great couture house. She had honey-coloured hair, a thin face with high cheekbones, and a mouth that gave us a bright, blank smile.

She looked me up and down with frank amusement, waiting for an introduction.

'This is Miss Helston – Rachel Helston.'

'English. Well!' Her tone was coolly polite.

'Rachel, this is my wife, Irene.'

'And are you on holiday here, Miss Helston?'

Dominick ran his hand over his smooth hair. 'Rachel is the daughter of Rupert Helston, the biographer. You remember you read his book, *The Maimed Princess*, and admired it. They live in Issandre.'

She gave me a long, thoughtful look, but she addressed Dominick. 'Ah, so that's where you're staying. You really should have let me have your address, though of course I could always find you through Brunton. He has told you, I believe, that your holiday will have to be curtailed. This is what I really came to remind you.'

'Brunton,' said Dominick to me, 'is my agent.' Then to Irene: 'What has my holiday got to do with him?'

'Foix again,' she said. 'He has just announced that he's going into the hospital in October for an operation on his leg. That means the London Classic Orchestra will be without its conductor for the American tour. You have been invited to take his place and we have accepted for you.'

Dominick looked angry. 'I suppose I could be allowed to say "Yes" or "No" to my own invitations. I don't see why –'

'The series starts at the end of October,' Irene continued calmly.

I was edging as inconspicuously as I could towards the door. Irene's voice stopped me. She put out a hand and her fingers were hot on my arm. 'Don't go,' she said. 'But Dominick must.'

Someone knocked on the door. 'Mr Rond?'

'I'm coming. I'm coming,' he called impatiently and looked at me.

I felt a swift rush of pity at the sight of his strained face. 'Good luck,' I said and immediately wondered if musicians, like actors, were superstitious about that phrase. But Dominick smiled.

The door closed and Irene and I were alone. She had moved to the mirror and was making up her mouth with a pale cyclamen lipstick.

'I must go,' I said desperately. 'I shall disturb everyone if I'm late.'

'They won't even let you into the hall if you're late.'

I dived for the door.

She was leaning against the dressing-table, looking at me. 'You'll be late, anyway, so you may as well stay and hear what I have to say. If you still want to hear the rest of the concert after that, you may be able to creep in somewhere.'

I said quickly, 'Before you say anything, please don't misconstrue what you saw when you came in. I mean, well we . . . Dominick and I . . .' I was floundering and her eyes watching me in the mirror, embarrassed me; they were quizzical, without pain or surprise.

She turned, playing with the gold cap of her lipstick. ' "Misconstrue"? What *do* you mean?'

'I don't want you to think that we . . . that I . . .' I was making everything so much worse.

'My dear Miss Helston, I hope I'm sufficiently understanding to allow my husband his amusements.'

'If it seemed that way to you, then I'm sorry. It's not in the least like that.'

She began to walk backward and forward across the room with a curious flowing stride. She's not calm at all, I thought. She's no calmer than I am. Only she has poise and it helps to hide her agitation.

She said, still walking up and down, 'Don't you think I'm perfectly aware of what's happening? Dominick has been on his own down here for twelve days. He's lonely and you offer consolation. I appreciate that, in my absence, he found someone to lean on – he always has to lean, you know. In fact, I have a rather pretty little speech I make to the women who "mother" him when I'm not around. Shall I make it to you?'

'No, thank you.'

Something in my tone must have annoyed her, for I saw her face sharpen, grow more taut. 'Do you realize that I've been staying in Paris for two weeks, but Brunton didn't contact me – I'd never have known about this concert if it hadn't been for the fact that I read in the newspapers that Foix was ill and Dominick was taking his place. There was also,' she added, 'the letter.'

I said disinterestedly, 'What letter? Whose?'

She shook her head. 'I don't know. It wasn't signed.'

The door handle was large and ornate. I ran a finger over the brass pattern. I said, because she was waiting for me to speak, 'You mean, someone sent you a notice about the concert?'

'I wouldn't put it that way. I'd say that someone decided it would be in the interests of both my husband and me if I came down here to Avignon. "Just to see for yourself" the letter said.'

'See – what?'

'That Dominick was in danger. That was how the writer worded it. The letter said that "a certain young woman" would be at the concert and if I watched, I'd see for myself what was happening.' She broke off. Then she added irritatedly, 'It seemed so stupidly melodramatic, but then anonymous letters are, aren't they?'

'Dominick came down with George Bannock just to spend a holiday with us. What possible danger could he be in?'

She did another restless turn of the room.

'I suppose the letter referred to the obvious one from which every man, temporarily parted from his wife, can fall into.'

I said angrily, 'Then it was a cruel and meaningless letter to write to you.'

'Oh, not meaningless. There was a postscript. It said, "She turns vindictive when thwarted." '

' "She." Just "*she*"?'

'I suppose the writer didn't want to be too blatant. But, of course, it all became quite clear to me when I walked into the room just now.'

I felt the blood throbbing in my throat. The awful thing was that I knew I looked guilty.

'You're quite wrong if you think there's anything between Dominick and me. For heaven's sake, I like him, but that's all. I know he's unhappy because he talked to me – oh, and don't look like that! I said 'talked' and that's what I mean. People do unburden themselves to strangers.'

She gave a small, bitter laugh. 'I'm quite sure you aren't his mistress, in spite of what the letter infers. I know my Dominick. *That's* not the danger. The danger is that he might imagine he's come to the end of the search. The search, my dear, for someone who can take his mother's place. My God, how I hate her – and being dead has made no difference. No woman should make her son her whole life. But then, no son would let his mother do that unless . . .'

I waited for her to finish the sentence. She didn't. Nor did she need to. 'Unless,' she could have said, 'the man is by nature a celibate and needs no other kind of love.' That, however, was by the way. Something else had sprung at me. Such a letter could have been sent only from one house.

'Do you know the Comtesse d'Arachenne?' I asked.

My question surprised her. 'I've met her on several occasions. She moves in musical circles.'

'So perhaps you know her handwriting.'

For the moment I had the initiative. I questioned. Irene answered.

'No, I don't think I ever saw it. And I don't see that it has any connection.'

'It could have,' I whispered. 'It could have. The anonymous letter – '

'Oh, Miss Helston, don't start playing detective. And your idea, as I can guess it, is preposterous. The letter wasn't written by an old woman. The handwriting was firm and strong, and in fact, extremely masculine. Also, it was written in English, although this could have been out of courtesy to me.'

Or because the writer was English.

Max? I shrank against the wall feeling like a puppet manoeuvred by strings too strong for me. Of course, Max Lambert, who came to our house and watched and saw . . . Saw me with Dominick, heard what the family so innocently called him – 'Rachel's Shadow.'

The letter, dictated by the Comtesse d'Arachenne, written by Lambert?

The rise and fall of violin music seeped into the room. I watched Irene. Since her first contemptuous state, she had scarcely looked at me.

I waited until I felt I had complete control of my voice, then I said, 'The letter was clever, since it libelled no one by name. Whoever wrote it knew that I would be here and that you would come. It – it reckoned on just what has happened – your misjudgement of a situation.'

Even as I said it, I felt a stir of guilt. Had I encouraged Dominick? Could I have acted differently? But how? *How?* When a man clings to a life line you don't even know you've thrown him, what could you do? I'd had no previous experience, no yardstick to help me cope. Perhaps I'd behaved stupidly. Perhaps I should have been harsher with him – and I certainly shouldn't have come to his dressing-room tonight. I stood there feeling helpless and very young. I also felt sick with a growing fear.

*When in doubt, run away*. It was child's logic, but that's just what I did. I wrenched open the door.

'Stop being a silly girl,' Irene called after me. 'Dominick is no use to you and whatever kind of husband he is, I won't let him go.'

The voice followed me as I ran just as a voice had followed me when I had fled from the Comtesse at Sonnengarde.

## CHAPTER TWELVE

I raced down the stone corridor, pushing past an astonished usher. There was no sound of music. I swung round a sharp corner, gave a cry and stopped dead.

'Oh, God!' I cried. 'Not you!'

'I'm sorry you mind so much,' said Max.

I put my hands out blindly and pushed him. 'Let me get by.'

It was like pushing a rock.

'You've got to pull up some time. If you race along like that, you'll probably end by getting run over. There's heavy traffic outside. And we don't want another accident, do we?'

I flung away from him. The damned passage was far too narrow for two people to pass if one chose to block it.

'Leave me alone.'

He looked at me with cold interest. The cleft between his eyebrows deepened. 'What's frightening you. Or rather, who?'

'No one. And now –'

'Oh, come! You don't rush blindly from a concert you came sixty miles to hear just for the hell of it.' He waited. Then he said, 'Very well, if you won't tell me, you won't. I'll take you home, since you obviously don't want to hear "The Swan of Tuonela." '

'I have a car.'

'The rest of the family will need it.'

'If I don't want to wait for the family, I'll get a train.'

'It's too late. You don't get country trains to run like the Metro in Paris.'

He stood aside. My wits must have suddenly atrophied because I could have escaped from him quite easily, and I didn't. Instead, I had managed to find a bit of courage. I threw back my head and tried to look at him levelly. 'Why are *you* here?'

'I had business to attend to in Avignon this afternoon. And I stayed to hear part of the concert. I happen to be a little tired, so I thought I'd go back to Issandre before the rush for cars starts.'

It was, I decided, a poor excuse, but I couldn't argue about it. He took my arm and began propelling me along the corridor, past the doorkeeper, and into the street.

He was right. The pavement was narrow and the traffic was using the road like a race track.

'You can let me go now,' I said. 'I'm not going to take a flying leap into the road.'

'Here's my car.'

It was neatly parked to the left of the hall.

I said meaningly, 'You talked about not wanting to be caught in the crush after the concert, but you wouldn't have had any difficulty – you aren't even in the car park.'

I didn't expect him to answer me and he didn't. The lamps along the street were very bright. I said stiffly, 'Well, good night,' and tried not to look at him. But my eyes flicked his way quite involuntarily. It was the narrowed, contemplative look he gave me that made me say accusingly, 'You knew Dominick's wife would be there tonight, didn't you?'

'I'm afraid I don't know her.'

'You had no need to, all you had to do was . . .'

'Go on. Was what?'

I could ask him, point-blank, if he wrote that letter at the Comtesse's dictation. But what would be the use? Of course he wouldn't admit that he had. Nor did I believe he was here just because he'd had business today in Avignon. He knew about the letter and curiosity and bitterness had made him remain and watch to see what happened.

I leaned against a lamp-post and felt helpless because he was so plausible. My limbs began to shake in the dreaded familiar way they had last time I'd met him.

I heard my own voice protesting, once more, trying to put myself right with Max Lambert. 'I'm being hounded for something I didn't do. I wasn't with Paul when he died. *I* didn't cause that accident. If someone did, then find her. She's around somewhere. Perhaps – perhaps if you camp up at Maladieu, she'll come back – for her mantilla. They say guilty people . . . Oh, God, what's the use?'

Max took a cigarette and lit it. He stood quietly, and I might almost have thought he was enjoying standing on the street corner with me, facing the ancient rampart walls, honey-coloured in the floodlights.

Why couldn't I keep calm when I talked to him? Why did I argue with him so much, anyway? Common sense should have made me avoid him, yet every time we met I began all over again, trying to justify myself and, I suspected, making everything seem worse. I wasn't particularly literary-minded – we had enough of that with Father – but I did recall one salient sentence of Shakespeare's. 'The lady doth protest too much, methinks.' And that's just what Max Lambert probably thought about me. It was an extraordinary thing, like being caught up in something you couldn't resist; like gambling, or drinking. Why did I do it? I wasn't helping myself. Short of finding the girl who had been in the car with Paul, nothing could help me to humble Max Lambert, if that was what I wanted.

'Shall we go home?' Max said.

The question was ludicrously intimate.

Up to now my feelings had been concerned with Paul and Maladieu and Sonnengarde. But something crept in that I didn't want to analyse. I only knew I felt acutely miserable.

Max held open the car door. 'Now that we've stopped being inquisitors, get in.'

My throat felt dry; my heart pressed tightly against my ribs. 'I've no intention of coming with you. My family are here.'

'I know. I've talked to them in the foyer. They were asking if I'd seen you. I said I thought I'd caught a glimpse of you going to the dressing-room.'

'So you did know where I was going. All the time, you –'

'I told them that if I found you and you'd had enough of

the concert, I'd run you home. So they won't wait around for you?

I said furiously, 'Oh, of course you said that to them! You knew I'd gone to see Dominick, and you knew that Irene would be going, too. You guessed that there'd be some sort of scene and I'd be upset, and probably not want to stay. You were going to enjoy it to the full by running me home and having me sit miserably by your side. Does watching someone else's unhappiness ease your own – is that it? What are you doing to us both? Or are you such a devil for your own punishment as well as mine?'

'Maybe I am.'

The way he said it, half lightly, hurt. Stupidly, irrationally I felt the pain stab me in the pit of my stomach. I put out my hand to the old, dry bark of the plane tree at my side and held on to it. 'I have no intention of going home yet. And I know of no journey I'd loathe more than one back to Issandre with you.'

He said smoothly, 'As you wish.'

I half turned to go. Then I blurted out: 'One thing. Paul didn't live long enough to regret his friendship with you. That, at least, he was spared.' The words were out, ugly and bitter and, had he but known it, springing from the new pain in me that I didn't understand. I stood frozen with shame. I had given cruelty for cruelty. Twice I opened my mouth to say 'I'm sorry.' But no sound would come. For a second we stood with only a couple of feet of ground between us.

Max's movement towards me was so swift that I was unprepared for it. His fingers dug into my arms, his mouth came down on mine. I couldn't move. His lips pressing mine were without passion, and certainly there was no gentleness. He was telling me, without words, that he was branding me in the most personal way he knew. *This girl killed my friend. Remember it, remember the touch of her . . . always . . .*

As suddenly as he had seized me, he let me go.

A couple came by, arms round each other, laughing. Max walked abruptly round to the far side of his car and got in. I was running across the street as I heard him drive away.

When I reached the old rampart wall, I stopped and leaned against a tree. Some men playing *pétanque* looked up and saw me and said something. I turned my head away. For the moment I couldn't move. My breath was ragged and my limbs shook.

In olden days on the Continent of Europe, the manner in

which a man kissed a woman's hand indicated his feeling for her – adoration, homage – or dislike. Each had its own gesture. So it was, I had discovered tonight, with a kiss.

I had asked for it.

A hurt for a hurt. . . . Well, what had he expected of me? An angelic turning of the other cheek? I, who had scarcely cried when Paul was killed, burst into helpless, muffled weeping.

The men playing *pétanque* were still watching me. I began to walk on. The moon lay on the water. When the weeping stopped, I saw the reflection of the lights in the wide sweep of the Rhône, the shuttered faces of the old houses, the half-bridge of Avignon. My brain was clearing; I could now think and a pattern was emerging.

Why, among all the gifted biographers of France had the Comtesse chosen an Englishman to write the biography of her family? Would the book ever be published? But then, what did it matter to her, if that wasn't really the object of the commission? The fee they were paying my father must be a handsome one, for he pressed a hard bargain, but whatever it was would be chicken feed to a rich banking family. Why had my father been chosen?

The swift answer came. So that Max could seem to help him and, by that means, infiltrate into the house, mix with the family. He could talk to them and in that way learn what he could about me – the people I cared about, the things that mattered to me.

I had to talk to someone, and I could only think of my father. I'd tell him about the letter. I would get him to consult Monsieur Duhamel, our solicitor. I knew nothing about French law, but I was certain that there must be libel laws.

Until this moment I had wanted to bury the horror of that night at Maladieu. Now, I suspected that others had no intention of letting me.

I didn't realize how long I'd been walking until I began to feel dizzy with tiredness. I went back to the concert hall and waited for the family to come out. The foyer seats were deep and comfortable and I sat quietly enough, but my fingers betrayed me. They plucked and pulled at my evening bag, so that I frayed the silk. I could have wept at the destruction, for Elise had given me this bag one Christmas and I loved it.

Time dragged in the quiet foyer. An usher, a programme seller, and then a man who was probably the manager all came out and looked at me. The bright forced glance I gave them must have assured them that I wasn't feeling ill.

The family appeared together. Father saw me first. 'Where did you get to?'

'I'm just not musical,' I said. 'I went for a walk.'

'You should have stayed. The second half was more comprehensible, at least to me, than the first. It had more tunes in it.' He tossed his programme on to a red plush seat. 'Dominick is driving back with George.'

'Dominick's wife was there tonight.'

'I know. I caught a glimpse of her. Attractive woman. He's a fool if he breaks with her. Oh, well, that's their problem, not ours.'

On the way home I sat in the back with Lucia and Elise. I knew this road so well with its open fields and old walls and streams. Presently the impregnable rocks of the lost world of Maladieu became visible, black against the luminous sky.

The speedometer leaped to seventy and in another quarter of an hour we were home. I wondered if George was far behind us. However late it was, I had to see Dominick tonight. I had to find out if he knew about the letter. And then I would tell my father.

We separated when we reached home. Father and Francis went down to the pottery for a final look at the great Persian panel, which was now completed and needed only to be polished. Elise and Lucia went to bed. I sat on one of the chairs on the veranda and waited for Dominick.

Twenty minutes later the car turned in at the drive. George put it away and saw me. 'You young people don't appreciate the beauty of bed,' he said. 'Wait till you get to my age, you won't want to sit up half the night communing with the stars.'

He went into the living-room and poured himself a stiff whisky. 'I need it after playing cheer-leader to Dominick,' he said and grinned at me. 'Good night.'

From the seat down in the garden under the walnut tree, Dominick called softly, 'Rachel?'

When I joined him, he drew me down to his side. He laid his head against my neck and took one of my arms and tried to put it around himself. 'Hold me,' he said, 'hold me close, darling. That's what I need after the strain of a concert.'

I resisted and leaned my head away. 'I don't feel like a comforter. And anyway, the evening was a success for you. You should be dancing with joy.'

He jerked upright. 'I suppose it's Irene.'

'What's Irene?'

'Making you angry. I'm sorry you had to see her tonight, but it wasn't my fault. And it doesn't matter.'

'It does to me.'

He asked quickly, 'What happened when I left you? What did she say?'

I told him about the anonymous letter.

He knew nothing about it. For a moment he seemed a little shocked, then said, 'No one takes notice of anonymous letters.'

'Irene didn't ignore it. And she knew perfectly well, after she'd seen us together in your dressing-room, to whom it referred.'

He said helplessly. 'Who could have written it?'

'Someone who lives here; someone who hates me.'

'Don't talk like that. No one could hate you. Rachel, why are you looking at me like that?'

I turned my face sharply away. I didn't want to tell him any more than he already knew about Paul. I said. 'The letter was written by someone who has seen us together and who knows how you feel about me.'

'Who could?'

'You've made it obvious to the family,' I said, hating the sharpness of my tone.

'But we've done no wrong, God knows!'

'The point is, the writer insinuates that *I* have.'

'What wrong could you do? You haven't an evil motive in your whole being. Rachel, please, ignore the letter. Let the horrible business die.'

I had a feeling that he wasn't as upset about the letter as he should have been and it puzzled me. I turned to him. 'I want to see it,' I said. 'I want you to get it from Irene.'

'How can I?'

'She has read it. She has no more use for it – or – or has she?'

The shutters in Lucia's room were pushed back and the light streamed out, shining on to Dominick's face. That was how I caught the wary look he gave me.

'I want to see the handwriting,' I explained.

'We'd both do well to forget it. Let loose the hare and you start the hounds running.'

'The hounds are already on the scent,' I said bitterly. 'Did you see Irene after the concert?'

'Yes.'

'What did you tell her?'

'Well, nothing much. We just went through all the old arguments.'

Something evasive in his tone made me ask, 'At the risk of sounding an egotist, did you talk about me?'

The few seconds' silence was an admission.

'You did!'

He edged away from me. 'You may as well know, I told her the truth.'

I took a long, slow breath before I asked, 'What truth?'

'That I'm in love with you.'

'Oh, Dominick, you fool!'

'She asked for honesty and I gave it to her.'

'And involved me.'

'Well, you *are* involved, aren't you?'

'No, I am not. Must you make me say things that sound cruel? Can't you accept facts without having them put into words?'

'Accept what?'

A swift memory flashed through my mind of the bitter thing I had said tonight to Max. That had been an instinctive reaction after a hurt. Now I must hurt for a different reason – for my own self-preservation.

'I've told you already. You know. I don't love you. I can never love you, and you had no right to bring me into your quarrel with Irene.'

'It seems that you were involved before I talked to her,' he said reasonably. 'The letter did that.'

And Dominick had played into the hands of whoever wrote it. I got up abruptly, unable to bear the weight of him against me. I walked to the flower-bed and began pulling the dead white trumpets off the tobacco plant.

Dominick rose and pulled me towards him. 'You've been hurt, Rachel. When Paul –' He saw me wince. 'I'm sorry to have to talk about him, but you must see that when you have a void like that in your life, there's only one thing to do, to compromise – to make the best of what's left. You're not doing that, are you?'

I said evasively, 'Let's not discuss me.'

'All right. But just answer these questions first. Are things here so wonderful? Do you want to spend your life running a home that isn't your own, looking after people who aren't even related to you? Well, do you?'

'Not for always, of course not. But there's a lot to be said for a happy family life, even if it isn't your own. And I have things to get over before I can start feeling again.'

'I'm asking for nothing more than you can give – what you give, in fact, to the family. That's all I want.'

'Perhaps *I* want something more.'

He drew me towards the seat and then, as I resisted, sat down and, with his arms round my waist, laid his head against my thigh. 'You mean you want love. At the risk of sounding conceited, perhaps that would come.'

I looked down at him without answering. He clung to me and I put my arms round his head and held him against the silk of my dress as I would have done Nikki. There was no passion in him. And certainly none in me for him.

Then, without a word, I pushed him gently away and walked down the path between the shrubs until I knew he could no longer see me. I leaned against the wall of the pottery and let the scented quiet seep into me.

## CHAPTER THIRTEEN

There was no valid reason why that night should have been so horrible. The worst of the shock of Paul's death was over. But I had a dream and it terrified me.

It was pitch-dark in my dream room. There was the girl without a face lying naked on a blue silk bed, her skin as luminous as a water nymph's. Paul leaned, laughing, over her. Then I heard the snap of a light being switched on and the crystal chandelier above the bed burst into brilliant, dancing prisms. The girl was still there – only now she had a face. Mine. It was Paul who lay faceless against me. Somehow in my dream, I knew he was dead.

I woke crying out. 'It wasn't I . . . it wasn't I . . .'

The dream seemed to have drained the energy out of me. I lay and waited for my body to become recharged. Then, when I could, I got up and went downstairs to make myself some tea. The kettle took ages to boil. I looked out of the window, hugging my body with my arms.

It was nearly dawn; the moon had gone and the dim shimmer of silver that lay over the guest huts and the pottery was from the first light of morning. I supposed the mistral must have been blowing a little, for I saw the low branches of the bushes toss and sway at the end of the path.

I made my tea, took it up to bed, and sat in the quiet drinking it. Today, I would tell my father about the letter.

After two cups of tea I slept and woke only when I heard Francis calling down to ask Peppina where his flamingo shirt was. Francis went in for bright colours during working hours.

Peppina's corn-crake voice rasped, 'It was torn and I have cut it up for dusters.'

'My shirt – '

'It was not decent any longer. You have so many visitors in the pottery. What do you want them to think with all that hair on your chest?'

'It's golden and I'm proud of it.'

'Then no one else is proud of you. Tsch!'

'You're a devil, Peppina. Where is my tiger shirt?'

'It is where it should be, in the drawer of the chest in your room.'

I heard Francis go grumbling and whistling back to his room. The small altercation over the banisters cheered me. The day was beginning so normally.

I was very late for breakfast. When I arrived on the veranda, Father wasn't there.

'He's taken Dominick to the station for the Avignon train,' Elise said. 'He had an early call from his agent, Brunton. It's about this American tour. Dominick says he'll be back this afternoon. You're to pick him up on the five o'clock train.'

One by one they finished breakfast and left me among the debris. Alone, I tried to take an interest in the newspaper and couldn't. I stared out at the riot of bougainvillae and marigolds and remembered something Dominick had said the night before. 'Is life here so wonderful that you want to stay, running a home that isn't your own, coping with people who aren't even related to you?'

But I loved them. I watched Nikki stretched flat on his stomach, stroking Clèry who lay in the sun with her paws in the air. I loved Nikki most of all. What did I want? Or was it too soon after Paul's death to ask myself such a question?

I had been so certain of my love for him. Now I questioned its depth. Had I been touched by the charm, or by the man I believed I saw beneath? If the latter, the laugh had been on me because I had never really known Paul. I had loved his gaiety, his generosity, his way of making me feel I mattered more than anyone else in the world – things that were sweet and flattering and on the surface. Was that why, although I could think of Paul with sadness and an ache of longing, it was without the terrible pain of having lost my whole world? Perhaps there would never be anyone else about whom I could feel like that; or perhaps somewhere in my life, I had missed the real person.

I put my head in my hands. My coffee grew cold and an exploring ant crawled over my bare instep. As I brushed it away, a distant commotion startled me.

'Rachel! Rachel, come here.'

I ran to the edge of the veranda and saw Francis standing like a fair and angry young bull, one foot on the flower-bed crushing a splendid orange lily.

'The panel,' he said.

'What about it?'

'What about it, hell! It's in pieces – a thousand bloody pieces on the pottery floor.'

I tore past him down the path. Clèry took a flying leap out of my way. Nikki scrambled to his feet and ran by my side asking, 'What's happened? Rachel, what's happened?'

I took no notice of him and I didn't stop running until I reached the pottery. I pushed open the door of the display-room.

Sunlight shafting through the great wall of window glinted on silver and crimson and green. The Persian horse and horseman in all their glory lay scattered like outsize pieces of confetti on the concrete floor.

I stared down at the ruin of Francis's most ambitious work. 'How?' I whispered.

'How the blazes do I know? I came in and found it like this.'

Nikki, who had followed me, gave a long-drawn: 'O-o-o-h! Oh, Francis!'

He wheeled round. '"Oh, Francis" be damned! Did you touch it?'

I said at once, 'Of course he didn't.'

'He can speak for himself . . . *Did* you?'

'No,' said Nikki.

'He's much too small to move something as heavy as that,' I said. 'Look, the leg of this bench is bent right over. The weight of the panel must have been too much for it and it just buckled.'

'The bench is made to hold things as heavy as that and you know it.'

I said, crushed, 'Well, I suppose a thing can become weakened with time.'

'It's a new bench and do you think I didn't test it for strength?'

Lucia said very softly, 'What he means, Rachel, is that someone could have deliberately pushed that leg in so that the panel slipped off.'

'How can you even suggest such a thing?' Elise shot round angrily. 'It's wicked. And, anyway, how could anyone have got in? The door is always kept locked when we're not around.'

Lucia said imperturbably, 'But some people have access to the key, don't they? All of us, for instance.'

We looked at one another. Outside a supercharged car roared past; the electric clock on the wall gave the small grunt with which it always announced its chiming of the half-hour.

Francis kicked at the pieces. 'Sweep it up, someone. I can't.' He strode to the door. 'And don't let me come back and find one single blasted chip.'

'Where are you going?'

'To ring Avignon and tell them. And then to start again.' He looked round at us furiously. 'Every one of you is going to work overtime on it. Do you hear, every bloody one of you.'

'Oh, shut up,' said Lucia. She went to the window as the door slammed after Francis and said over her shoulder to me, 'You were in the garden last night, weren't you?'

'Yes.'

'But of course you didn't see anyone.'

'Only Dominick.'

'He went to bed about twelve. I saw him from my window. But you went for a walk, didn't you, down the garden?'

I said steadily, 'I came as far as the pottery. I even tried the door.'

Her eyes; her voice mocked. 'Did you? And you saw no one and heard no one?'

'The table could have collapsed any time between when we locked up and this morning,' Elise said, 'so why should you think Rachel saw anyone?'

'I'm only asking. And it's obvious, isn't it? Someone could have been jealous of Francis's winning the competition with his mosaic, couldn't they? Strong motives like that make people do violent things.'

Elise cried, 'Oh, stop it! The damage is done and it's no use holding an inquest. Francis has a tracing of the design and he can work from that. It's not as if he had to draw the whole thing over again.' She went out to fetch a dustpan and brush.

When she came back, she got to work on the pieces. Lucia began to say, 'Since Francis isn't here to tell me what to do –' and then stopped and looked at Elise.

I had been going to find a broom to help sweep up, but something made me stop, too.

Elise was standing looking at something she had picked up from the wreckage.

'Rachel . . .' She held a small object in her palm.

Lucia was quicker than I. She darted across the room and touched the tiny thing in Elise's hand. 'It's Rachel's ring. Where did you find it?'

'Among those pieces,' Elise said and stirred them with her toe. It was an old Georgian ring of garnets and amethysts set in a star. Aunt Solange had given it to me years ago. I loved it and I had worn it last night.

I took it from Elise and slowly brushed the cement dust from the stones. 'But I left it on my dressing-table. I remember –'

Elise was looking at me with gentle, puzzled eyes. There was nothing gentle about Lucia's expression.

'Or did you only *think* you left it there? Perhaps, when you came in here last night, you dropped –'

'I did *not* come in here last night.'

'All right. All right, if you say so.'

'I do say so.'

Elise started sweeping again. 'At any rate, I'm glad I found it. It would have been awful if you lost it. You're so fond of it, aren't you, Rachel?'

I slid the ring on my finger for safekeeping and demanded, 'How did it get there? How *could* it when I left it in my room?'

'Well, it hasn't got wings,' said Lucia.

I walked out of the pottery.

Francis had just finished telephoning Avignon when I reached the house. He said, 'Luckily I gave them a date for the panel well in advance of their wanting it. The hall isn't ready yet, so there's time to make another. Father's furious, but after damning and blasting my carelessness, as he calls it, he has locked himself in the studio and stuck the 'Don't Disturb' sign on the door.'

I held out my hand and the little ring gleamed in the sun. 'Elise found this among the bits.'

'Your ring? When did you drop it?'

'I didn't,' I said. 'I left it on my dressing-table last night.'

'Then how do you explain – ?'

'I can't.'

'Well, you must have scooped it up with something this morning without realizing it and managed to drop it in the pottery.'

I said miserably, 'But Francis, I didn't. I know I didn't!'

'It can't have walked there – '

'That's what Lucia said. I believe she thinks *I* did it – smashed your panel, I mean.'

'For Pete's sake, don't let's start our imaginations running wild.' He thrust a hand through his sandy hair, so that it stood on end. 'I suppose the damned table collapsed, and that's an end to it. I'm lucky there's time to do another. You coming back to the pottery? I want all the help I can get. There are dyes to be mixed and everyone can start cutting tesserae.'

I went along the veranda to my bedroom and stood at the french doors. Since I always slept with them open, how easy for someone to put their hand in and whip the ring off the dressing-table!

Some time during the night, while I'd been asleep, who had come along the terrace? Who had perhaps stood at the door raking a torch around to see what he could find of mine to put among the wreck he'd made of the Persian panel? Who knew that my bedroom was on the ground floor? All our friends in Issandre, but we could rule them out; the family . . . and Max.

Had Max stood just where I was now standing, watching me asleep, hating me for a vindictiveness of which I was innocent?

'I'll come later,' I said.

A wild thought flashed through my mind that perhaps I had done this thing after all. Perhaps the shock of the tragedy at Maladieu had had the effect of making me walk in my sleep. Perhaps I *had* broken the panel because subconsciously I did envy Francis. But I knew that not even some deep, unknown urge would have sent me sleepwalking to the pottery to destroy the lovely thing Francis had made.

For the first time since I'd come as a child to Issandre, I felt uneasy at sleeping in that ground-floor room.

# CHAPTER FOURTEEN

Halfway through the morning Father called on the house telephone – another sure indication that no one must disturb him at the studio. Voices on the telephone he never minded. Faces and people moving across his vision broke his concentration.

'Max has a couple of books for me,' he said. 'I gather he's busy this morning with some work sent over from London. So will you go across and collect them?'

I said carefully, 'I'll have them collected for you.'

He missed the point. 'Good.' He rang off.

Nothing would have induced me to go to the Château and I stood by the telephone wondering whom I could send. If Peppina appeared in their drive, she would probably be shooed off the estate as a vagrant before she had a chance to explain. Nor did I dare take anyone from the pottery, although this was one errand I was sure Lucia would willingly do. Not that I had any idea whether Sonnengarde was still the attraction or whether, now, a man came first. To my knowledge she had been out with Max three times this past week and, for all I knew, there could have been other meetings. I knew, though, that Francis would be furiously angry if I took Lucia away from the work on the new Persian panel.

There was only Nikki to send, and he loved running errands. I called him and sent him to fetch the books for Father.

I was tidying the living-room, wondering why men thought the floor was the place for newspapers and flower bowls for cigarette ends, when the telephone rang. Before I could get to it, the ringing stopped and I guessed my father had answered it on the extension in the studio.

Barely a minute later I saw him striding down the drive. I wondered if he had decided to give himself half a morning off.

It was some time later when I realized that Nikki had been far too long fetching the books from the Château. I became suddenly alarmed. I had no clear idea in my mind as to what might have happened, but I acted swiftly.

One of the cars was parked under some trees. I ran to it, started the engine and drove with a rush down the drive and out past the lines of silver olives to Sonnengarde. As I approached the gate, I had a moment of dread about driving up the long elm avenue.

I need not have worried about that.

Three people stood just inside the great wrought-iron gates. My father, Nikki and the Comtesse d'Arachenne.

Nikki was beating his fists against my father's arm. I pulled the car to the side of the road, got out, and walked through the gates.

All three watched me as I approached. I was intensely aware of a kind of aura of anger. My father, black-browed, was shaking off Nikki's frantic little fists; Nikki himself was crying and the Comtesse was tapping impatiently with a gold-handled stick I felt certain she used more to intimidate people than because she had need of it. Her hair was like frost in the sunlight; her mouth was tight and drawn down.

'Rachel!' Nikki made a small, swift movement towards me.

My father grabbed him. 'Oh, no! This time you don't go running to her to protect you.'

'Protect him from what?' I tried to avoid looking at the Comtesse, but she forced me. She lifted her hand. I saw the flash of a thin steel blade. Its handle was set with jewels, crimson and sapphire.

Puzzled, I said, 'A dagger?'

'Which I use as a paper-knife,' she said.

I remembered I had seen it myself, glittering in the sunlight after she had pushed back the shutters in that great room.

With a sinking heart I looked at Nikki. He was standing very straight and trembling violently. His hands looked too heavy for his thin little wrists and wisps of black hair stood straight up on top of his head like black pins on a pin-cushion.

'That,' my father said, 'was lying on the Comtesse's desk. And this' – his hand clamped down on Nikki's neck – 'this delinquent I took from the gutter – '

'He isn't – '

'This delinquent,' my father went on, 'stole it.'

Nikki's frightened face lifted to mine. 'Rachel, I didn't.'

'Be quiet!'

'I won't.' With an eel-like movement he twisted out of Father's grip and flung himself at me. 'I didn't steal anything.'

I looked from my father to the Comtesse. I loathed having to speak to her, but for Nikki's sake I had to. 'Perhaps you will tell me what proof you have that he stole your paper-knife.'

Her face was very white like that of someone who never

walks in the sun; the thin, blue-veined lids dropped over her eyes. I suspected that the slowness of her answer was intended to prolong our agony, Nikki's and mine.

'I found the child crossing the lawn. He had slipped the dagger into the top of his shorts – obviously to hide it. But I saw the gleam of the hilt. He ran when he saw me, but my gardener caught him and held him while I went into the house and telephoned your father.'

'I – I ran,' Nikki said between hiccups, 'because the man said . . . I was . . . trus – trus – pussing.'

'Like hell you did!'

'Father, please let Nikki tell me what happened.'

'A man gave it to me.'

'You mean, the dagger? What man?'

'I don't know. I – didn't see him.'

'What about that?' said my father. 'A man he didn't see gave him a valuable jewelled dagger. It beats the Santa Claus story, doesn't it?'

I ignored the sarcasm. I crouched down so that I was on a level with Nikki and took his two hands in mine. 'Tell me what happened – about the man – about everything. Slowly, now. Just tell me.'

'You told me to fetch some books for P-Papa, but I couldn't reach the bell. So I just went around the house. I was going to see if there was a b-back door li-like we have. And some big glass doors were open. And then a m-man called me. He said, "You're tr-truspussing." And I said I'd come for some books. And he said, "What books?" and I said I didn't know, just b-books. And he said, "Try a better lie next time." And then he said, "I forgive you for tr-truspussing b-but the C-Comtesse won't. If you'll b-be a good boy and r-run, you shall have a gift to take away wi-with you. Look, it's on that d-desk. T-take it. The dagger, I mean." And I went and took it and then he said, 'Now s-scramble." And I d-did.'

'This man. Who was he?'

'I – I don't know.'

'Oh, come, Nikki! You saw him, he talked to you.'

'I t-tell you I d-didn't see him. It was awfully dark in the room. And there was a door to another room and that was open. I think the man was in there. I mean, just in-inside the door.'

'That's damned likely,' said my father.

I said, 'And his voice? Nikki, think. Think! Wasn't there something, some little thing, about it that was familiar – I mean that you recognized?'

He gave a miserable little shake of his head. 'He talked like I do when I put my hands over my mouth to make it sound sort of hollow. You know.' He warmed to his explanation, cupped his hand and raised them to his mouth. 'Like this.'

'That'll do,' my father shouted. 'We don't want further demonstrations of your brilliant imagination. You stole that dagger and I – '

'I didn't. Papa – '

'And from now you can stop calling me that. I'm not acknowledging a thief as my son. Nor am I harbouring one in my house. The law knows how to deal with young criminals. It has places for them.'

'Oh, no!' I held Nikki to me. 'You can't give a child a home then throw him out when you think he's done wrong.'

My father turned his black eyes on me and the fury in them shook me. Then he turned to the Comtesse. 'Forgive us for this, Madame. We will continue our argument at home.'

Forgive us? I looked at her. I was quite certain there was sadistic enjoyment behind her mask of anger.

'There are men in your house, Madame,' I said. 'There is Max Lambert. And there is your servant, Morven. One of them could have spoken to Nikki.'

'My servant was at the top of the house. Monsieur Lambert was working in his room. And neither of them would have the impertinence to offer one of my valuable possessions to a child to take away with him.'

Something held me back from walking away. It was so small, just a feather of proof that Nikki's story could be true.

'I'm sure,' I said, 'he honestly believes someone told him to take the dagger from your desk. He quoted the voice as saying: "You shall have a *gift*." Children don't use that word. They say "present." '

'The word is the same in French. Do you mean to tell me the child pretends the voice spoke to him in English?'

'It sounds very like it. Did he, Nikki?'

'Yes – but it was funny, like I told you – sort of hollow.'

The tip of the Comtesse's stick moved slowly, digging in the earth. I had a feeling she could have slashed it across my face, only violence was not her way. She said to my father with exaggerated composure, 'As you say, Monsieur Helston, this is for you to investigate. You will do so? But kindly get off my property. I am busy. I have much to do.'

My father, who had never bent to anyone in his life, made

a poor attempt at a bow. 'You have my assurance, Madame, that the boy will be suitably punished. You heard me say that I'll not harbour a criminal in my house.'

*'He's not . . .'*

'I'm afraid my daughter has an obsessional affection for the child. But it will make no difference to my decision.'

'There's nothing obsessional . . .' I began and gave up.

The Comtesse had already turned her back on us. It was an ignominious dismissal of us from Sonnengarde. We had gone a few steps, when she called, 'Monsieur Helston.'

My father swung round half-anxiously, half-eagerly. 'Madame?'

'I shall have some more material for you. I have unearthed very old letters and there are the books this child was supposed to collect. Monsieur Lambert will bring them to you.'

I heard Father let out a long, heavy breath. 'Thank you, Madame. I'm glad you don't hold this wretched business against me personally.'

'I do not use spite against myself, Monsieur Helston. And you are useful to me.'

I had never before heard my father ingratiate himself but, seeing him standing there like a chastened giant, my fury got mixed up with acute distress. I felt helpless and alien as I stood near him, and I couldn't bear it. I put my arm round Nikki and swept away. My father caught up with us outside the gates.

Our voices clashed. I said, 'I know it looks black against Nikki. Oh, I know it! But how *could* you say the things you did to him in front of her?'

At the same time my father was shouting, 'And a nice mess this could have landed me into! She had every right to take the whole commission away from me, and all you can do is to . . .'

Our words hit against each other, but neither gave in.

'Don't! Oh, p-please don't,' Nikki wailed.

With an arm still around him I swung left, towards the olive grove. My father shouted after me. 'Do you intend to leave the car here?'

I'd forgotten it. I turned to see him getting into the driving-seat. He slammed the door and started the engine. We walked on, keeping in the shade of the olives.

Dismally I realized that I had no proof that two people were wrong and Nikki right. As someone in Monsieur Briac's shop had said on that first occasion, 'There's always a beginning to delinquency.'

Nikki broke away from me and rushed into the trees. I caught up with him as he flung himself on the ground. He sobbed into the dark earth. 'Don't let him send me away. Rachel, I'll d-die if I have to go.'

I knelt by his side, pulled him towards me and cradled him in my arms. 'You trust me, don't you?'

'Y-yes.'

I put him from me and took his face between my hands. 'There's only you and me now. Father isn't here, so you've no need to be afraid. Will you tell me the truth?'

His solemn, streaming eyes met mine.

'Did a man tell you you could have that dagger?'

'Yes, Rachel, he did. He really did.'

I dropped my hands and leaned against a tree, staring into the soft, luminous green light.

'Rachel, Papa won't send me away, will he?'

'Wait a minute. Let me think.'

Think. Remember that other day at Issandre. A bar of chocolate and a packet of macaroons had appeared in Nikki's basket. But the man who accused him vanished after making his accusation to Monsieur Briac. Again today, Nikki hadn't seen the man who had told him to take the dagger. A child's mountain of lies? Or the truth? And if so, what was the meaning of the coincidence of two invisible men?

I looked at Nikki. He sat cross-legged and, as he watched me, his neck stuck out of his shirt like a fledgling bird's.

I said, 'Think back. In Monsieur Briac's shop did you see anyone you knew?'

'No.'

'Monsieur Lambert, for instance?'

'I don't think so. I was watching Monsieur Briac grinding coffee. I didn't see anyone.' He paused and then said anxiously, 'Rachel, you are angry, aren't you?'

'Yes. But not with you.' I was going to believe his story for the time being, anyway.

When we reached home, I took Nikki to the pottery, called Elise, and explained that he was in disgrace.

'Oh, not again!'

'I'll tell you about it later, though you'll probably hear it from Father first. He's very angry. Keep Nikki by you till lunchtime, will you?'

I went to my room and lay flat on my bed. I was always

able to think better that way.

Two weeks ago the Comtesse d'Arachenne had said to me, 'I shall find a way to punish you. And I shall see to it that it will be punishment far more bitter, and hurt you more deeply, than any physical violence.'

Suppose the whole sequence of events since the tragedy of Maladieu was her form of punishment for me? Suppose, by sending Nikki for the books this morning I had played right into her hands?

Had they seen Nikki come to the house, the Comtesse and Max? Had the plan occurred to them to implicate a little boy who was very young for his age and not in the least quick-thinking? The idea was outrageous, but it nagged at me all the same.

Even the shutters could not keep out the oppressiveness that hung over the valley. I turned restlessly on the bed. Just suppose I'd hit the truth. Just suppose . . . *Keep away from imagination; stick to facts.* Very well, then. What were the facts? That things were happening to people I cared about, so that I became deeply implicated. What was the object? To break up my home life; to have fingers pointed at me? Rachel is championing a little delinquent. Rachel is an opportunist. She caused one man's death because he no longer wanted her, and now only a couple of weeks later, she has fastened herself on to a married man whose future promises riches and fame . . . Rachel has been devoured with jealousy since Francis won the mosaic award, so she destroyed the Persian panel. . . .

Max watching; Max reporting to the old woman sitting in her high-vaulted, shadowy room; Max talking to our friendly, gregarious family. Max taking Lucia out, driving, lunching, getting her to talk. Because, like so many men, he found her beauty irresistible, or because he wanted to learn all he could about me – whom I loved . . . what I loved . . .?

Then, through the mass of bewildered thoughts, came the realization that I hadn't told my father about the letter to Irene. And now, after the scene at the Château, he would be in no mood to listen.

I got up, went to the doors and pushed back the shutters. I could see movement in the pottery. Peppina, looking like a blackbird, was bending over the rosemary bed in the tiny herb garden.

Would my father send Nikki away as being out of his control? Could he do it? Law – French, English or any other –

had never concerned me much. Now it became dreadfully important because I had given Nikki my promise that I would not leave him.

If Father meant what he'd said and the blow fell, could I take Nikki with me to Paris and throw us both on Aunt Solange's hospitality? I knew she liked having me visit her. But she had never met Nikki or shown any desire to have him stay. Her beautiful apartment was not furnished for the amusement of small boys, nor could her life with its cultural interests, its sophistication, be adapted to a child.

Suppose I took a cheap apartment somewhere? But I had no money except for the allowance my father made me. And what work was I fitted for? The designing and making of mosaics. But how many jobs were there in that field? Then could I go as a housekeeper? But who would want a girl with the encumbrance of a supposedly delinquent boy? I hadn't been helping Nikki or myself by that impulsive promise not to leave him.

Nor was I helping myself by remaining here. Hot and untidy, I went to the wardrobe for a fresh dress. As I took it off its hanger I saw the little rawhide suitcase Paul had given me. I hadn't looked at it since the night I had put it there, at the back, in the dark.

I lifted the case out and snapped it open. I would never wear the nightdress or the slippers, nor would I ever use the brush and comb. But I would find someone to give these things to – a friend who was getting married or had a birthday. I thought of Elise. She would never know where they came from, but I had a feeling that one day, soon, she might want pretty bedroom things. She and Francis were very close and the brother and sister relationship of their childhood was developing into something that was intriguing even Father. Elise would look so pretty in the sea-green nightdress. I folded it and put it back in the case and snapped the lock.

I stood stroking the rich cream leather. Paul. The Paris memory was still poignant and yet it was paradoxically unreal. I might have taken part in some vivid play that had run for a week before the curtain had been rung down on it for ever.

# CHAPTER FIFTEEN

That afternoon I was to pick Dominick up at the station. My father, using the big car, had gone into Issandre to see Monsieur Duhamel, his solicitor.

We had had a tense and divided lunch with Nikki relegated to the kitchen to eat with Peppina. Elise was on my side and refused to believe Nikki would steal even a currant from a bun. Francis offered a middle-of-the-road 'He-could-be-on-the-other-hand-he-mightn't-be' kind of philosophy. Lucia was bored. My father and I knew each other's opinions too well to argue any more. George took no part in it. He wolfed crayfish in white wine and kept putting gentle fingers on his right shoulder which was severely sunburned.

I was going into Issandre a little earlier than the time when the train was due because I wanted to get some magazines and a book of designs which Madame Geraldine at the bookshop had ordered for me.

When I went out to the garage to fetch the runabout, I found Max in the drive dragging a sack out of his car.

He saw me and said, 'I believe Francis wants all the stained glass he can get, so I've collected this for him.'

I was not usually so graceless, but I passed him without comment.

He stopped, pulling the sack on to the grass. 'There were some broken windows at the back of the Monk's Chapel. They were so overgrown with ivy that nobody could see them from the outside. I found them when I was prowling around, so I picked up the pieces and brought them over.'

'I could have wished you hadn't.'

He let go of the top of the sack, and the glass inside made a little silvery, clattering sound.

'Perhaps Francis will think otherwise.'

'Does the Comtesse know you've brought it here?'

'No. But it's of no use to her.'

'You'd better take it back. I can easily believe that someone – Nikki – or I – will be accused of stealing it.'

'Don't be so damned silly.'

I felt like an adolescent in front of him and that made me

more angry. 'I suppose being a lawyer gives you a sense of superiority.'

'You're being very childish.'

Childish? Yes, I was, but it sprang from bewilderment because I had no idea how to handle the situation in which I found myself. I could understand why children, wrongly punished, hit out with their fists. They had no command over words. Nor had I. Every time I talked with Max, I was certain I said the wrong thing, or perhaps the right thing in the wrong way.

'Well?' Max asked impatiently. 'What do you want me to do with this stuff?'

'Take it back.'

'After scrabbling in centuries-old dust to get it? I don't like wasting my time. Things should have a reason.'

'I can quite believe it.'

There were footsteps coming towards us from behind the hedge. 'Thank heaven,' Max said. 'Here's Francis. Now perhaps I'll get some sense out of someone.' He raised his voice and called, 'I've brought you some stained glass I think might be useful. Where do you want it put?'

'Good Lord, where did you get that?' Feet apart, Francis opened the sack and peered in delightedly.

'From the Monk's Chapel.'

'But I thought we weren't allowed to have it.'

'Oh, Max has the magic touch.' I hated the acidity of my tone.

They took no notice of me. Francis's bland face beamed. 'Thanks a lot. We love working in stained glass. I'll take it across to the pottery.'

I told myself as I went to fetch the runabout that there was nothing sinister about that sack of coloured glass. Max had been quite open about it; Francis had accepted it, not I. There was no way in which this, too, could be used against me or those I cared about. Yet, so wary and frightened and cautious was I, that even this simple gesture seemed fraught with malevolent intent.

It was market day. I joined the stream of traffic into Issandre and parked the car in the shade by the station. I sat watching the people, laden with chickens and strawberries and fat white geese. I knew some of them by sight and normally I would have given as many as I could a lift, but I was in no mood for town talk. A painter friend of ours passed by. Down the centuries, the artists of Provence had learned the magician's trick of carrying more canvases than seemed humanly possible. I leaned out of the car to suggest giving Victor a lift. Instead, when he glanced at me, I merely waved. Afterwards I felt horribly mean.

But I was too troubled to want to chat with anyone. I kept picturing my father closeted with Monsieur Duhamel, making some decision that might mean the end of Nikki's life at the Villa – and, if it came to that, of mine, too.

Avoiding the eyes of people to whom sheer ordinary neighbourliness should have obliged me to offer a lift, I stared fixedly at the scudding clouds blown by the mistral from the north-west.

I was aware of the roaring of the train only after it had stopped. I looked back and watched the exit.

Dominick came, walking quickly through the barrier. His fair hair was bleached by the sun; his skin was only lightly tanned, for he had spent far too much time indoors playing music to me while I worked.

He got in beside me and threw a bulging brief case into the back of the car. 'I had to buy that in Avignon in order to bring back a couple of music scores Brunton forced on me.' He gave a big sigh. 'This is wonderful – being back, I mean.'

'Was Brunton pleased about the concert the other night?'

'Oh, yes. And too full of plans for more.'

As we drove out of Issandre and into the country, I was so busy wondering what Monsieur Duhamel had said to my father that I hadn't much to say to Dominick. My preoccupation must have been very obvious, for as we turned into the narrow side road which was a short cut to the Villa, he said, 'Now you can stop the car and tell me what's the matter.'

I pulled up under some trees, but instead of telling him, I asked, 'Did you see Irene?'

'So that's the trouble.'

'Not entirely,' I said. 'But tell me.'

He began reluctantly: 'I wish we didn't have to talk about her.' He shot me a glance. My expression must have been uncompromising for he said, 'All right. She was there at the hotel with Brunton when I arrived. He knew that I'd left Irene, but he had decided that it was policy to pretend nothing was wrong. Her father has put a lot of work his way, and you know, money and influence talk. Irene behaved like a charming wife, excited over the proposed American tour, making plans for me as if it were her one concern. Oh, God, it was awful! And worse when Brunton left because then her mask fell off and we burst into one of our everlasting rows.'

I watched a bird dive into a field. 'And then?'

He paused for a second. 'Why should there be any more?'

I said wearily, 'Because there is, isn't there?'

'All right. There is. She mentioned you. She laughed about it. She – no, let's drop it.'

'Tell me. I'll only make guesses if you don't.'

'She reminded me of the letter. She said, "You'll get so involved and I'll have to rescue you." She went on talking and talking until I felt coiled up like a tight spring. That was when I hit her. Rachel, for the first time in my life, I hit a woman. She was more shocked than hurt. But it was terrible. She said . . .'

'She said what?'

' "You never used to be violent. This is what she has done to you. It's her influence. The letter said she was . . ." '

'Go on! Go on!'

' "That she was – evil." '

I said in a tight voice, 'You didn't have to tell me *that*.'

'I'm sorry, but you asked. Rachel' – his voice grew placating – 'since it isn't true, it doesn't matter, does it?'

It wasn't true, but it did matter. I sat behind the wheel and stared at the light-drenched landscape. 'Did she show you the letter?'

'No.'

'Then you've no idea whether – what happened up at Maladieu – about Paul's death, I mean – was mentioned in it?'

'What do you mean? What could have been said? I don't understand.'

He looked so bewildered that I knew he was speaking the truth. He knew nothing very much about the contents of that letter.

'Rachel, what happened up there?'

'Never mind.' I said gently. I no longer wanted to talk about it. Instead, I said, 'Two things have happened since you've been away. Francis's Persian panel has been destroyed. And Nikki has been accused again of stealing.'

He said swiftly, in a voice full of consternation, 'Tell me about it all,' and reached out and took my hand.

I sat very still, feeling the sympathetic curl of his fingers round mine.

When I'd finished, he said, 'You don't believe it, do you – about Nikki, I mean?'

'No.'

'Then, since I have faith in your judgement, nor do I.'

His arm stole round me and it was the most comforting thing I had known for a long time. I forgot to be angry with him. Tears sprang to my eyes so that the countryside was starred with gold.

'Oh, Rachel!'

I laid my head against him and my shoulders shook. I heard myself saying stumblingly, 'I'm sorry. I'm sorry. Crying isn't my way . . .'

He held me without a word.

The last time I had cried, I had been standing near the bridge at Avignon. I began to shiver. Dominick held me closer.

The relief at being able to let go was so strong that I clung to him. Absorbed in my grief, I gave no thought to the fact that I would be misunderstood. It was some moments before I realized that he was covering my face with little stabs of shy, embarrassed kisses.

'What am I going to do?' My voice came muffled from Dominick's shoulder. 'I shouldn't have promised never to leave Nikki, should I? But I have. And if Father sends him away – '

'Nikki can come with us.'

I lifted my head from his shoulder and looked at him, stupefied. 'Us? You and me? But there's no question – '

'It's the obvious solution since you made the boy a promise you feel you should keep. I don't see how you're going to manage on your own.'

'Nor do I. But it's my problem. There'll be a job somewhere for me. In Paris or nearer home, in Orléans.'

'And who'd look after Nikki while you're working?'

'I'd find a way. It won't be *that* difficult.'

'And you're not *that* stupid,' he retorted.

I pulled away from him. 'Oh, don't try to complicate things.'

'If you'll just stop and think you'll realize that I'm trying to make things easier. You don't love me. I've told you I understand that. I'll settle for what you *can* give.' Then the matter-of-factness dropped from his voice. 'Don't you see? There are two of us needing you.'

We had changed roles. Now it was Dominick whose head lay heavily against my shoulder. He was nuzzling my neck like a puppy. I sat staring with wet eyes at the sun on the golden fields. Although I felt mean not to give as I'd been given, I didn't put my arm round him or encourage his need.

I sat still, looking ahead of me. 'I give you nothing. You

can't want that state of affairs all your life.'

'What you are is enough for me. Rachel, tell me. Are you bothered about the conventions of the thing? I mean, Irene might be vindictive and not give me a divorce for years. If it's that – '

'No, it's not that.'

'Well then, what?'

'Two things,' I said. 'First, I'm thinking of Irene. I think she loves you in her way. Then again, you and I have nothing in common. I'm not musical.'

'I might say "Thank God for that!" '

'And even if Irene didn't love you and I decided to live with you, I'd fail you. I'd fail because, if I didn't grow to love you, I'd be restless and probably leave you. And if I did grow to love you . . .'

'Well?'

I took a deep breath and plunged into honesty. 'I'd want more than you could give me.'

He raised his head, his eyes hurt. 'Am I such a dead loss?'

I did then gather him into my arms. 'Idiot,' I said softly. 'Of course you aren't.'

I prayed he'd leave the subject. He didn't.

'You want love, don't you, Rachel?'

(Dear heaven, what a stupid question!) I moved my arm from around him and glanced at my watch.

'Not yet,' he said and covered my wrist with his hand. His voice became very gentle. 'You loved Paul. The accident must have seemed to rip your world from under your feet. I know I'd be very much second best, but can't you accept it? Can't you see it could work?'

One thing I saw very plainly. Dominick, for all his gentleness, had the obstinacy so often found in weak people. There could be danger in his persistence, for in the way of escape he was offering me lay my own temptation.

I had been staring too intently into the sunlight and my eyes began to hurt. I shut them and felt Dominick stir in my arms. This patience of his was touching. I was withholding my answer, but providing I had my arms about him, he was content to be silent and wait. I was going to have to be truthful or the days ahead would be full of the same cycle of questions.

'You aren't looking very far ahead, are you?' I said as gently as I could. '*I* am. I can even see that, eventually, if you had your way, we might be married. I don't know how you'd feel about me after some years. But I know what would happen to me. One day I would wake up and I'd want to smash every mirror in the house. I'd turn aside from myself when I was trying on a new dress or a hat. You know why? I'd be afraid to see that I'd grown old and that I'd spent all those years without ever being a wife.'

'You give love in everything you do.'

I said half-angrily, 'You *don't* understand, do you?'

'Madame. Monsieur. I take the garlic to market. Fine garlic. But please – you buy?'

Dominick and I turned together and saw the basket thrust under our noses. Above it, a small impudent face grinned at us.

'No,' I said. 'Thank you. No garlic.'

The boy looked at me. *'Dommage!* And it is such beautiful garlic!'

As he scuffed away, I began to shake with laughter. Love and garlic! I turned to Dominick. His face was quite grave and I realized, all of a sudden, that in the two weeks he'd been with us I had never heard him laugh.

When we arrived at the Villa, I turned in at the drive. Max and Lucia lay under the walnut tree. Lucia's lovely face rested sideways on her arms as she looked at him. And Max watched her. I felt that they were enclosed in their own world, absorbed in each other and a sudden raging anger seized me.

'Look out!'

Dominick shouted just in time. I had missed by inches the left-hand stone pillar of the gate.

Lucia heard the car and lifted her head a little, letting it sink back on her arms when she saw who it was. Against the blue of her shorts her legs were honey-gold. She had kicked off her sandals and her toes were curling and uncurling with sensuous delight like cats' claws.

'You see,' Dominick said as we passed them, 'once people get to know your family, not even the luxury of the Château can keep them away.'

I didn't answer him. I stopped the car and let him get out, then I drove it into the garage. It was cold and dark and I wished I could have gone to sleep in there for a hundred years and wakened to find no one left who remembered the night at Maladieu.

My father was crossing the lawn. In a flash the bath of self-pity in which I had been drowning, gave way to healthier action. I ran to him. 'What did Monsieur Duhamel say?'

'Not what you've obviously been wishing him to. I don't have to keep that child under my roof. The French law doesn't force any man to be a martyr. But – '

'But what?'

He stood frowning over my head. 'If I go to the police and tell them I can no longer control a child I've made mine, if I tell them that he's rapidly growing into a delinquent, I can be rid of him. But because I'm well known, the papers will get hold of the story. I don't want that. Publicity of the right kind is all very well, but to be held up as a poor disciplinarian, a man who can't control a child of seven . . . I'm damned if I'm going to have that.'

'So . . . Nikki stays.'

'Nikki does *not* stay. Duhamel tells me there is a kind of school somewhere outside Orléans – a disciplinary institution for want of a better word – where people who can afford it send their children for correction if they're difficult to handle and they want to keep them out of the hands of the police. It'll be a hell of an expense, but it's a solution. A child can stay there as long as the money comes in to pay for him. And if *they* can't make a decent citizen out of him, then the police step in.'

'And if Nikki goes, then how long – ?'

'He won't come back here,' Father said with emphasis. 'He'll stay at the school until he's old enough to work and fend for himself.'

'How *can* you do this to him?'

'I'm spending good money on a child who isn't even mine. This school doesn't take beans for payment. I consider I'm doing as much as any man could. The alternative is to hand him over to the French authorities – and no child is going to make me a laughing-stock.'

'Suppose the school finds him absolutely honest? After all, there's nothing else he can be accused of – he never gives any trouble. They might send him back.

'They won't. The place is run by an ex-police inspector, his wife who was a prison nurse, and a schoolmaster. There's also a psychiatrist there. They've all had years of experience. They understand that shock might make a child behave well for a time. In my opinion, characteristics are innate. But we'll see.'

'I shan't let Nikki go.'

My father, the most genial of men when everything went his way, gave me a single frozen look, turned his back and began to walk away. 'Don't talk damned nonsense.'

'Mother would never have let you do it.' I hurled my words after him.

His footsteps stopped for a moment, but he didn't look round. When he walked on, he was like an angry bear lunging across the lawn towards the studio.

Keeping busy, making jobs for myself round the house, trying to stop myself thinking by activity did no good at all. I kept visualizing Nikki at that school. What would happen to him, a child so much younger than his years and sensitive to a degree, among rich young toughs who would probably bully him? In my imagination he was being shouted at, disciplined, and punished out of all proportion to the little sins he might have committed. It wouldn't be that those in charge of the school were sadists, it would be that experience had taught them that small misdemeanors in children who were potential delinquents were auguries for their future crimes. The more I thought about it, the more the school became a kind of Dickensian nightmare.

I had also something of my own to regret. At tea-time, when my father came up the veranda steps, I went up to him.

'I'm sorry,' I said. 'I shouldn't have brought Mother's name into this.'

He shrugged his big shoulders. 'Oh, I'm sure I'd have had the same tussle with her . . . Has Peppina made meringues for tea?' He sat down at the head of the table and looked at the empty chair by my side. 'I gather Nikki's in the kitcnen with Peppina.'

Someone, I think it was Elise, said, 'Yes, Father. You said that's where he must always eat from now on.'

I had to listen all over again while Father told the rest of the family his plans for Nikki. Elise protested and so did Francis, but Father quelled what might have been a small riot had the three of us been strong enough against him. Dominick remained silent, watching me, and George said, 'Best thing that could happen. Make a man of him!' Childishly, I hoped the raw, sun-scorched spot on his shoulder would be agony by night-time.

When I came back to the veranda after helping to clear away the tea things, I found Dominick alone. A music manuscript covered with the hieroglyphics of dots and dashes and tiny notations, lay on the table. But he wasn't studying it. He had his head in his hands. He looked up when he heard me and the vine shadows across his face made him look haggard.

I laid a hand on the manuscript. 'Is it so difficult?'

He said, 'I had a letter from Irene this morning. She insists on coming on this American tour in October. How do you stop a woman from gate-crashing your life? Because, if she does come, it will be a fiasco.'

I sat down in the chair opposite him. 'You'd better go to Paris, or London, or wherever she is now, and talk to her, hadn't you?'

'There's only one thing that'll stop her.'

'What's that?'

'You know perfectly well.' He raised his head and looked steadily into my eyes. 'If you come too.'

'That's impossible.'

'Why is it? Rachel, give me one good reason.'

I watched a fly with small iridescent wings, crawl across the table. 'I've already given you more than one.'

'All you've done is to tell me you don't love me. I've accepted that. So let's start from there.' He reached over and touched my hand. 'I was listening during tea to your father's plans for Nikki. You hate the whole idea, don't you?'

'You know I do.'

'Then I've got a solution. Come and live with me for a year – just one year. And bring Nikki. I'll look after you both. It would only be fifty-two weeks out of your life.'

I said bewilderedly, 'And then? Then, what?'

'If, when the time is up, you can't bear the life, I'll let you go. That's fair enough, isn't it? It'll give you both a breathing space – you to make some sort of preparation for earning your own living and Nikki – well, it'll save him from that school.'

I said brokenly, 'Must you be so good?'

'I'm being an optimist. I believe that when our year together is up, you'll stay because you'd be happy with me. And if you weren't, then at least you'd have given me a year of yourself.'

I shook my head at him. 'I can't do it. It wouldn't work.'

He frowned at the manuscript before him. 'The whole point is, you don't want to leave here, do you? You want to find some way to compromise. You're torn between fighting for Nikki and fighting for yourself. This is your little world and you cling to it, don't you, Rachel?'

I said, 'Circumstances make me stay.'

'You could break away. Elise could take your place. But you don't want to go.'

I said resentfully, 'How do you know what I want? You

don't really know much about me, do you? All you've ever done is to fall in love with your image of me.'

'That's not true,' he said painfully. 'I've lived in this house with you for nearly three weeks. That's the way to know people.'

'You're quite wrong. How do you know how much I'm hiding even from my family?'

I was nervy and near to quarrelling and hating myself for it.

Dominick said peaceably, 'All right, prove I'm wrong. Take Nikki and get away. Out of France. Go to England. Listen, Rachel – I've got a flat in St John's Wood. I took it when I walked out on Irene. She never goes there. If you really want to save Nikki from that school, go to London, to my flat. Get yourself a job. With your knowledge of French, there should be something you could do. I have a woman who cleans for me; she'd look after Nikki.'

I said gently, 'You have preposterous ideas, don't you? Even if I said "Yes," there's the question of a school. And I'm sure I couldn't get Nikki out of the country if Father chose to stop me.'

'There's a way over that, too. Take the ordinary ferry from Calais to Dover. You don't need to carry suitcases. I'll give you money for new outfits, which you can buy when you get to London.'

'The whole thing's mad. I *can't*!'

He was feeling in his pocket. 'Here are the keys to the flat. There are two.' He was busy taking them off a ring. 'And don't dismiss the whole idea on an impulse. Think it over. If you decide not to go, then you can give the keys back. But take them now.' He pushed them across the table.

A shadow passed across us. I glanced up and saw that Lucia had come silently on to the veranda. She perched on the rail fanning herself with the little ivory and black lace fan she had found in an antique shop in Châteauroux. The vine cast shadows over her face, giving a mystery to her smile.

My hand went quickly over the keys lying on the table. I slid them into my pocket, hoping she hadn't seen. If she had, I wondered whether it would amuse her to tell Max.

'Francis is impossible,' she complained. 'I've struck for an hour. *I* didn't destroy the Persian panel, so why should he use me like slave labour?' She looked at Dominick over the rim of her fan. 'It's odd that you didn't notice anyone around that night when you came back from the concert. But, of course, you didn't go near the pottery, did you? It was Rachel who went down there.'

He said, 'The accident could have occurred any time after all of us were asleep.'

She smiled at Dominick. Then she looked at me. 'He thinks it was an accident.'

He appealed to me. 'Well, wasn't it?'

I said in a hard voice, 'Lucia believes that someone was jealous of Francis's success in the competition and deliberately ruined the panel.'

She jumped down from the rail. 'But we're not holding an enquiry among ourselves. We're such a nice family. We just have our suspicions.' She sauntered past us, running one finger along the curlicues of the table edge. 'And don't ask me who I think smashed that panel because I won't tell you. I'm one of the nice family. I don't tell tales.'

We sat in silence until she'd walked away, then Dominick said, 'I thought the panel was too heavy for the table and it collapsed?'

I said explosively, 'The panel, Nikki's supposed thieving, the letter to Irene . . . If I knew for certain what I suspect, then I'd have the answer to them all.'

'What do you suspect? Tell me what – ?'

'No,' I said. 'But there's one thing you can do to help. You can get hold of that letter someone sent to Irene. Or, if she won't part with it, ask to see it and study the handwriting. That would help me tremendously.'

'I'm sorry,' Dominick said, 'but she has destroyed it. She told me so.'

## CHAPTER SIXTEEN

Issandre was *en fête*. Every year the two rival massed bands marched, one from the south, one from the north of the town, to the Square. Torch bearers preceded them and their personal colours hung from gaudy banners with streamers flying: north – red reindeer on blue; south – green dragon on white. The youth of the town followed, setting off firecrackers, singing and shouting, their arms round their girls or each other.

Thousands of small coloured lights were strung between the trees of the Square, the shops kept their lights on, and the tricolour usually hung limply from the old Bell Tower in the hot air of the fête nights.

In the centre of the Square was a plinth on which stood a statue of Issandre's first mayor. Every year, for this one night, the fat man with his stone regalia was hauled off by crane to be dumped in some storehouse. In his place was set a golden papier-mâché donkey. For days before the fête the town's chosen painters worked hard giving him a fresh coat. As Elise remarked, 'After all these years of coats of gold paint, he must be a much fatter donkey than he was when he first appeared.'

Every year since we were children, Father bore us to the fête and, because he was a celebrated man, tables were always reserved for us at the Café Chinois, so that we had a fine view of the dancing and the fun and Father could be seen by all those who wanted to come up and speak to him.

For the first time, I tried to avoid going. I was tired; I had a headache; I had a lot to do. Every protest was overruled. I went to the fête with the rest of the family.

The donkey was floodlit. His ears gleamed like long arrowheads of gold. At his feet people flung flowers, and someone had hung a garland of stephanotis around his neck.

'It's all so pagan,' Dominick said.

'It probably *is* pagan,' I told him. 'At any rate no one seems to know the origin.'

'But the way they throw flowers at it! As if they're worshipping it.'

I laughed at his solemnity. 'It's only fun,' I said. 'If anybody worshipped him once, they don't now.'

'I do,' said Lucia. 'He's gold.'

At our table, we collected friends. Pascal, who owned the Chinois, miraculously produced other tables and joined them to ours. We drank coffee and cognac and danced. Francis found Ginette Valois, the daughter of the town's most successful notary, and bore her off to dance.

My father never danced; he preferred to hold court, which he did magnificently. Lucia, Elise, and I could scarcely sit down before someone dragged us up again, though dancing on stone with a crush of people wasn't easy even on our strong feet.

I found myself singing with the rest while the bands played alternately. I joined hands with strangers and whirled in a local folk dance. Such was the influence of it all that the past three weeks vanished as if they'd never been. I was carefree again.

At last, laughing and exhausted, I sat out and watched. Rockets of coloured lights split the sky and rained down in red and blue and purple stars; the golden donkey was knee-deep in flowers.

The wife of the local rag-and-bone man made leis of wild flowers every year and sold them at the fête. Father bought three and hung them round our necks. Mine was made of bougainvillaea she must have snatched from someone's wall. I touched the cool purple petals.

And then I looked up and saw Max.

Father caught sight of him at the same time, hailed him, and insisted that he join us. All the happiness went out of me. I was too aware of him sitting at the round table next to Lucia and turned my chair so that I wouldn't have to look directly at him.

Elise was saying, 'You don't have fêtes like this in England, do you?'

'Oh, I think they keep up some old customs in certain places.'

'But not in London.'

'No, not in London.'

'Max,' Elise said, 'you've never told us where you live. Do you have a big house with a garden? Do you live near Westminster Abbey? Do you stand up in Court and defend criminals?'

'The answer to all those questions,' he said laughing, 'is "No." I live in a flat in north-west London. It has a balcony but no garden. I live alone, but I'm looked after by someone called Mrs Strangeways. She's very fat, has bright pink cheeks and cooks like an angel. And my legal specialty is corporate law.'

'You're having a long holiday.'

Max smiled into Elise's pretty inquisitive face. 'I've left one company and am joining another later in the year.'

She continued, 'I wonder why you aren't married?'

He said, with amusement, 'That's quite a point, isn't it?'

They were still talking when Ginette Valois's brother Bernard dragged me off to a dance again.

We were swept with the crowd three times round the Square: jostled; managing a few dancing steps; bumping into the trunks of the plane trees; walking when the crush made dancing impossible or the noise too great to hear the band; then dancing again.

On the fourth time around, as we passed the tables where

the family sat, cars which had tried to get through the Square, had been halted.

Bernard said, 'Don't they know they can't use the Square during a fête? What are the police doing – letting them come through?'

I started to say, 'They're probably tourists and they mightn't know.' Then I gave a sharp cry and stopped dead. 'That car . . .' I broke from Bernard's arms and fought my way through the dancers to the pile-up of cars caused by the whole little world of Issandre dancing in the streets. All I wanted was to be able to recognize the man in the car. Pushing my way through the crowds, I practised my questions:

'You saw me up at Maladieu on the night of the accident, remember? You saw me come up the hill, didn't you? I wasn't there when you arrived, was I? . . . Thank you, thank you! Now please, will you just pull into a side street and wait while I call someone so that you can tell him?' I'd go, then, and find Max.

The cars began to move on. I raced towards them and dashed out into the road. *That's the one, the second car up. Go on, quick before the gendarme moves them on . . .Go on! . . .*

We were at the corner of the Square. I flung myself at the huge car. I know I touched one of the windows.

At the same moment some youths came racing by, shouting and scrapping. I was flung backwards as they fought past. A group of people broke my fall. 'Hey! Hey!' they cried and righted me and held me, laughing.

'I'm sorry,' I said and pulled away.

The car was turning the corner. Again I shot into the street after it.

Another car hooted and the scream of tyres mingled with the music and the voices. Something like a steel band clamped down on my wrist.

'You bloody little fool!' said Max and dragged me on to the pavement.

'Let me go!'

He held me all the more tightly.

'That car . . . I must get to that car.'

'Whichever one you're talking about, it's gone now,' he said. 'The *gendarme* has cleared all the traffic out of the Square.'

'Damn,' I cried and turned to him in helpless fury. 'You did that on purpose. You didn't want me to stop that car! You wanted –'

He seized my shoulders and shook me. 'You little idiot! Before you stopped that car, the following car would have stopped *you*, and for good and all. So, unless you had suicidal tendencies, I think I've done you a favour.'

The anger went out of me. I said despairingly, 'But it was the same car that I saw up at Maladieu on the night – '

'What are you talking about?'

I cried in a frenzy of impatience, 'The one belonging to the man who took Paul to hospital. I caught a glimpse of the mascot on the bonnet. It was the same . . . the same as on that car I tried to stop.'

'Well, they can be bought by the thousand.'

'But this was unusual – a silver unicorn with a man's head.'

'Was it?' He looked away, eyes narrowed in a way he had and which I couldn't explain. It could have been boredom.

I was sorry now that I'd tried to explain. That narrowed look could have meant a sudden interest, an idea I'd given him, a scheme forming. I could be playing into his hands, trapping myself by expansiveness. With this man, one had to be cautious and secretive and all the things I was not. But, to mark my own sincerity, I had to drive home to him the fact that I'd desperately needed to stop that car and identify the owner. I had to shout at him because of the din in the Square. 'It was just a chance that the driver you prevented me from stopping was the man who found Paul at Maladieu. If so, he might have proved to you that he saw me coming up the street *after* the accident; that I had nothing to do with it.'

'I'm sorry, I'm afraid I must argue that one, too. You could have run away and then decided to come back.'

I said bitterly, 'You have an answer for everything, haven't you?'

'I wish to God I hadn't.' He turned and walked into the crowd.

This time I looked before I crossed the road. Father said when I reached our table, 'Bernard's been searching for you. He says you leaped out of his arms while you were dancing and disappeared.'

The lei around my neck had been bruised and crushed in my tussle with Max. I took it off and laid it on the table.

Bernard broke from the crowd and saw me. 'If you'd been chasing a criminal, you couldn't have shot away from me quicker than you did!' He was laughing.

'I'm sorry. I thought I saw someone I knew, but the car went on before I could speak to him.'

His eyes were merry. 'So you ran from my arms to another man? All right, I forgive you. Let's dance. Put that lei on again. It looks good against that cream dress.'

I put it on and danced. But I no longer felt like joining in the singing. And I didn't see Max again that night.

## CHAPTER SEVENTEEN

From my bedroom window I watched a man walk up the drive. Then I closed the shutters and fastened them.

Peppina was at the door as I came out of my room and, with the sunset blazing behind him, the man on the step looked like the Demon King in a pantomime. It was Morven.

He had handed an envelope to Peppina and was saying, 'It is important that she receives it at once.'

'She shall, Monsieur.'

Our front door was closed only at night. Peppina left it wide open and came down the hall, turning the letter over and looking at something on the flap. She saw me and said, 'It's a message for Lucia from the Château. Tsch! There'll be no holding her now! Do you know where she is?'

'I'll find her,' I said.

I made myself look at the envelope as I took it from her. The handwriting was large and thin and wavy. On the back, was printed in ornate letters 'Sonnengarde'.

Peppina lingered, her eyes bright with curiosity. 'What does the Comtesse want with Lucia?'

'I don't know.'

'It is Monsieur Lambert's doing, of course. You know, I do not believe he comes here to help your father. It is Lucia. *Dommage. Dommage!*'

'A pity for whom?'

'For Monsieur.'

'Then you're wasting it,' I said shortly and left her.

It was nearly dinner-time and long past the usual hour for working in the pottery, but Francis had set himself a dead-line for finishing the Persian panel. Somewhere in his sweet and seemingly easy-going nature was a touch of iron. We all knew it and respected it.

I found Lucia in the pottery sulkily mixing more colour for the tesserae. Francis was using mostly stained glass for the panel, but he needed some opaque colours for the peculiar old background tints. Lucia looked as if she would like to throw the whole pot of dye at him. I went over to her bench.

Francis saw me. 'If you take her away from what she's doing, I'll break your neck! She's already wandered off twice this afternoon.'

'I'm just delivering this,' I said and laid the letter on the bench.

Lucia picked it up, looked at the writing, turned the envelope over and saw the word on the flap. It took her only a moment to tear open the thick envelope; her fierce little fingers shook with excitement.

The note was short. When she had read it, she held it out to me. 'Since you're so anxious to know what it says and who's written it, here, read it.'

I backed away. 'I don't want to.'

She said with amusement, 'Her Christian name is Monique. I wonder if you can guess her surname?'

I didn't answer.

She looked across the room at Francis. 'You can finish the dye yourself.'

He made a dive for the jars on her bench. 'Don't leave them like that, you little fool. You'll ruin them.'

'That's too bad.' Her voice was soft. 'You see, I've an important date tonight and I have to get ready for it.' The way she paused for magical effect, she might really have been my father's daughter. 'I've been invited to Sonnengarde,' she said.

Lucia came down to dinner in the raw silk dress Madame Olivette in Issandre had made for her from a Paris pattern. Madame's clients included several from the great villas of Arles and Avignon, for she was Balenciaga trained and could have made a fortune had she remained in Paris. But Issandre was where her brothers and sisters, aunts and cousins lived, so back she had to come to our little town.

She had never made anythng more lovely than the sapphire silk Lucia wore. It outlined her perfect figure, yet it wasn't brash. Against the rich colour her skin looked like velvet. With the dress, she wore pearls which had been my mother's and which she had borrowed from me and never returned. I made a note to get them from her tomorrow.

When Lucia chose, she could be enchanting. I saw the eyes of the men at dinner that night drawn to her like a magnet. She had enormous reserves of charm which she never bothered to use with us. But this was her great occasion. We were just part of the prelude before the act; before her entry into the Château. I remembered what she had said some years ago: 'One day I shall go to Sonnengarde. And it won't be as a tourist.'

When we had finished dinner and Elise and I were clearing away, Lucia said, 'I'll take the big car.'

'Oh, no, you won't,' Father said. 'You dented the runabout the other day through sheer impatience. You won't take either. You'll walk, like anyone else. It's only a matter of a few minutes.'

She looked down at her sandals which were little more than thin straps. 'But I can't arrive on foot!'

George said, 'I'd run you there, only my car's being oiled and greased.'

Lucia ignored him and walked out. George turned to Father. 'I could run her there in your car.'

'Let her be.'

It was odd the way Father alternated between indulging Lucia more than any of us and then behaving unreasonably where he would have been indulgent with us. I sometimes felt that he was ashamed of the fact that she was his secret favourite. But then, Father was a man very susceptible to beauty.

After Lucia had gone and Elise and I had helped Peppina to wash up, the men suggested that we all go into Issandre. I was the only one who wanted to stay home.

Dominick said immediately, 'I'll stay too.'

'You'd be on your own,' I said. 'I've a heap of things to do, dull things; chores; household bills to check. If I finish them all reasonably early, I'll join you. I suppose you'll be at the Chinois?'

Father said they would and they left noisily. As soon as the car disappeared I was sorry I was staying home. The café life in Issandre was fun.

For company I turned in to Radio III. Someone was playing organ music. The sombre tones did nothing to lighten my mood.

I was looking through the little pile of bills for which I always had to write cheques for Father to sign when the telephone bell rang.

I lifted the receiver: 'The Villa Daphnis.'

The voice was a man's and he spoke in halting English with an atrocious accent. 'A woman whom I gather is a servant of yours has just stopped me and asked me if I'd seen a dark child wandering on the road. I hadn't. But when I was passing the Château just now, I saw a small boy in the grounds. I believe there are no children there, so I thought it could be the boy your servant was looking for.'

'Thank you, but I'm sure my brother is here.'

'You'd better make certain, hadn't you?'

'Who are you?'

The voice said impatiently, 'I've told you, a passer-by who was stopped by your servant, and I'm in rather a hurry, but I thought you ought to know.'

'It's kind of you, Monsieur.'

I replaced the receiver and went into the kitchen.

Peppina wasn't there. Sometimes in the evening she would go up to the Villa Oisan. She and Monsieur Cambé's servant, Albertine, had formed a kind of reluctant friendship, forced on them by the fact that they were the only two women of the same age and occupation living in the area. But Peppina wouldn't have taken Nikki with her without telling me.

I ran out into the garden calling, 'Nikki, Nikki, Nikki.' My voice rose each time until at the third call I startled some sleepy birds.

I searched the pottery and the guest huts. My father's studio was locked and anyway I knew Nikki would not go in there. He was too afraid of Father.

I didn't stop to close the door of the house. I just ran down the drive and across the road. The olive trees threw black shadows across the path and as I raced, I kicked up little stones which lodged in my open sandals.

'Nikki.' My voice rose hollowly into the night. I called, listening, then called again. Only the silence beat about me.

When I came to the gates of Sonnengarde, I walked on the grass in the shadow of the elm trees. The great house was like some black stage-set out of a melodrama. I stopped and listened again. There wasn't a sound.

'Nikki.'

I was certain now that he had been caught trespassing and they – and I knew who 'they' were – would be waiting for me to rescue him.

There was a beam of light on the far lawn. Cautiously, still keeping to the shadows, I crept round the house until I reached the terrace which ran the length of the south wall. Now I saw that the light came from tall open windows on the ground floor.

'Nikki.' My toe caught the base of an urn at the terrace steps. I winced with pain and leaned for a moment against the stone pillar.

This time I heard voices coming from the lighted room. The Comtesse's? Max's? Nikki's? Morven's, even?

With a wild fear that even my heartbeats might be heard and give me away, I crept up the steps and along the terrace, keeping close against the magnolia-covered wall.

I thought desperately: It mustn't be Nikki in there. Whatever happens, it mustn't be . . .

It wasn't. I was close enough now to see between the thick glossy leaves of the magnolia. Lights blazed from a chandelier and a standard lamp in the far corner.

Monique d'Arachenne sat in the high carved chair. Lucia, in a smaller chair, faced her. There was no sign of Nikki. That was all I cared about. I breathed a swift sigh of relief and backed away from the window. I was going to leave them and search the grounds. But before I was quite out of earshot, I heard my own name.

The Comtesse was saying in her formal stilted French '. . . Rachel. You think I do not know her because I have only just come to live here. But I do, my child, I do.' The pause was momentary. 'It is painful to have to say this, but it is for your sake.' Another pause. Then: 'Your sister Rachel is not to be trusted.'

I clutched at the magnolia so tightly that some of the rough leaves came off in my hand. I leaned forward and peered into the room.

The fascination of that still, black-clad figure with the diamonds in her ears, was spellbinding. I would have had to be pried away from the wall.

Lucia's hands rested lightly in her lap; her ankles were crossed; her dress was splayed round her like a fan. 'But Madame . . .' It was a courteous protest and meant nothing.

The Comtesse continued, 'Let us not talk about your sister. I have important things to say to you.'

Lucia's head lifted slightly. I knew that in spite of her apparent serenity, she was taut with excitement.

'You think it strange, since you have not met me before, that I should be taking an interest in you? The old have whims, my dear, *and* wisdom. I may seem shut in in my own world, but I have contacts outside who keep me informed.'

'Max?'

'He is interested in you and I approve his taste. You have distinction.' The dry, pedantic voice grew momentarily warm. 'And how I love beauty!'

The magnolia leaves were cold against my neck. I had to go on listening, for I had a wild hope that I might hear something that would throw the light I needed on all that had happened. Here, in this conversation to which I was blatantly listening in, it was possible that I might learn whether it was the Comtesse and Max, or Max alone who was harming me.

I edged closer. The leaves rustled and stopped moving.

'You know, of course,' the Comtesse continued, 'that Paul was my only son. What you may *not* know is that I married my cousin. The name d'Arachenne is not merely mine through marriage; it is the name of my family, too. Unfortunately, I have no love for those on my husband's side. Our banking business makes us rich, but I am rich in my own right. I have decided, now I have lost my son, to leave my estate away from my husband's family.' She paused, leaned her head back and half closed her eyes. 'I intend to make Max Lambert my heir. He has been good to me – so very good – and so helpful. In spite of our strict French laws of inheritance, I know there is a way to make Max my heir and I will find that way!'

Lucia said on a breath, 'Max heir to – all *this* . . .' and could not keep the excitement out of her voice.

'You like money, do you not? And all the things it can buy? But of course you do. It is burning on your beautiful, ambitious little face like a dark light. You mustn't mind my frankness.' She chuckled. 'It would please you, would it not, to become mistress of Sonnengarde?'

Lucia said, 'I don't understand.'

A flash of irritation showed on the Comtesse's face. She dropped her stilted, formal way of talking. 'Come now, don't play-act with me.'

'I'm sorry, Madame, but I really don't understand.'

(*Oh, but she does!* I wanted to shout into the room. *She understands perfectly. And you know she does.*) I was in a fever of impatience for them to come to the climax of all this. My hands were clenched and holding my breath had become painful, but I was afraid of missing a single word through the disturbance of my own breathing.

On the Comtesse's finger was one huge solitaire diamond. It glittered as she swept her hand round the room with distaste. 'This house has been inhabited far too long by a miserable recluse, and now by me, ailing and old. After me, I want to see Sonnengarde become alive again with youth. It is mine to give; it is yours, *ma petite*, to take.'

'Madame!' It was a whisper, yet it filled the room with awe and triumph.

'You will marry Max Lambert,' said the Comtesse and leaned back in her chair, her face alight with something that, had I not known otherwise, I would have believed to be joy for Lucia. 'We will arrange it. I have a strong will and money; you have magnetism and ambition. You and Max are already friends. He is young and I have urged him to go out and find companionship with people of his own age; to be gay.' She smiled. 'And when he met you, my dear, he needed no further encouragement from me. You are old in wisdom where men are concerned. It is something some women are born with. Only a few, of course, but you are one.'

Lucia didn't move. Her beautiful gaze was fixed on the old face framed by the red cushion.

The white head nodded with pleasure. 'So a friendship has begun between you. Propinquity will make the final fusion. You understand? The idea pleases you?'

Lucia was on her feet. She turned her head slowly, looking about her, up at the chandelier, around the walls at the tapestries, at the magnificent furniture. At Sonnengarde. She was assessing her inheritance.

I had seen and heard enough. I turned blindly, feeling sick with a misery so strong that it shook me. At the Comtesse's next remark I stopped.

'And that brings me back to your sister Rachel. You must be very careful of her, *ma petite*.'

Lucia laughed. 'Oh, yes, Madame, I will.'

'She killed my son.'

Lucia breathed. 'The accident . . . at Maladieu . . .?'

'We will not speak of it now. And you must tell no one, do you hear? I have my reasons for not wanting that – er – intrigue made public knowledge, but I do not wish to discuss them with you. All I ask of you, for your own sake, my child, is that you are careful of Rachel. You will have what she wanted so desperately, and because of that, she'll destroy you, too.'

Lucia said slowly, 'Rachel . . . and Paul?'

'You must find a way to get Rachel out of the house; in fact, out of your life. Do you hear?'

'Father would never let her go.' Lucia stopped, thought a moment and then added, 'Unless . . .'

'Unless what?'

Lucia said slowly like someone thinking it out as she spoke, 'Father is making plans to send Nikki to some corrective school. Rachel is very upset about it. She even threatened to leave home and take him with her. I don't know if she meant it. She probably didn't, though she does adore him.'

'Then you must see that she does take him away, mustn't you? I promise you, you will have no peace of mind once Rachel knows that you and Max will inherit Sonnengarde.'

'I'm stronger than Rachel. I can manage her.'

'You don't begin to understand, do you?' A note of exasperation had crept into the old voice. 'A girl who has once tried to kill – and succeeded . . . Come here.'

She rose from her chair and Lucia went and stood before her. The old woman put her hands on her shoulders and kissed her cheek. 'You will be, through Max, like my own daughter.'

Lucia said with charming wistfulness, 'It would be wonderful.'

'Then listen to me and do as I say, or it will all be spoiled.'

'I will do as you say, Madame.'

'Good – then get Rachel out of your house, out of the lives of all of you.'

'If I can.'

'You can!'

For a moment they looked at each other. Then I heard Monique d'Arachenne laugh. 'The prize is a good one, is it not, *chérie*?'

'It is the kind of prize I have dreamed of,' said Lucia.

Someone touched my shoulder, I started around with a muffled scream. A hand was clapped over my mouth.

'Aren't you in enough trouble without adding to it first by trespassing, then by listening at windows?' said Max.

I twisted out of his grasp. 'Where's Nikki?'

'Hush.' He pulled me away from the open window, whispering. 'What's this about Nikki?'

'You know perfectly well. Where is he?'

'In bed and fast asleep, I should hope.'

'Then why did you phone me and disguise your voice, pretending you were a Frenchman with a pretty bad English accent?'

'What am I supposed to have told you?'

'That Nikki is here in the grounds.'

'Really?' His face was completely in the shadow. To say that I was afraid of him was an understatement.

My voice shook with pleading. 'Where *is* Nikki?'

'How do I know? And we can't stay here.' Hand on my wrist he led me down the steps into the deeper shadow of the trees. 'Now, what's all this about?'

I had nothing to lose by telling him. I only wished we were somewhere where there was light so that I could watch his face for the evasions, the half-truths. I wished, too, that I could be more calm, but as I told him about the telephone call my voice came jerkily, between short, sharp breaths as if the air of Sonnengarde was too rarefied for me.

When I had finished there was a long silence. I thought he wasn't going to say anything. Then he spoke, and his voice was grave. 'You can believe me or not, as you like. But I didn't make that call.'

'Then who did?'

'How the devil do I know?' The moonlight revealed the deep lines of his face. 'But I can promise you one thing. Nikki isn't here. I've come past your house and he was in the garden with Peppina. It must have been some silly hoax.'

'Nothing that's happened has been a hoax,' I said angrily.

'What do you mean by that?'

'You know perfectly well. And I suppose you know, too, that Lucia is with the Comtesse.'

'Is she?'

We stood in an uncomfortable silence. I wondered how he would react if I said, 'A marriage is being arranged in there.' But perhaps he knew. Or at least he must know of Madame la Comtesse's bright plans for his inheritance. He was devious. Lawyer-like, he betrayed nothing. But I knew too much, and the odds were against him. So, in a way, it was I who had the strongest weapon without quite knowing how to use it or what to do to force an evasive man to admit the truth.

I must have moved without knowing it, for I was aware of the edge of light streaming from the Château touching my face. Max was looking hard at me. 'Well, what's on your mind? What are you trying to tell me?'

'I'm quite sure you know. And when Lucia and you . . .' I couldn't go on.

'Lucia and I – what?'

'Go and ask her,' I shouted. 'Ask them both.' I hated him. An impotent rage mixed with despair made me cry out, 'And for

God's sake, leave me alone!'

He stood directly in front of me. There was no way of escape except up the steps again. Or so I told myself. I had no clear idea why I didn't run to the right or the left. It could have been that the lighted windows were magnets too strong to resist. All I knew was that I had to go back and torment myself by more listening, although I had surely learned enough.

I fled on to the terrace, making no attempt this time to move quietly, and pulled up dead at the open doors.

The Comtesse had returned to her chair. There was an open jewel case on the table. Something glittered darkly like rubies.

She was saying, 'If you will come tomorrow, I will take you round the Château. There is so much history here.'

'They are so beautiful.' Lucia's voice was dreamlike.

'Beautiful? What?' Monique d'Arachenne gave her a puzzled look. Then her eyes followed Lucia's gaze to the table. 'Oh, you mean the earrings. Well, I have told you. They will be my wedding present to you. But you must be very clever and very careful. If Rachel – '

'If Rachel – what?' I heard my own clear, hard voice with a sense of shock. I hadn't intended to walk in on them. But the courage that had failed me in front of Max, surged back, forcing me through the french doors so that I stood like a white-faced fury on the Aubusson carpet.

The Comtesse's voice came like a whiplash. 'Mademoiselle, I have not invited you to my house.'

'Oh, yes, in a way, you have. Or someone here did. He telephoned me telling me that my brother Nikki had been seen in the grounds. You knew that would bring me here faster than anything.'

'If he is on my property, then this time I telephone the police.'

'But he isn't and you know it. That call was deliberate, wasn't it? It was made to bring me here as quickly as I could come. Why?'

'You are not in a position to ask *me* questions, Mademoiselle. Now go.'

From the moment I had stepped into the room I had seen the shades of expression cross her face – triumph, hate, malice. But not even a hint of surprise. That was why I knew she had been expecting me. She had known I was outside listening.

I noticed for the first time, a large, ornate mirror on a table set at right angles to the french doors. In it was reflected part of the terrace and the climbing magnolia.

I had a moment's triumph. By being too bold, too frantic to make me suffer, she had made her first mistake. *Lucia was a witness to all she had said about me*. She would testify. Madame la Comtesse had trapped herself.

I looked at my sister. 'Are you coming?'

Her hand rested on the table near the jewel-case and she said with charming formality, 'If the Comtesse wishes me to.'

'I do *not* wish.' The ancient head was lifted, the eyes blazed at me. 'But now perhaps Mademoiselle Helston will go before I call my servants.'

'Lucia and I will both go.'

'Your sister will leave when I tell her.'

'Lucia . . .'

She turned her face from me.

Short of dragging her away, there was nothing I could do. I was hit by despair at that young, so lovely face turned from me, but I'd no intention of showing it. 'Before I go,' I said to the Comtesse, 'I would like to point out that slander is a serious offence.'

'Then I suggest you try to accuse me of it. Believe me, you'll harm yourself, not me. Now go.' She shivered violently. 'And close that terrace door after you.'

I said with scorn, 'How uncomfortable you must have been this last half hour, Madame, with the night air and the flying insects.' I dodged a white moth. 'I'd be sorry to hate anyone as you hate me.'

She passed a hand over her brow; her voice lost its power and became an old woman's. 'I had a son, Mademoiselle. Your fury at his change of heart robbed me of him. There is nothing more I have to say.'

Something snapped inside me and my poise fell away from me. 'I loved Paul. I went to Maladieu that night to meet him *because* I loved him; because I didn't receive the letter he wrote me. I found him dead. Have you not pity for me?'

'None.'

I had known she hadn't, but the way she said the word was like a blow in my face. I should have left her, but emotion was too strong and tore at me in waves so that, beside myself, I cried, 'And so because you have no pity, you try to turn my sister against me. I'm one of those who hear no good of themselves when they listen at doors. But I'm glad I did. Glad, do you hear? Because now I'm forewarned. You would harm me in any way you could, wouldn't you? You've tried already. None of the things that have upset me this past few weeks have been just chance – *none* of them. They've been manoeuvred by you, haven't they? Well, now I know. And so will others. I can't stop you hating me in the quiet of this place. But I won't let you sit planning how you can destroy my peace of mind, part me from my family. . . . Lucia,' I turned to her, 'for the love of heaven don't go blindly into something that may sound like all you ever wanted, but which will end by being a nightmare. Don't listen to her. It isn't you she cares a damn about. The whole idea is to harm me, somehow . . . somehow . . .'

From her big chair, Monique d'Arachenne was looking at me strangely, her eyes hooded. 'My child, I think I should pity you. Guilt and frustration have made you a little mad.'

I swung around on my sister. 'I've got to talk to you . . . away from here.'

She gave me a long, bored look. 'Oh, do go! And stop making scenes.'

I turned and walked out of the room. I was shaking so that I had to be careful how I put my feet down. The air was warm and seemed to choke me; the frogs had started their croaking. To me it sounded like a pagan chorus mocking me.

I met nobody as I walked past the olive grove. The moon was a small, brilliant arc. I knew that tears were running down my face. I wasn't crying because of the Comtesse's words, or for anything I had overheard her say. I was crying because the girl who had been my sister for thirteen years had looked at me as if I were a detested stranger.

## CHAPTER EIGHTEEN

I hurried home at an even faster rate than I had sped to the Château. I wanted the family; Peppina, Nikka – even Father. I wanted more than anything else in the world to feel them round me. It was fantastic that I, who was the one who really belonged, should be the one most needing the reassurance of knowing it.

I found Peppina sitting like a black shadow on the veranda steps. She rose when she saw me and said accusingly, 'You go out, all of you. And nobody tells Peppina. I look for you. Tsch! The house is empty. And again Nikki cries.'

'You have put him to bed?'

'Of course. Of course. Your father tells him again tonight about the school. *Le pauvre petit*, he shivers and trembles, like this.' Great shudders twisted her body. 'I tell him he does not go to school, but with you. I say, "Rachel will look after you, *mon gars*." '

'I'm sorry I left you without telling you. But I couldn't find you.'

'Then you did not look far,' she retorted. 'I was in the wood with Nikki because he had seen Clèry there and he was afraid she would get lost in the dark. He is such a *child*! Now,' she added briskly, 'I will make you coffee.'

'I could do with it. I'll come and get it.'

As we entered the kitchen, her small black-currant eyes swivelled around at me. 'You have been crying again. Rachel, what makes you unhappy?' Her voice had softened; I was her child once more.

I sat down in the rocking-chair which had once been my mother's and which Peppina loved. 'I can't see a way out.'

'Ah! So we are back to Nikki.'

'Partly. Or' – I rocked myself slowly – 'perhaps wholly. I mean, if I could prove he didn't steal those things, I could clear up a lot of other things, too.'

'What else is there?'

I said, 'Who broke Francis's panel.'

'That was an accident. Those tables, they are' – at a loss for the word, she made a twisting movement with her hands – 'so – so – '

'They're built to carry heavy weights,' I said. 'It was deliberate. And those other things . . .'

She pounced, sharp as a knife cutting through my hesitation. 'What other things?'

It wouldn't help to tell her. 'Oh, small, odd things that have been happening,' I said vaguely.

'You tell me.'

'Not now. Not now,' I said.

'You are unhappy because of Nikki. Well, then, you do something about it.' She laid her hands flat on the table and looked at me. 'You go away with Monsieur Dominick. You let him protect you. He is kind and he – '

'Wait a minute. How do you know anything about that?'

'I see. And what I do not, I feel here,' she thumped her flat chest.

'You've been listening at keyholes.'

'Perhaps. But then, it is because you do not tell me things, so I must find out for myself.'

'Oh, Peppina!' I leaned my head against the old green cushion. 'Well, since you've heard so much, you probably know, too, that what you suggest about Dominick is impossible. I don't love him.'

'Oh, love!' She shrugged her shoulders. 'Today you lie in a man's arms and you say, "It is so beautiful! It is my heart's desire." Then one day you say, "Ah, but I am tired of washing his shirts; I am tired of his liver; I am tired of his feud with the president of his business." Ah, *love*!'

Peppina was a natural cynic. I didn't answer her. She persisted. 'Or perhaps there is someone else I do not know about. Is that it? You tell Peppina.' She came coaxingly towards me and, resting against the stove, looked down at me. 'Is it, perhaps, Monsieur Lambert?'

'*No!*' Then I demanded more quietly, 'What in the world gave you that idea?'

'It would be better for him to love you than Lucia,' she said. 'Him, I like. He is so quiet, so strong.'

'You're quite wrong. He's weak. He is completely under the Comtesse's thumb.'

'That I do not believe. No woman's thumb would hold that one down.'

'Oh, yes, it would.'

'You are so young. You do not know people.'

'I do! I do!' I broke off and made a small gesture of hopelessness. I'm changing, I thought. I used to be calm, now I shout to make my point. I seem to be for ever defending myself and what I believe, and in between I look over my shoulder like a criminal. . . .

Oh, I was most certainly not being punished by violence. That crudity was not for the people at the Château.

Peppina was studying the shining inside of a saucepan. She said with the elaborate casualness she displayed when she was consumed with curiosity, 'There is something in this house that I do not understand.'

'I think we all understand. Nikki is to be sent away.'

She shook her head vigorously and put down the pen. 'It is more. Once you were all happy. Now the house is troubled. Your father and Monsieur George do not notice. They notice only what goes on in themselves. They are wrapped up in their own comfort. The rest of you . . .' She shook her head and a hairpin fell on to the floor. She picked it up and stuck it back into her black knot. 'The other day I heard Francis say to Elise, "Who could feel spiteful towards me so that he breaks my panel?" And Elise says she doesn't know and bursts into tears. Francis says, "What do you think? Who . . .?" And Elise only says, "Let it be, Francis, let it be." And he says, "But perhaps I know." And she just cries all the harder. Then he goes and kisses her and I hear no more.' She sighed and rubbed her skinny arms. 'And then there is Nikki, and there is you and Monsieur Dominick. None of you happy. *Eh bien*, why? Tell Peppina.' She thrust her face close to me. I couldn't look into her tiny, loving eyes.

Francis . . . Elise . . . What were the secret thoughts they would not even tell to each other? That Nikki broke the panel. Or that I had done it out of jealousy because my competition design was not even placed?

As I was leaving the kitchen, Peppina called after me. 'You had better go and find Monsieur Max.'

I stopped dead.

'He came a little while ago and he asked for you. I told him I didn't know where you were and I think he is waiting somewhere.

Max in this house! I was so angry, I was speechless. I turned and walked towards the living-room and flicked on the light. The room was empty.

Nikki was calling from his bedroom.

I ran up the stairs. His door was open and his bedside light on. He sat up in bed, his hair on end and his eyes too bright for sleep. At the far side of the bed stood Max.

I asked indignantly, 'What are you doing up here?'

'I heard Nikki crying and came to see what was the matter.'

'Peppina was in the kitchen. Why didn't you call her? And what do you want here, anyway?'

'You.'

My heart turned over. Love and hate had the same effect; they melted limbs, silenced voices.

'I'm sorry,' Max said. 'But Nikki sounded upset, so I thought I'd better do something about it.'

Nikki said, 'I wanted some lemonade. I couldn't sleep.'

'Oh, Nikki, you know you can! You're just –'

'Papa is sending me away. Rachel, don't let him. I want to stay with you. You *said* I could stay with you, always.'

I looked at Max. 'You know what it's all about, don't you?'

'I'm afraid I do.'

I said scornfully, 'I don't think fear comes easily to you.'

I scooped Nikki in my arms. Over his head I said, 'Hadn't you better go now?'

'I came to see you.'

'What did you want?'

'To try and make sense out of what you told me earlier this evening in the Château grounds.'

'The Comtesse will tell you more than I can.' I leaned my cheek against Nikki's black hair. 'I can't get him to sleep with you here.'

His eyes didn't leave my face. Once again my limbs felt as if they were melting. 'I'm sure,' I said curtly, 'that Lucia will be waiting for you.'

To my amazement he burst out laughing. 'So you're human, after all!' He walked round the bed and paused in front of me. 'You wrong me,' he said. 'But then I'm beginning to believe we're wronging each other. God help us!'

If I'd wanted to reply, he gave me no opportunity. The door closed and I was alone with Nikki.

I sat down by the bed and urged him to sleep. With my hand touching his, I sat very quietly, but my thoughts raced.

Somehow I'd have to escape the tension, the menace that emanated from Monique d'Arachenne and threatened to destroy me. If I could think quietly about it all, I would find it hard to believe it was happening. But it seemed such a long time now since I had felt quiet inside myself, and it *was* happening. People did destroy one another.

And now a second need to escape was added. I had to be free of Max. I had to have release from the awful paradox that now swept me whenever I saw him.

Dominick had said, 'Give me a year. After that you'll be quite free to leave me if you wish.'

Just three hundred and sixty-five days out of the thousands I would probably live. For Nikki, a reprieve. For me, an escape.

Up from the deep wells the psychiatrists grandly call the subconscious, a thought rushed over me like a tidal wave. I gasped, fought it, pushed it back. Sitting by Nikki's side, I stared at nothing. The thought won through, became definite, formed itself into words:

*Love is first in the imagination. We project it on to the man or woman most resembling the image.*

Walking into a crowded room; looking up from a chair into a stranger's face; seated next to someone in a plane, you see him . . . you see her. . . .

And I had sat on a fountain's rim in the grounds of Sonnengarde and a man had offered me kindness – until he found out my name.

Now, with a desperate sense of self-preservation, I knew I had to despise Max Lambert, to think the worst of him. Because if I didn't, I would have to face the fact that I loved him. How did it happen? How could you hate and love? The paradox was beyond me. I sat in the small quiet room and gave comfort to Nikki and could find none for myself.

I'd no idea how long Nikki had been asleep, but eventually I left him and went down to my bedroom. I sat at my bureau and rested my head on my arms.

When I heard someone at my door, I called, 'Who is it?'

The door opened and Lucia entered. She held her head high and my mother's pearls looked real on her. She might have already been mistress of Sonnengarde.

She stepped up to the window and said over her shoulder, 'That was a stupid exhibition you made of yourself in front of the Comtesse.'

I was surprised at the power she possessed to hurt me. I said as firmly as I could, 'I chose to let you know that I'd heard everything that had been said.'

'Then you must have been beautifully entertained.'

My control broke. 'You let her. You let her say those things about me. How *could* you?'

Lucia turned. Her eyes were quite blank. 'What things?'

'You know perfectly well. She accuses me of Paul's death. I'm vicious and revengeful. I'm to be hounded, by all kinds of sinister manoeuvres, out of Issandre. Lucia, you heard her. You were a witness.'

Her violet eyes didn't flicker; her gaze was as wide as a cat's. 'I don't know *what* you're talking about.'

'Lucia!'

'You know' she considered me – 'you're getting altogether too intense about things. Making that scene at the Château and behaving ridiculously about Nikki – as if he belongs to the family.'

'He belongs as much as Elise or Francis or you.'

'Oh, I don't belong,' she said. 'I've just been living here until such time – '

'Until – such – time – ?'

'As I can go back to the way of life I was born to.'

'Your grandiose ideas don't interest me.'

' "Like to like," ' she said softly. 'But then you know, don't you, Rachel? You had your ears pinned to the door of the drawing-room at Sonnengarde. You heard that I'm going to marry Max.'

I said barely audibly, 'Always providing he asks you.'

'He will.' The table lamp flung shadows across her so that part of her face was light and young, the other dark and sly and too wise. Something in my expression annoyed her. She burst out. 'Oh, for heaven's sake, you don't really believe Max has been staying at Sonnengarde all this time just out of sympathy for an old woman and kindliness and generosity and all those sweet virtues, do you?'

'No, I don't. But I expected you to. You don't seem to respect him much, yet you're prepared to marry him.'

She gave a breathy laugh. 'If Max wrote his mercenary little plan on cardboard and hung it round his neck, it couldn't be plainer. He stayed after Paul's death to ingratiate himself with a rich old woman who doted on her son.' She flicked me a contemptuous look. 'Or, isn't it obvious to you? Don't you get the picture? He's there, at the Comtesse's side, cashing in on the backwash of her loss. Oh, but then, you must have heard about that, too, when you listened at the door. He's heir to the Comtesse's fortune.'

If she had wanted deliberately to sicken me, she wouldn't have changed a word of her cynical little speech. I leaned against the tallboy, the palms of my hands sore where my nails dug into them.

'And you dare think of marrying Max after saying all that?'

'I'm not marrying Max, I'm marrying Sonnengarde.' Her voice took on a kind of dreamy gentleness. 'From your conventional standards, my character's horrid. But nobody in all its history will ever have loved that glorious place as I will.'

'It could turn sour unless there's some feeling for the man who gives it to you.'

'Only mediocrity is sour,' she said.

'Have you thought why the Comtesse is doing this? Has it occurred to you that she might not care a hang for you?'

'Oh, I'm sure she doesn't. And I don't mind. She's got to leave her money to someone and I suppose it gives her a sense of power to have arranged two people's lives. She probably sits planning in that enormous bed of hers – you haven't seen it, of course, but I have. It's a museum piece, all crimson brocade and black carved wood. She says that generations of d'Arachennes were born in that bed – I suppose that makes it historic. But I shan't keep it. I certainly won't ever sleep in it. I shall have a bed of wrought iron and a coverlet of white fox skins.' She spread her arms wide. 'You know, the Comtesse belongs to another age – there are still some French aristocrats who are like that – she even talks in an old-fashioned, stilted way. Well, she's probably the last of them in her family. When I get to Sonnengarde, I'll make her servants sit up and snap out of the nineteenth century.'

'Lucia, listen. *Listen!*'

She sighed, turned from looking at her lovely shadowed face in the mirror. 'Well, what is it?'

'Monique d'Arachenne is evil. Shall I tell you what I believe to be the truth? Nikki never stole any of those things he's accused of taking. *She* arranged that, she and – and someone else – planned those two supposed thefts as part of my punishment because she believes I was responsible for Paul's death.'

'*Your* punishment? *You* aren't being sent to that corrective school in Orléans.'

'She's hurting me through someone I care very much for.'

'Oh, really, what a bore you are over that thieving little gutter brat.'

I slapped her face. I'd never before done such a thing to anyone. My hand just went out and before I realized it, there was the impact – my palm against her golden skin.

She sprang back, rigid with fury. 'I'll never forgive you for that.'

'I don't care, and I'll do it again if you ever repeat what you just said.' I seized her by the shoulders. '*Won't* you believe me? All that's happening here is part of a plan to persecute me – and I'm not being melodramatic. Or perhaps I am. But then melodramatic things happen in life. I know; I *know* the Comtesse is at the back of the supposed thefts, *and* the broken panel *and* the letter to Irene – '

'The letter?' she wrenched my hands from her shoulders.

'You didn't know about that, did you? It was sent warning Dominick's wife against me – but it didn't mention my name.'

'And I suppose it was anonymous.'

'Yes.'

'How silly. The police can always trace such things.'

'Irene destroyed it.'

In a bored voice, she said, 'Well, you've asked for it. It's the stupidest thing in the world to play around with a married man.'

'I'm not . . .' I began, and then gave up. 'Oh, what's the use? I'm tired of talking, of trying to make people see the truth.'

She gave me a strange, perceptive look. 'Perhaps we do see

the truth and it's you who don't – or won't – or can't.' She walked lightly past me. Her scent was like a cloud of sandalwood around us both. She paused by the bedside table and played with a little Meissen china box. 'There's a much simpler explanation for all this melodrama of yours. You're jealous. That's it, isn't it? You may as well be frank and admit it. You're in love with Max yourself.'

I left her in my room, laughing at her own accusation, and went downstairs.

The garden was quiet and dark; sequestered as a cloister. It would have been a wonderful place in which to think had I known where to begin.

## CHAPTER NINETEEN

In the morning my father went very early to his studio and put the 'Don't Disturb' sign on his door. At lunch, he had Peppina take him a tray. In the afternoon, I knew he was going into Avignon to meet an artist, now a very old man, who had painted portraits of the d'Arachennes half a century earlier.

I should have known that it was never any use trying to talk to Father when he was preoccupied. But I had waited ever since breakfast for him to be available and I was too tense to wait any longer.

I found him in his studio putting papers in order before leaving for Avignon.

'I've got to talk to you, Father.'

'Well, don't choose now.'

'I must.'

He looked, frowning at me. 'I'll be back about five o'clock. You can talk to me this evening.'

'Listen, please. I'll tell you quite quickly.'

'If it's more money for housekeeping . . .'

The look I gave him was enough. He added, vaguely alarmed, 'Well, you'd better tell me. Only make it brief.' He brushed cigar ash off his shirt and reached for his coat.

'First of all you've got to promise not to refuse to listen if I mention Nikki.'

'If you're going to beg me to change my mind – ' he began.

'I'm not. Nikki is only incidental in this.' I pulled my chair up close to him. If he tried to escape before I finished, he'd have to knock me over to do so.

First of all I reminded him, very briefly, of the two thefts for which Nikki had been blamed. Then quickly, without giving him time to protest, I mentioned the broken panel. 'Francis hasn't told me, but I don't think he believes it was an accident.'

'Of course it was. It was just his sheer carelessness not to have made certain the bench was strong.'

'They found my ring among the broken pieces.'

'Did they?' he asked absent-mindedly. 'Well, you shouldn't wear jewellery when you're working in the pottery.'

'I didn't. I left it on my dressing-table.'

'You mean you thought you did. Really, Rachel, what's finding your ring got to do with the broken panel?'

'*You* ask Francis if he really thinks it was an accident.'

'If he had any other ideas, he'd have told me. And come to that, what's in your mind? He didn't break the damned thing deliberately.'

'He could have an idea that someone did.'

He gave me a curious, doubtful look. 'Who? And why?'

'Jealousy. And that makes me the most likely suspect.'

He began fidgeting with the papers on his desk. 'I've never heard such nonsense.'

'And then,' I went on relentlessly, 'there was the anonymous letter to Dominick's wife.'

'What letter?'

'Someone wrote to her telling her that Dominick was running around with a girl who was no good to him.'

'Mentioning no names, I suppose.'

'No.'

'Well then, why are you looking at me as if something ought to click in my mind? Nothing does. So Dominick's wife received an anonymous letter. What do you think I can do about it?'

'I know it referred to me.'

He threw up his hands. 'Lord above! Where do you get your over-sensitiveness from? Certainly not from me and not from your mother. For heaven's sake, girl, see sense. A young man in Dominick's position, with a great career before him, world appraisal, and with a marriage breaking up, must have dozens of women fighting to become the second Mrs Dominick Rond.'

I said helplessly, 'Can't you understand?'

He ticked the things I'd told him off on his fingers. 'Nikki is twice caught stealing; a mosaic panel gets broken; Irene Rond receives an anonymous letter. Where's the common denominator?'

'Here,' I said. 'I am.'

His voice boomed. 'You? What the hell . . .?'

'Please don't blow up, Father. Listen. There's something else, something that I think makes the whole series of happenings a deliberate attempt to harm me.' Then I told him briefly about the conversation I'd overheard last night on the terrace at Sonnengarde.

He listened quietly enough and when I'd finished, he turned an unexpectedly troubled face towards me.

'You do see now, Father, don't you that I –'

'You overheard two people talking and got hold of the wrong end of the stick. You walked in upon a private conversation and accused the Comtesse –'

But I hadn't told him that bit yet. I stared at him. 'How did you know – ?'

'Lucia told me in confidence. She's very troubled about you.'

'That's the illusion to end all illusions!'

'It's true. She told me exactly what happened.'

'I'm quite certain she didn't,' I cried, 'or you wouldn't be so calm about it.'

'I've no reason to doubt her story. After all, no one forced her to tell me.'

I said explosively, 'What *did* she tell you?'

'That the old Comtesse has become very fond of Max and she wanted to meet Lucia because he was attracted to her. She sent for her and you went to the Château, looking for Nikki, and happened to listen in on their conversation and put some wild construction of your own on their words.'

I lifted my hand and slapped it down on the desk. 'And that's that! Such a charming, simple explanation.'

'It was. The Comtesse is old and lonely and she has taken a great interest in Max and Lucia. The old often become sentimental. She hopes they'll marry.'

'Hopes! That's putting it mildly. She's using Max and Sonnengarde as a bribe to Lucia in return for her efforts to harm me. I'm to be hounded out of Issandre, I'm to be –'

'My dear,' Father said with alarming gentleness, 'you had a shock when Paul died. I'm afraid I didn't realize how hard it had hit you. The rest of the family knew nothing about your affair with Paul. I thought I was doing right in persuading you to keep quiet about it. Perhaps I was wrong. You're not by nature secretive and the strain of having to act that way has obviously added to your distress. We've all noticed that you're behaving oddly these days.'

I cried in a fury of frustration, 'Who wouldn't act oddly when things press down on them – hideous, insinuating things? Father, can't you see, other people are being involved, but always in a way to hurt *me*. *I'm* the one – '

'That's enough!'

'No, it *isn't* enough.' I leaned over the desk, storming at him. 'You don't want to listen to what I'm trying to tell you, do you? Why? Do you think I'm mad?'

I saw a look in Father's eyes that scared me. He wasn't given to feeling anguish, but there was pain in his eyes now. 'Of course you aren't mad. I think this – er – distress of yours is a temporary thing brought on by shock.'

I whispered, shakenly, 'You don't usually use the wrong word, Father. You don't mean "distress," you mean – '

'Don't try to put words in my mouth. I mean what I say. But I warn you, Rachel, if you aren't careful, this can develop into a persecution mania.'

I shot up from my chair as though it were going to be pulled from under me. 'Don't say that! Don't!'

He glanced down at my hands which were gripping the corner of his desk so tightly that my nails scratched the polish. I realized that, to him, this was another sign of what he feared was happening to me. My head throbbed and hot pins pricked the skin all over my body.

He got up out of his chair, came and laid both his hands on my shoulders. 'I'm going to get Courcelles to have a look at you. He's one of the leading specialists in Avignon, and – '

'I don't want a doctor.'

'I don't care what you want. Something must be done before the whole thing gets out of hand. It's for your good,' he said more gently. 'I can't have my own daughter cracking up.'

I said bitterly, 'You're doing your best to crack me up.'

'I'm not, and one day, when you're your normal self again, you'll realize that. You probably only need a short course of treatment.'

'I'm not lying on any psychiatrist's couch.'

He said reasonably, 'I've told you, you're too sensitive. That's what's brought this on. You've got in this state because an old and ailing woman uttered threats to you after her son was killed. We all do silly things when we're desperate with grief. Remember how I shut myself up for days and drank like a fish after your mother died? But I got it out of my system. The old Comtesse got it out of hers by wild talk to you. You've shut your shock up inside yourself and put the lid on. That's as dangerous as covering up a volcano.' He put an arm round me and I saw him surreptitiously looking at his watch. 'I must go or I'll be late for my appointment. We'll talk some more tonight. Don't worry. You'll probably feel better about everything now that you've talked it out.'

He strode across the studio to the door. Opening it, he called back to me, 'If Max comes, tell him I've gone into Avignon and let him into the studio. There may be some things he can do to help me – sort out that pile of notes, perhaps. And ask him to lunch.'

Fortunately he didn't hear me laugh. If he had, he might have had more proof that I was most certainly not normal. I felt my way round the desk and sank into his chair. Hands in my lap, I laid my face against the cool pile of papers and laughed and cried and shivered until I exhausted myself.

Dimly I heard someone calling me. I took no notice. No one came into the studio to disturb me.

Dominick had said, 'Give me a year.'

Give him a year. His year. My escape. A year to break the subtle stranglehold they had on me. They? Monique d'Arachenne and Max Lambert, working together like demon allies.

And Father had said, 'Ask Max to stay to lunch.'

I had no idea of the passing of the time. When I was calmer, I sat up, blew my nose, and brushed the tear stains off my face. But I didn't leave the studio.

I had an empty feeling. I felt I had no part in the life around me. I supposed there was a great deal to be done – there always was in a household such as ours. But in some way I was not connected with it. I no longer spoke the same language as my father, with its terrible, clear reasoning that was so far from the truth.

When I'd been a child in our Wandsworth Common home, we'd had a cleaning woman who was full of old wives' remedies and old wives' sayings. Although I was so young then, there was one she repeated so often that I learned it parrot-like and never forgot it. 'There's none so blind as they that won't see,' she would mumble when she was at cross purposes over something. There was none so blind now as my father – and yet, oh, God, the plausibility of every single one of his arguments! Indeed, it would be easy to believe that I was on the verge of some maniacal obsession; that nothing was as I had experienced it except in my sick mind. Easy, that is, had I not remembered Monique d'Arachenne's words to me as she banished me from Sonnengarde, and known perfectly well that she had spoken them from cold hate and not wild grief.

I was being punished without violence. So far the anguish was mental. But if I didn't break this way, would she, in her vindictiveness, turn to violence? If so, against whom? Against me – or those I loved?

'She'? 'She,' I kept saying. But suppose the Comtesse d'Arachenne's words to me had been, as my father said, wild and unmeant? Suppose the danger was from Max . . .

The more I thought about it, the more obvious it seemed. A man with a fanatical belief in the absolute truth; a man harsh in his judgements, strong in his hate, would be far more likely to resort to violence than a frail old woman. Futile to say, 'But a man like Max, intelligent, clear-thinking, wouldn't behave like that.' The fact remained that people did. The mind was a delicate thing and hatred could temporarily destroy sanity.

I found I'd been technically turning over the pages of a very old illustrated volume of the history of France under Louis XIV, the Golden King. I flicked through the closely printed pages with the occasional coloured illustration.

The one that stopped my thoughts had eight small pictures. They illustrated the crests of the great families of France. Oriflamme was the first, the ancient banner of the French kings; three tongues of fire with silken tassels. I looked quickly down the page. Stags and shields and birds were painted in the heraldic colours – argent and azure, sable and vert. I sat staring at the last of the eight illustrations.

In blue and silver, it depicted a unicorn with a flowing mane and a silver pointed horn. A unicorn with a man's face. The mascot on the car at Maladieu that, for one bright second, had stood out like a thing of living silver against the black rocks. The heraldic beast of the d'Arachennes.

After the dumb despair that had slowed down my reactions, the startling fact that I had come upon the first real link in the chain of events since the night up at Maladieu, set my heart racing. I took such a leap out of my own limbo of desolation that I felt momentarily faint.

The stranger up there on that lonely rock-bound road, who had called himself a doctor, had owned a car that could probably belong only to a member of the d'Arachenne family. And on the night of the fête I'd touched that car; I'd been on the point of recognizing the driver – only Max had pulled me away.

Aware that I had no right to do such a thing, I tore out the illustrated page, folded it, and put it in the pocket of my dress.

Then I went out, locked the studio door, and hid the key in its usual place, under a red stone behind the lily bed.

Peppina was agitatedly scuttling round the house. She was looking for Nikki. 'He's hiding,' she said sadly. 'He thinks we are all, like his Papa, angry with him.'

'He has probably gone to play with Eugene and Jacques up at the Villa Oisans,' I said and, instead of joining in the search for him as I would normally have done, I left her. I was busy wondering why the man who had stopped to help at Maladieu had not recognized Paul. In fact, had affected not to know him.

'Rachel,' Peppina was calling. 'Rachel.'

'You must wait,' I said and ran back to the studio.

Somewhere in the text of the book I'd opened there could be a reference to the heraldic banners of the great families. I had no idea what purpose it would serve to find it, but I wouldn't rest until I did so.

'Rachel!'

I was almost out of earshot.

I unlocked the studio door with impatient fingers, went back to the desk, picked up the book, and searched the index.

The paragraph I was looking for was short. The banner of the d'Arachennes had first been seen carried into battle against the English at Agincourt. From that time on, the family had proudly displayed their crest. It appeared in stone over the great portico of the door of their Paris house; was emblazoned over the tomb of Auberon d'Arachenne in Chartres Cathedral; was painted on the doors of their carriages . . . *And poised, in gleaming metal, as an insignia on the bonnet of a Mercedes.*

I put the book back on the desk and saw through the window, Francis and Elise in the garden. He was brushing something, probably cement dust, from her cheek.

Who had driven that silver-crested car up the wild road to Maladieu? There was a possibility that the whole thing was coincidental. I had no idea whether heraldic beasts could be copied by the thousand for anyone to buy. I intended to find out. But I willed that unicorn to be exclusive to the d'Arachenne family.

And if I found that it was, then what? Search for the owner of the car and demand to know why he hadn't told me he knew Paul? And where would that get me?

## CHAPTER TWENTY

A long sky-blue Dauphine came sweeping around the drive. I watched it without interest, for we had so many visitors who came to see the mosaics. The car however, did not turn left towards the pottery, but drove straight up to the house.

I watched, through the trees, and saw a woman get out and ring the bell. She waited, looked around impatiently, then peered through the open doorway into the hall.

When I realized that there was no one there to answer the bell, I ran across the lawn. The woman wore a dark rose-coloured dress and beautiful crocodile shoes. It was Dominick's wife.

She turned and saw me at the same moment that I recognized her. 'Mrs Rond . . .'

She gave me a cool look. 'Good afternoon. Is Dominick in?'

'I'm afraid not. But if I can help you . . .?'

To my surprise a trace of a smile touched her lips. 'I was rude to you when we met in Avignon.' She moved to the veranda and began to stroke Clèry who was perched on the rail.

'Mrs Rond, I think –'

She cut me short. 'I really came to see you, not Dominick.'

'All the way from Paris? You must be tired.'

'Oh, I'm staying in the neighbourhood.'

'Please sit down. And let me get you some tea.'

She sank with a natural grace into one of the rattan chairs. 'I'd like a long soft drink, please. Lemonade or orange, I don't mind. But not for the moment. Let me talk first. But won't you sit down, too? You make me a little nervous standing.'

I sat down.

She turned from Clèry who flicked an offended tail. Lucia's fan lay on the table. Irene picked it up, spread it out, and fanned herself. 'Are you in love with Dominick?'

Oh, no, not that all over again!

'I told you the truth about that on the night of the concert.'

'Is he in love with you? . . . Oh, don't bother to answer. He is. He made that very clear.' She brushed aside my protest. 'Very well, then. Let's start from that. I want to ask you a few things. First, do you understand music? Are you prepared to listen and discuss it with him for hours on end?'

'I don't know a thing about music,' I said, 'and it's quite unimportant whether I do or not. There's no question of my caring for Dominick. But he told me that he came down here to get away from music; that he doesn't *want* to talk about it. He needs a rest from it, Mrs Rond.'

'Oh, that's a temporary mood. Dominick could no more refrain from discussing music than he could stop breathing. Another thing' – she put the fan down and her fingers twisted restlessly in her lap – 'any wife of Dominick's would have to cope with being the liaison between him and his agent; he hates the business side of his work.'

Clèry gave a colossal leap into my lap. I stroked her absently. 'Why tell me all this? There's no need – '

'I think there is. You see, I'd like you to understand. The very fact that Dominick believes he is in love with you makes it necessary for you to see my side. You may not realize it, but I'm in danger of losing him. He's very persistent when he wants something; he could wear you down. I don't want to have to fight you and *you* would not be happy with him.'

'He won't wear me down.'

She gave me a shrewd look. Then she leaned her head back against the green linen cushion. 'My life as Dominick's wife isn't a normal one, you know. It's the kind of existence people have together when they're past any physical desire. A life without anything more than affection, with the knowledge that there will never be children, never be a real family life.'

'But in spite of that, you love him, don't you?'

'It surprises you? Yes, I love him. I've been through hell, the hell any normal woman would suffer. We've quarrelled and parted more than once. But we've always gone back to each other. I've had to face the fact that I'd rather live with Dominick as he is than live without him.' She shut her eyes and then opened them again quickly. 'All this had to be said. Now I've said it, it's up to you, Rachel – he calls you "Rachel." You can take him from me as easily as you're stroking that cat. Perhaps I'd be a tigress about it and fight to get him back. Or perhaps I'd have too much pride to fight for someone who no longer wanted me. I don't know how I'd react.'

'I shall never take Dominick from you.' Then I added honestly, 'Whatever happened, I could never love him the way you do. If you came here because you are afraid of me, don't be. Please don't be.'

A light spread over her face, softening the sophistication, so that for a moment she looked almost gentle. 'Do you know, I believe that,' she said. 'And I can't understand who was vicious enough to send me that letter. It *was* vicious, you know.'

'Dominick told me you destroyed it.'

'I took it out of my bag one morning, tore it into tiny pieces and threw it into the Seine.' She thought what she had told me would please me and smiled. 'Now, may I have that lemonade?'

'Of course.'

I went to get it for her. As I collected the bottle, the tumbler, and the ice, I doubted if the problem that tore at Irene and Dominick would ever be solved. The question was far more fundamental than Dominick's temporary feeling for me. Because Irene was his wife and a normal woman, would she be able to sustain their sexless relationship? Or would there come a breaking point?

I didn't know. One never knew the depth of someone else's strengths or weaknesses. All I *did* know, was that the gods were good to Dominick. He had the most lasting thing they could give him – his career. Nothing could take his music away from him. And, in the final sum of his life, that was all that mattered to him. It was his wife I pitied.

Irene and I drank lemonade and talked, like two casual friends, of all kinds of things, carefully leaving Dominick's name out of our conversation.

Only when she was about to leave, she said, 'You can tell him I called. Say I'm staying at the Parthenon in Issandre.'

'He will go to see you,' I said. 'I know he will.'

'That letter was wicked.' She touched my hand. 'You are honest and kind. If ever you are in England, please come to see me.'

'I will.' My fingers closed over her hand. We smiled at each other.

She turned and got into her car. The door closed and the

blue Dauphine skimmed down the drive like something that had wings.

'Rachel, I keep calling you.'

Irene had been gone for some time and I was lying on the far side of the walnut tree, hidden from the drive. I was still thinking about the heraldic beast of the d'Arachennes.

'Rachel.'

I scrambled up from my hiding place and saw Peppina in the drive. 'What is it?'

'It's Nikki. I cannot find him. He said to me today, "I will not go to that prison" – that is what he calls the school. He said, "I will run away." Oh, I laughed at him and told him not to be silly, that we all loved him. He said, "Rachel said she wouldn't let me go. She promised, but she didn't mean it." And now he's run away. I know he has! I've looked everywhere. Or do you think perhaps Monsieur George has taken him on his car drive?'

George had left before tea-time, taking Dominick with him to les Saintes Maries. The great cellist, Scaram, lived there in retirement. Dominick wanted to meet him. I knew they hadn't taken Nikki. But no one had seen him for some hours and now it was half-past five.

Naturally nervous, he never strayed far from our garden unless we knew where he was going. And he'd said nothing about going up the hill to play with Jacques and Eugène Cambé.

I called the others from the pottery and we became a search party. We went through every room in the house, the garden, the olive grove. We rang the Villa Oisans; he wasn't there; we combed the field at the back of the house in case he had fallen asleep in the long grass.

'Nikki! Nikki!' The quiet countryside was filled with his name.

I was halfway up the hill with the vineyards on my left when I saw Max. He came striding towards me and said peremptorily, 'I want you to come with me.'

I cut him short. 'Nikki's lost.'

'He'll turn up. Now come –'

I said furiously, 'You don't care whether he turns up or not, do you?'

He had been gripping my wrist. He let go. 'All right. I'll help you look for him. Then you'll do what I ask. Where have you searched?'

'Everywhere.'

He said impatiently, 'Of course you haven't, or you'd have found him. Well, go on looking here. I'll go to the top of the hill. He may be somewhere around the vineyards.'

Elise, Francis, Peppina, and I met, made a plan of where we would look, then parted and began our more systematic search.

Lucia lay under the walnut tree and shut her eyes. When Francis called to her to get up and help, she rolled over on her face and lay supine under the leaves.

We didn't stop to argue with her. I guessed that, lying like a golden statue, she was dreaming of Sonnengarde.

My search ended at the edge of the vineyard. Sometimes Nikki went up there and watched the vine pickers and nibbled grapes. I asked them, 'Have you seen Nikki?'

They stopped their singing, raised themselves from their picking, and said he hadn't been near them all day.

There was no need to panic, I told myself, and straightway panicked. If we didn't find him by nightfall what would we do? The police would have to be told and that would land Nikki into greater trouble.

Eventually I came to the path that ran along the top of the vine-covered hill. The buildings where the wine was pressed and bottled and matured came into view. Edouard Cambé greeted me. No, he hadn't seen Nikki, but then he'd been in his office wrestling with figures for most of the afternoon.

'The vaults,' I said. 'They fascinated him when you showed him round. Could he be hiding down there?'

We crossed the courtyard. I heard the drone of machinery that worked the wine presses. The great door of the building was open and the rich smell of grapes reached out to me in waves. We went into the first room. Some of the men recognized me and I asked them, 'Have you seen Nikki?' The same question; the same answer. 'No, Mademoiselle.'

'All the same,' said Monsieur Cambé, 'we'll make sure. He could have slipped by without anyone noticing. He's such a little fellow.'

We went through an archway into the pressing-room. Here, men were busy on the day's yield, feeding the presses that bled the grapes.

There was a ladder leaning against one of them. I thought in panic that if the room had been left empty for a few moments Nikki could have climbed up there unnoticed. If he reached the top, the wine fumes might have rendered him unconscious and he could have fallen into the vat.

'Monsieur Cambé' – I stared at the ladder. 'If Nikki –'

'Oh, don't worry. The men have been here all the time, they'd have seen him if he tried to climb up to one of those. And he wouldn't, anyway. He's not stupid.'

It was I who was stupid to imagine such a thing, the noise of the presses, the snap-snap of the great blades of the machinery roared in my ears, unnaturally loud.

'We'll try the cellars.'

The stone steps were worn with generations of feet. There was a sweet, mildew smell.

There was also the clear, high sound of a little boy's voice. 'I'm *not* sleepy and I *can* walk.'

I ran forward.

'I'm not carrying you for those reasons,' I heard Max's brisk voice reply. 'I happen to know small boys. They're like eels. If I put you down, you'll start to give me a chase round the wine bottles. There must be thousands of them and I'm in no mood to play hide-and-seek.'

Max came out of the dimness and he had Nikki wriggling in his arms.

'You've found him,' I cried unnecessarily.

'Actually, I didn't,' Max said. 'The cellerar saw him behind some *sapines*. I suspect he has developed a taste for wine rather early in his life.' He glanced down at the boy. 'I only hope you'll learn how to carry your liquor when you grow up.'

'Put me down. I feel silly being carried.'

'You'd feel sillier if you got lost in that maze of cellars.'

'What's a maze?'

Max said to me, 'You can tell him later.' He strode out into the air. I followed.

Elise came running along the path. 'You're looking here, too. Oh' – she caught sight of Nikki – 'he's found. Thank heaven for that. Darling, what did you want to scare us like that for? Max, where did you find him?'

'Down among the wine.'

'But he could have been there all night. And we might never –'

'Well, he's found and no harm's done.' I spoke briskly, more to hide my own relief than to check Elise.

I took Nikki's hand. 'We'll go home now.'

He leaned away from me. 'Not to Papa. Please, not to Papa! He'll be so angry.'

I said matter-of-factly, 'Papa doesn't even know you've been missing.'

Max put his arm between us. 'Let Elise take him.' He prised Nikki's hand from mine firmly.

'I don't want to go with Elise. I want Rachel.'

'You'll have Rachel – later,' said Max. 'You told me once that you were seven. That's almost being a grown-up, so let's see you behave like one.' His tone was firm but not unkind.

I said, 'We're all going the same way.'

'Oh, no, you're not. You're coming with me – this way.' He turned me towards the path between the vines that led to the road.

Nikki darted to my side. 'I'm coming, too.'

Max took hold of him and turned him round. 'Go with Elise,' he said.

She gave him a doubtful look, took Nikki's hand and said, 'Come on. Francis wants help in the pottery. Let's hurry. I'll race you down the hill.'

I watched them run down the path between the vines. Then I turned to Max. 'Why did you help me find Nikki?'

He said in surprise, 'I don't see the reason for the question. Someone's lost, so we find him.'

'But it was the last thing you really wanted to do, wasn't it? I mean, help me. Unless there's some motive behind it – something – '

He said briskly, 'Come off the drama, Rachel.'

The colloquial command had an odd effect on me. I felt as if I'd been holding my breath for a long time and his words released it with a wonderful sense of relief.

'Now,' he said, 'you and I are going to Maladieu.'

'Oh, no, I'm not.'

'You're coming – '

'Can't you leave me alone? Oh, thank you for finding Nikki, but don't spoil my gratitude – '

'I hoped I might be going to earn it.'

I gave him a swift, angry look. 'By taking me to Maladieu? I wish the earth would open and swallow that place up.'

'If it did, then there'd be no proof.'

'No proof of what?' I demanded bitterly. 'That I caused Paul's death?'

'No, proof that you didn't.'

I swallowed and stared at him, open-mouthed. 'You mean that? You mean you believe – ?'

'Don't you get it?' he asked roughly. 'I'm on your side.'

'You're – on – my – side?'

'That's what I said.'

'You – you don't have to shout at me.'

'I'm sorry. That's not because I'm angry with you but with myself.'

'Go on. Please, go on.'

'I can't. I don't know enough yet. Only, we'd better get going. Nothing in a crisis remains static. We may even now be too late.'

I had no chance to ask. *Too late for what?* We might have been taking part in a race. We were running so fast down the hill towards the road that I needed all my attention not to fall headlong in trying to keep up with Max's long legs. The workers in the vineyard stopped and stared at us.

Then we reached the flat road and I was able to collect my thoughts, some small snake of suspicion crept into my mind. This could be a trap and I could be an idiot for trusting him. I ought not to go to Maladieu with him. But a bit of me persisted in its dogged wishful thinking. 'He said he was on my side. He could mean it. He just *could* . . .' And I'd take a chance.

The sun had moved around a little since he'd parked his car under the trees and the bonnet dazzled my eyes. Max opened the passenger door, gave me a brief push and shut me in.

I watched him stride around the front and get in behind the wheel. 'Perhaps,' I said, watching his strong-boned hand reaching for the starter, 'you'll tell me why you want to take me to Maladieu?'

'To find someone,' he said. 'The only person who can prove the truth of what you've always protested.'

'That I wasn't in the car with Paul?'

'That's it.'

'You believe me now? Max, you really believe me?'

In the flashing side glance he gave me, he must have seen the joy on my face. I breathed one word to him. 'Who?'

'You mean, who can prove that I was mistaken and that I've got a hell of a lot to ask your forgiveness for?'

'Never mind the forgiveness. Who?'

'You'll find out if we aren't too late.'

I was sitting uncomfortably in the car, unrelaxed, leaning forward with my hands gripped together. I was so seething with questions that I didn't know which one to ask first. 'At least tell me *something*.'

I watched his face. He looked older, more grave. But he didn't answer me.

'Why are we going to Maladieu?'

'I told you. To find the one person who can prove, not only that I've been wrong, but that I've wronged you. Don't ask me anything more yet. I'm not trying to be mysterious, but let's see what happens up there.' He jerked his head towards the hated place.

I sat by his side in silence. He had said just now that he had to ask my forgiveness. How easy was forgiveness going to be? Part of me didn't want to forgive him because I was afraid that would release me from bitterness and free me for loving him. And that was just something else that was going to hurt.

We came to the steep road that led to Maladieu and drove up it past the Hostelrie Sainte Bérénice. I glanced back and saw that the garden was empty of customers. There were brand-new umbrellas in yellow and blue, and dazzling white wrought-iron tables. The garden had been tended to and I wondered how much money had been spent on the place. Gaston Bigorne was nowhere to be seen.

The road narrowed and, at the top, where the cannon balls of old battles had opened up the towers to the winds, was a small square. The impregnable rock-face rose above us.

The tourists had all gone. The place where we stood seemed to have sunk back into its uneasy, violent past. It waited furtively for the medieval orgies in the Hall of the Seigneurs; the clandestine meetings of kings and mistresses in the Court of the Troubadours.

Max pulled the car up under one jagged wall. He held out his hand to me as we stood in the dry dust and the silence.

'I'm sorry if you don't trust me, but you'll have to try. Come on.'

We went into the first great rock hall which was the Court of the Troubadours. I shivered in the chill of cold stone. The place was light enough, for somewhere down the centuries enemies of Maladieu had also blown up the great doorway. Our footsteps echoed through the high arch into the next court. Here we met darkness and the quiet was broken by the flutter of wings as the blind bats heard us and floundered among the cracked columns.

As children, we had played in the outer court, but had been warned never to go far inside for, where the stone palace ended, the caves began. 'They go right into the earth,' my mother had said, 'and if you strayed, it might be hours before anyone found you.'

Max was ahead of me. 'Don't dawdle.'

But we had reached the far side of the Hall of the Seigneurs. Here the actual caves began and I stood irresolute at the entrance. 'I'm not going in there.'

'You're perfectly safe with me.'

As safe as a rabbit without a burrow! 'No.' I shouted have turned and run back out into the sunshine. But I was too late. Max seized my hand, dragging me towards the high cave entrance.

'I said I wasn't going in there.'

'Be quiet!'

He must have thought I was going to scream, for his other hand came down over my mouth. I wrenched my face away, but he still held my hand and the grip was too strong for argument.

'I'd better show you that I don't intend to harm you, hadn't I?' He stood in front of me. 'This way . . .' he said.

The opaque blackness of his head was between me and the cave walls. '*This* way,' he said again and for the second time since I had known him, he kissed me. His lips were cool and light on mine, his touch unexpectedly gentle, substantiating his promise: *I don't intend to harm you.*

That was all. And I had to pretend that I accepted it as just that. I didn't dare let an atom of feeling come to the surface. I kept my arms at my sides, my lips closed and unresponsive. He was merely offering me reassurance and I was afraid of a movement that would let my love show through. I only hoped he couldn't feel the hard racing of my heart.

As gently as he had touched me, he let me go. I leaned against the rock and there was a strange luminous light before my eyes. I knew it couldn't come from any place in that dark, underworld cave. Yet the light was there before my eyes as if a door was opened and the moon shone through. I stared at it as a man in the desert would stare at a mirage. Translucent, magical, the light flooded through my whole being. Max believed me. I no longer needed to be afraid. That I wanted more from him than just his belief in me must be my secret. After all, suspicion had been a mutual thing between us and all I could ever hope for from him now was a mutual trust. It was Lucia, not I, who was close to him.

Lucia and Max . . . But at least he no longer hated me and, like the beggar at the feast, I had to be content with that.

I blinked two or three times, and the light that seemed to

come from the corner of the cave towards which I'd been staring in stunned silence, seemed to spread. The moonlit door, the symbol of my own escape from despair, had been made by my own tears. I brushed my hand across my eyes and the magic was gone. I was back in a black cave.

Max was moving cautiously forward into the deeper darkness, but I remained leaning against the wall.

'Where are you, Rachel?'

I pushed myself away from the rock and went towards the voice. I put my hands before me until at last they touched the rough surface of his coat.

There was a snap of spring against metal. The flame from his cigarette lighter illuminated the cave.

At first I thought it was just another black void. Then, as my eyes became accustomed to the dark corners, I saw in one what looked to be a rough bed. I went over and peered more closely. The mattress was poor and the sheet was unbleached. There was a good quality red and black rug flung back and a large box stood by the bedside.

The lighter flame flickered and waned before I could see what was in it. 'Someone sleeps here,' I said. 'But how can they? the air . . .'

'Keep your voice down,' Max said. 'And if you promise to move quietly, I'll show you how it's possible for someone to live and breathe here.'

He walked carefully, feeling his way.

How deep did they go, these caves that had a curious, heavy atmosphere of strange rites and old sins? I had a sense of walking downhill, deeper into the earth.

Once or twice I stumbled. Max saved me from falling.

'It's so dreadfully stuffy.'

'It's the smell of a million years,' he said.

I suppose if I had had a watch and a torch and could have timed our black journey through the caves of Maladieu I would have found that the whole walk lasted only a few minutes. It seemed like hours.

When Max stopped, I sniffed the air. 'There's another smell. It's like cooking – roasting . . .'

'That's right. I noticed it, too, when I came here earlier.'

'Where can it be coming from?'

I heard a very soft scraping of stone. Then I saw light. Not daylight but the artificial light of a room. I crept forward, peered through the gap made by the removal of the stone and gasped.

Max hissed, 'I said, "Be quiet." '

'It's a kitchen. And there's . . .' I covered my mouth with my hand, watching.

Gaston Bigorne and a woman sat sprawled in chairs. She was furiously slicing carrots and tossing them into a basin. Her black greasy hair fell over her sullen face. She and the man were obviously quarrelling. I couldn't quite hear what they said for the kitchen was large and they were at the far end.

Max leaning over me, watched too.

'Then the kitchen of the Hostelrie must be built right into the rock,' I whispered.

His hand went past me and he moved the stone, which was on the wide ledge, back into its place. The lighter snapped on again.

'But who sleeps here?'

'Damn, my lighter's given out. Rachel, where the devil are you? Hang on to my coat. The way back's tricky, the rocks point out this way and you can scrape your face against them if you aren't careful.'

We didn't speak again until we were outside in the little square. The air rushed at me, sweet and warm and thyme-scented. The sunlight burned my eyes and I put my arm across my forehead to dim it.

'Now tell me,' I said, 'who sleeps in that awful place? And why did you bring me here?'

'I'll tell you later.' He was striding to the car. 'Get in.' He wasn't bothering with niceties. I had scarcely sat down when the car started and I had to slam the door while he was turning to go down the hill.

I looked at the Hostelrie as we passed. '*Does* someone really live in that awful cave?' I asked again. 'And does he depend on that hole into Monsieur Bigorne's kitchen for light and air? Do they pass food to him through it?'

'Probably.'

'You could tell me what – '

'What it's got to do with you? You'll find out.'

'Where are we going?'

'That's the fifth question in a row.' The lightness of his tone relieved the menace of the journey. 'Hasn't it dawned on you yet that I've no intention of telling you anything until I'm certain I know it all myself?'

'At least tell me where we're going now.'

'To Sonnengarde,' said Max.

# CHAPTER TWENTY-ONE

During the drive away from Maladieu, I found it unnerving and not a little frightening that Max would not answer my questions. In the end, I gave up asking them and we sat in what was to me a bewildered silence.

I had scraped my arm against the rocks in one of the deeper caves and there was a scratched and bleeding spot near my elbow. I tried to concentrate on that, on wishing it didn't burn so much. I made quite a fuss to myself about that small raw spot in order to keep my mind off the questions Max wouldn't answer. It was like acting in a play without in the least knowing what the story was about.

When the car turned in at the Château gates, I began to protest.

'Max, please leave me here. If the Comtesse sees me, there'll be another scene and I can't face it.'

'I doubt if she'll be at her window. And, anyway, I'm with you.'

'Is that supposed to be reassuring?' But it was.

Without answering, he pulled the car to the side of the drive under the elms and laid his hand lightly over mine. 'Let's get out. Careful, don't slam the door and don't make a noise.'

I shot a quick glance about me. There was a path bordered by bushes to the left of the drive. I thought I caught a glimpse of a car there. I'd no idea where Max was taking me, but I no longer questioned. I walked unprotesting by his side until we came to the old stone fountain.

'We can talk here,' he said.

I flung myself on the grass. Max sat down on the stone rim and lit a cigarette. Sunlight filtered through the trees; somewhere a bird gave sharp, tentative little chirps.

It was I who broke the silence. I had a burning question and I could wait no longer to ask it. 'You really believe now that I wasn't with Paul when he died?'

'I've told you.'

'But someone was there and you know who it was.'

'Perhaps.'

I said, 'Let's start at the beginning. You stayed at the Château because you suspected me of being involved in Paul's death.

You wanted me to suffer for what you thought had been vindictiveness on my part.'

'God knows I've got faults,' he said savagely, 'but I had no wish to make you suffer. I stayed to find out the truth about that night. If the accident had been merely the result of a quarrel between you and Paul, then I'd have accepted it and gone away. If, on the other hand, someone deliberately tried to harm Paul, then I was going to find out who it was and which. But one thing you must believe, I never meant to hurt you – or, in fact, anyone. The truth was all I wanted.'

'But someone wanted more than that. Someone wanted to destroy me. You know that, don't you?'

'I know a lot of things,' he said, 'but too late to stop them hurting you.'

I looked at him quickly, too eagerly. 'You know that someone planned it so that Nikki should seem a thief, that someone broke Francis's panel and placed my ring among the pieces so that I'd be suspected? And about the letter to Dominick's wife.'

'Yes.'

'You do? You know all that? And you let it happen –'

'Wait a minute.'

But I rushed on. 'Max, then please tell my father. He thinks I'm imagining it all; that I'm ill. You see, I told him – I *had* to tell someone – that I believed Paul's mother planned to have the biography of her family written for one reason only. It would give you entry into our house. She couldn't harm me in the way she wanted unless she knew things about me and the people I cared most for. Someone had to infiltrate into our family. You –'

'God help me, I had only pity for her. She was demented with grief, and lonely. I tried to interest her in outside things; to take her mind off her own tragedy. I thought I was succeeding; that she was slowly taking an interest in people again. She certainly appeared to be by the questions she asked about you all.'

I said furiously, 'And she used the things you told her against me and against a child – Nikki. That's something for which I'll never forgive her.'

Max said very quietly, 'I think if you could see her now, you'd forgive even that.'

'But you did more than tell her about us, didn't you? You helped her. She had to have someone to carry out her orders.'

He looked at me in swift astonishment. 'Dear heaven, you've

been thinking that *I* was responsible? All this time –' He broke off. 'But of course, in a way I was. You're right. I talked about you as a family, told her bits of gossip.' He ran a hand over his hair, frowning. 'And now I've got to make you believe me – though God knows, when I think of how *I* disbelieved you, I don't deserve generosity from you.'

I made a small gesture of pushing his words away.

'Then – if *you* didn't – who – helped the Comtesse?'

'Gaston Bigorne,' he said.

I remembered the new sun umbrellas, the wrought-iron tables, the clipped grass, and the flowers in the freshly dug beds.

I had hated Max for not believing me, but *I* hadn't trusted him either. We had been enemies because circumstances had made us seem like that. Even now, I wasn't entirely certain of him. When you have been so hurt, the recovery doesn't burst on you like lightning; it comes slowly. There was still so much to know, so much to be explained.

'Forget Gaston Bigorne for now,' Max said. 'I want to talk about Paul.'

I no longer cringed at the sound of his name.

'You may have loved him,' Max said, 'but you never really knew him.'

'Oh, I did! He was idle and pleasure-loving, he told me so himself. He was awfully honest.'

'That's just what he wasn't.' Then Max said more gently, 'I'm destroying an illusion, Rachel? I'm sorry. But you've got to know. Paul was in trouble up to his neck.'

I clasped my hands round my knees, looking up into his grave face.

'He appropriated money – a very great deal. For some time the Banque d'Arachenne had been alarmed at discrepancies. Eventually the bank's detectives discovered who was responsible.'

'Not Paul? Oh, no, not Paul!'

Max didn't have to answer that. 'The day of old Fabian's funeral was also the day of Paul's reckoning,' he said. 'They were all down here, Artois, who is president of the bank, and Louis and Gerard, his two sons. Because our families had been close friends, they told me about it. They said, "At all costs, there must be no public scandal."'

'The Comtesse? She had to know, of course.'

'They kept it from her – they were afraid of how she might react. She was quite capable of believing so strongly in her son's innocence that she might defy them and proclaim it publicly – and that they didn't dare risk. But they had to act quickly and drastically to save the bank's reputation.'

'So the climax came when they were here for Fabian d'Arachenne's funeral?'

'That's it. On the night after the funeral when the Comtesse had been seen by a doctor and put to bed. Artois and his sons called Paul into the library and forced the truth out of him.'

'But he had a great deal of money of his own. He told me so.'

'Not enough. He was being blackmailed.'

'But . . . he *couldn't* be! He was always so much on top of the world. There was nothing scared about him.'

'He had a gift of pushing unpleasant things aside when he chose. It was very likely that he believed every payment that he made would be the last. I knew him so well, Rachel. He was always the glorious optimist. He believed in his luck as old kings believed in their divine right.'

'Who was blackmailing him?'

'He had had as a mistress, a very beautiful woman who was involved with a powerful narcotic ring. I am quite certain Paul knew nothing about it until some of the peddlers were caught. But he could have been implicated, so as the price for silence, one of the men who wasn't caught did the obvious thing – he blackmailed him.'

'And when his family found out, Paul would have been sent to prison. Paul,' I said unbelievingly, 'in a prison!'

'Oh, they'd never have done that. It would have meant exposure for the Bank and that was the last thing they intended. Their reputation in the world was too high for such a scandal to be permitted. The men of the family had it all planned. They would repay the money from their own fortunes. Paul was to disappear, take another name, another identity, and leave the country.'

'And he agreed?'

'He had no alternative. He was entirely at their mercy and he knew it. The precautions they took to get him out of France were elaborate – but with money so much is possible. Nothing, of course, must be done from the Château. They could trust no one, certainly not the servants. So Paul was to drive to some remote spot where he would be met. From that moment he would no longer be known as Paul d'Arachenne. That man was dead.'

'He went to Maladieu.' I watched Max's face. It was no longer grave and hard but curiously sad. What had he once said? 'Paul is like my brother.' I went on, 'So . . . so Paul didn't go up there to meet me?'

He shook his head.

'But he *did* meet a woman!' And then I cried accusingly, 'You knew all this from the beginning.'

'I wish to God I had. All I knew then was that Paul had misappropriated bank funds. They told me about it briefly and ordered me to keep it to myself. I told you, not even the Comtesse must know.'

I said unbelieving, 'How could they keep it from her? He was her son – '

' – Who could do no wrong in her eyes. They dared not let her know their plans. She would have fought like a tigress and probably have jeopardized the bank, her family name, everything. So, they had to let her believe that Paul was dead. They had no pity for her.'

'Later, I suppose, when things had calmed down, they would have told her that he was alive. But she'd never have forgiven them for making her suffer.' I paused, and then said, 'The man at Maladieu who found Paul; the one who said he was a doctor?'

'Was Artois d'Arachenne. He had gone there because that was where Paul was to change his identity, safely away from the Comtesse and from servants' curious eyes.'

'And when I came upon the crash, he didn't dare let me know he knew Paul. It must have been a terrible shock for him to find that Paul *was* actually dead. It was a dreadful irony, wasn't it? The make-believe that turned into a reality.' I watched Max's face. It was shadowed with suffering. 'You really cared for him, didn't you?'

'When he was a small boy, he was sent to the prep school I went to so that I could watch over him. He was a handful, but even then his charm disarmed those who had to punish him. He was at Oxford with me, too. I think it was there that I first realized his inability to see any wrong in himself. He did what he wanted, took what he wanted, and believed in the infallibility of Paul d'Arachenne. But you can't be responsible for someone like Paul without growing to care for him. He was like a brother I had to protect. He returned to France to join the family banking business and I studied law. But our families were still close and I saw him often.'

'And now the Comtesse has shown her gratitude for all

you'd done for Paul in the early days by putting you in his place.'

He stared at me. 'What on earth do you mean?'

'You don't know, you *really* don't know what she has planned for you?'

'Do you?'

'Yes.'

He gave me a blank look. 'Then you'd better tell me.'

'That night you found me on the terrace of the Château, listening at the doors, I heard the Comtesse say that now Paul was dead, you were to be her heir.'

'What the devil are you talking about?'

'I heard. She told Lucia.'

'Then she must have been out of her mind. She should know perfectly well she can't leave a solitary franc of the d'Arachenne money away from the family.'

I sat blinking into the sunlight. It didn't come as a surprise. I saw it all too clearly. Monique d'Arachenne hadn't been out of her mind at all. Her news had been bait for Lucia, who was to be an ally in my persecution. She had sent for my sister and had assessed her character with swift, uncanny accuracy. And Lucia hadn't questioned the Comtesse's plans. All her life she had had a dream and now it was coming true. To her, it was her right; her mysterious birthright.

Max rose abruptly. 'We can't stay here.'

'Where are we going?'

'To the Château.'

'Max, please.'

'To the Château,' he said again.

## CHAPTER TWENTY-TWO

There was a side entrance to the Château almost hidden by ivy. The walls were at least a foot thick and the door was heavy and creaked as Max pushed at it.

At the end of a narrow stone passage was another door and when we went through it, we came to the main hall.

Morven appeared out of the shadows.

Max said, 'Is Madame in the drawing-room?'

'Yes, Monsieur, but I do not think she'll see anyone.'

'Oh, she will.' Max put an arm across my shoulders and

led me towards the big double doors. He opened them without knocking.

Monique d'Arachenne sat upright in the big chair. Her face was chalk white and she was so immovable that she might have been dead. Not even the jewels at her throat sparkled with changing light as she breathed.

Lucia stood by the fireplace. We stared at each other like strangers. Her eyes were brilliant and the delicate nostrils of her nose were quivering like an animal sensing danger. She looked beautiful and primitive and wild.

I glanced at the Comtesse, expecting her to demand that I leave her house. No word came. She did not seem to see me.

Lucia lifted her eyes from my face and saw Max. The effect was electric. She seemed to cross half the great room in a single movement.

'Oh, no, you don't!' Max put out a hand and stopped her.

'Get out of my way.' She looked towards the windows. The shutters were drawn over them and Max could have stopped her that way, too.

He said, 'I have something of yours,' and put his hand in his pocket. When he brought it out again a piece of lace, soft and dark, rippled through his fingers. It was the black mantilla.

'I have never seen . . .'

'You dropped it up at Maladieu on the night you were there with Paul.'

For the first time Monique d'Arachenne showed some sign of life. She turned her head.

Lucia looked at her then back at Max. She said defiantly, 'What makes you think that I was there?'

'I saw you.'

'You couldn't have.'

'In the car, with Paul.'

'I wasn't – '

'Oh, for God's sake, don't prolong the ordeal by a string of denials! I didn't know at the time; I thought – well, I thought it was someone else of similar build, with the same kind of dark coat over her shoulders.'

She gave him a triumphant look. 'Someone – *anyone*!'

'Not anyone. You.'

I saw her stiffen. Her violet eyes blazed. Before she could speak, however, Max continued.

'You and I have met quite a bit during the past couple of weeks, haven't we? I'm a good listener; that's part of my training. And I discovered what I was quite certain must have been the case – that you had known Paul in Paris. After all, his family and your aunt Solange had been friends for years. Besides, what did it matter now that you had known him? The enquiry into the car crash was closed. You loved Paris, you said, and you talked about all the exclusive places you'd been to; places you don't go to without an escort. Once, you let drop his name. Sometimes an expression is more telling than words. Yours was when you mentioned Paul's name. You were never "just good friends" were you, Lucia?'

She said haughtily, 'Your deductions are ludicrous. What happened up at Maladieu had nothing to do with me.'

'But you were there. Shall I tell you how I know?' He waited, then, as she remained silent, he went on. 'On the day we went to the Manoir in Avignon for lunch the wind blew your hair about and you told me you hated being untidy. I suggested you wear a scarf. You looked at me in blank horror. "I never wear scarves," you said. "If I need something over my hair I wear a mantilla. I bought a beautiful one and then lost it the same night during that beastly storm." It didn't matter – your telling me that. You had no idea I'd found it.'

'Why in the world should it be mine?'

'Because not many girls wear mantillas. They're glamorous, but I shouldn't imagine they keep your hair particularly dry. Now' – his voice sharpened – 'you can tell me exactly what happened that night.'

Her small white teeth bit into her lip; her eyes were defiant. Then quite suddenly her stare faltered. I could never understand afterwards why she told us about it. Perhaps she was a little afraid of Max.

'All right. I *was* up there that night. And what's wrong with that? Of course I'd met Paul when I stayed with Aunt Solange.'

I looked across the room at Monique d'Arachenne. Her white, almost transparent lids hid her eyes; her hands gripped the arms of her chair. As though her own supremacy no longer mattered, she had ceded the initiative to Max.

Lucia took the mantilla and let it run through her fingers like dark, woven cobwebs. 'I *had* to see Paul again.'

Max made an almost imperceptible movement towards me. His coat sleeve brushed my bare arm. 'You and Paul had a love affair,' he said to Lucia. 'That's it, isn't it? And he grew tired of it, but you didn't.'

'Have you lived to the age of thirty-four without having been in love? Max, if you say "Yes," then I won't believe you. It's part of growing up.'

Max said relentlessly, 'This isn't a philosophical discussion. Keep to the facts.'

Lucia's head went up. She said defiantly, 'Why should I talk about my life to anyone?'

Why should she? I hadn't. All the time I'd been holding on to my secret love for Paul, Lucia had had a similar secret because neither of us had been certain of him; although knowing Lucia's nature, she had probably trusted him less than I. But she had a more practical motive for holding Paul – Sonnengarde.

Max was saying impatiently, 'If you won't tell me what happened that night, then *I'll tell you*. And I think it will be the truth.'

Lucia's eyes moved restlessly around the room. She seemed to speak, not to us, but to the tapestries and the portraits and the white jades in the gilt-garlanded corner cabinet.

'I had to see Paul. We'd been so close in Paris. . . .'She paused. 'All right! We were lovers. But I wasn't a fool. I saw to it that he promised marriage first – not that I had much faith in his promises. But, when I came home I wrote to him making plans for our wedding. I wasn't going to lose him because of those hundreds of miles between us.' She shot me a scornful look. 'I was waiting for the right moment to tell the family. Then Paul's letters ceased. That's why I had to see him when he came down here. I got the car out and arrived at the Château on the night of the storm, just as he was driving out of the gates, and I followed him. He stopped the car at the corner where the road goes up to Maladieu and got out. He was acting strangely, as if he wasn't certain where he wanted to go. He kept looking about him. I wondered for a moment if he'd seen me and wondered who was following him. Then suddenly he got back into his car. I ran up to it and got in before he could stop me. He was in a mood I'd never seen before, angry and tense. He tried to turn me out, but I wouldn't go. Then he drove on, up towards Maladieu. He was furiously angry, but I had a feeling all the time that something was frightening him and that I was just incidental. We argued and fought as he drove up that awful hill. That's when you saw us,' she said definantly to Max. 'I remember your car passing us, hooting. When we got halfway up, Paul stopped and pushed me out. He had such a strange look on his face that I was scared. I fell. I think I could have broken every bone in my body for all he cared at that moment. He locked the car door against me and shot up the hill like a madman.' She was folding the mantilla slowly. 'I seem to remember Paul catching his sleeve in this as he pushed me out of the car. When – when they – found him, he wasn't lying in the car, was he? So I suppose the mantilla got somehow dragged out with him.'

Max said, 'Surely you heard the car crash?'

'With the thunder going on almost continuously? Of course I didn't. I ran as fast as I could back to my car.'

'And when, later, you learned about the accident, you said nothing.'

'Why should I?'

'And because you didn't come forward and tell the truth of what happened that night, someone else had to suffer.'

'What do you mean? Who suffered?'

'Rachel kept quiet, too,' Max said.

I saw her face flame. Not all her distress could keep the touch of derision out of her eyes.

'You'd never be Paul's type, not in a thousand years. Why, he –'

'Let's stick to facts,' Max cut in.

'The fact being,' I said, 'that I was accused of quarrelling with him in the car.'

Max turned to the woman in the chair. 'I know now,' he said to Monique d'Arachenne, 'who set out to destroy Rachel and her relationships with those she cared about. You, Madame, God help you! You planned every move, didn't you, to harm Rachel? – a girl you believed had killed your son.'

I had a sudden wild idea that she had become deaf, for she made no sign that she had heard a word.

Lucia turned and faced her. 'Madame ...'

It was so quiet in the room that I heard my own heartbeats. We were like figures caught and held in a tableau.

Then very slowly the Comtesse turned her head. Was she going to vent her hate on Lucia as she had done on me these past few weeks? I held my breath.

Suddenly I saw that the Comtesse was not looking at anyone. She was listening, her head bent slightly sideways. I glanced quickly at Max. He had noticed, too.

The tempo in the room quickened without another movement being made. Then, everything happened at once.

The silence was broken by a sound outside. A car was revving up. Max moved with the speed of light. He caught hold of me and dragged me with him towards the door.

My stammered protest, 'Max ... don't pull at me!' was lost

in the sudden confusion.

He flung open the door. Monique d'Arachenne's voice followed us, shrill, pitched on a note of terror. 'Stay where you are. *Sacre dieu*, stay – where – you – are!'

Our footsteps sounded like an army on the stone floor of the hall. I was vaguely aware of Morven in the shadows, of a woman screaming at us from the high, vaulted room we had just left. I heard Lucia's voice, lower-pitched but angry, impatient, mingling with the cries.

Max didn't let go of me until we reached the car. Once more I was bundled in with an unceremonious push. The car lurched forward.

'For heaven's sake, what is it?'

I might have been pleading with the wind. The car accelerated and we roared down the drive under the whispering elms and turned left. Towards Maladieu.

'Why? Max, why are we going back there?'

'You'll see. You'll have to see for yourself, or you won't believe it.'

'Believe what?'

I'm certain he didn't hear me.

When we turned into the road that led up to the ruins, the sun had dropped lower and was perched like a blazing flower on a pinnacle of rock. Red-gold, fiery; Valhalla.

We drove up the steep road and my heart sank. I was dreading a return to that place.

'Oh, not the caves!' But the road led to no other place.

## CHAPTER TWENTY-THREE

Max drew into the high rocky square and turned off the engine before he spoke. 'You'll stay in the car.'

'And you?' My voice rose in alarm. 'Don't go back into the caves. There's danger. I don't know what it is, but –'

'But you've got an instinct about it?' A smile faintly twisted his lips. 'Instinct, the woman's weapon!'

'Don't joke about it!'

'Dear, sweet God, I'm not!'

'Then – you mean – there *is* danger in there?'

'Does it matter to you?' He had turned his head away from me, but his profile was set and bitter.

'Yes, it matters.'

'After all I've done to you?'

'You didn't mean –'

'To harm you? No, but that doesn't entirely whitewash me. I've a hell of a lot of faults, Rachel, and one of them is jumping to conclusions, then following them like a blind man following a tiger. I don't do it in my work, but by God, I make up for it in my life; my personal relationships. My older brother once said to me: "It'll take something colossal to teach you a lesson." '

I touched his arm. 'Max, it's all right,' I said. 'Really, it's all right.'

He said savagely, 'Is it?' Then he raised his head, listening. He reached for the door handle and his voice sharpened. 'Do as I tell you; stay where you are.' He swung himself swiftly and quietly out of the car and was across the square in great flying movements, his shoes kicking up the dust.

It was only then, when I turned my head to watch him, that I saw a car parked right across the broken arch that led into the Court of the Troubadours. Max scrambled round it, climbing over the bumper. To steady himself he put his hand on the bonnet. Something gleamed in the dying sun. It was a silver unicorn with a man's face.

I moved over to the driving-seat and sat staring at it until my eyes ached. The eerie silence had a sound of its own; pulsating, breathy. Blinking, with sun spots in front of my eyes, I looked back over my shoulder. I had an odd feeling that in ancient times this barren place could have been a natural arena and that at any moment the ghost lions would be let loose.

I was so steeped in my fearful imagination that when, out of the corner of my eye, I saw something move on the jagged line of rocks to the left of the crumbling palace, I gave a huge start.

A man had appeared from high up among the ruins of Maladieu and was leaping and scrambling across the rocks. Twice, he gave swift glances backwards; once he appeared to fall and to rise with difficulty as though he'd hurt himself.

My own movements were involuntary. I pushed open the door of the car and scrambled out. My legs were so unsteady that I couldn't move. I leaned against the car and, head lifted, watched the man's desperate flight.

Gaston Bigorne, of course.

Holding my breath, I watched him. He appeared to be making

for the north-western edge. And beyond that . . .? From this distance I couldn't see his face, but I was tense with fear for him. I knew that he was racing towards a place from which there was no escape, for the rocks culminated in a single high, inaccessible peak, which fell sharply thousands of feet into the valley. But then, it was the only way – the Palace of Maladieu itself blocked flight in the other direction.

A shout made me turn my head. From the place where the man had appeared, came two more men. I couldn't see their faces, but I was certain one of them was Max.

I was no longer just afraid. Terror seized every limb and every muscle. Not all were sure-footed and those wicked pinnacles were deathtraps for anyone who made a false step.

The car's body was hot where it touched my skin. It burned through me, but I couldn't move to ease the pain. I watched and became identified with the panic and the urgency.

The escaping man had reached the base of the highest pinnacle. I saw him hesitate, measure its height then put out his hands and begin to climb. But if he reached the top, he was trapped. He was not winged for flight.

He climbed to a point and then stopped and looked up. The rock face was sheer to the top. The red sun blazed behind him and he was like something carved in charcoal, poised for a moment against the last blaze of the sky.

He reached again, feeling for a hold. I saw him try to lever himself up. For a moment he seemed to be suspended. Then his arms went sideways, flailing, beating the air. He swayed. His face turned as he wheeled round and the sun illumined him enough for me to see the line of his dark hair, the contours of his face. Shock froze me.

I screamed.

*'Paul!'*

The next moment I heard three cries, sharp and terrifying, echoing among the crags. On the last terrible shout, the tangle of arms and legs disappeared, the sky became empty and there was only the grey peak and the sunset.

And then my legs would no longer hold me. I sank on to the dusty road and covered my eyes. The dust of my fall rose and was gritty on my hands, in my mouth. I stayed where I was, crouched in the road, and lost count of time. Eyes covered, I felt nothing, not even the discomfort of my own body.

Someone touched me; lifted me up.

Max held me. 'I'm sorry. I'd no idea it would be like this. Rachel . . .'

Words failed him as they failed me. I let him help me into the car and closed the door. I watched him move in front of the bonnet, pause only for a second, then get in behind the wheel.

I stared towards the caves. The sun dyed the silver horn of the unicorn blood-red.

We drove in a strange silence down the hill, away from the rock palace. Max was letting me get over my shock quietly and I was grateful. There were many things I wanted to ask him, but for the moment I was unable to speak.

Max slowed down as we passed the Hostelrie and drew to the side of the road. 'I'm going to telephone the police.'

I said in alarm, 'Not from here. Please . . . wait till we get home. A few minutes won't make that much difference.'

He was already out of the car. 'There's nothing to be afraid of,' he called over his shoulder. 'And it must be done at once.'

I watched him disappear through the door and prayed that Gaston Bigorne wouldn't come and find me alone. I wasn't afraid of him, but even in this moment of shock, the thought of his wet mouth and his little leering eyes revolted me. The tables and the bright new umbrellas looked like a display in a store window. I thought I saw someone cross the hall of the Hostelrie, but no one came out to me.

When Max returned, he got in behind the wheel. 'The police are on the way and the ambulance men will find Paul.'

'He's dead, Max. This time – he's dead. He couldn't fall from that height and live, could he?'

'No.'

'You saw Gaston Bigorne?'

'Yes. I had to ask him where the telephone was.'

'Did you tell him about Paul?'

'Only briefly. He's behaving with the innocence of a babe. But the questions are jobs for the police. Mine is to get you away from here.' The car gained speed, turned the corner of the narrow street and reached the high road. 'I'll answer everything they have to ask me at the Château,' he said.

I put out an unsteady hand and took a Gauloise from a packet in the glove compartment. I also found a box of matches, but my hand shook so much I couldn't strike it. Max took the cigarette and lit it for me.

I smoked so seldom that I coughed over this one. My spluttering brought me out of shock back to some sort of normality. 'Now,' I said, 'tell me.'

Max stopped the car for the second time, lit a cigarette, and sat back saying, without looking at me, 'You know now that it was someone else who died up at Maladieu on the night of the storm.'

'And yet, I saw . . .'

'What? Paul's face?'

'No, it was dark. All I could see when the lightning flashed was that he was terribly disfigured and partly covered by the rug. But I recognized his ring and the clothes he wore.'

Max corrected me. 'Paul's suit that someone else wore.'

'I suppose so. But who?'

'I don't know. I suspect the blackmailer. Artois himself, or one of his sons, could have killed the man. Perhaps they met him somewhere, stunned him, then drove him here, put him in the path of Paul's car and killed him, making quite certain that he was too mutilated for anyone to prove that it wasn't Paul. You remember, it was Artois himself who identified his nephew at the mortuary.'

Shuddering at the awful picture of that killing, I asked weakly, 'And Paul?'

'According to Bigorne, he returned to France secretly and called on his mother some hours after I found you on the terrace at Sonnengarde. She was a sick woman and there was his inheritance – it was too big a thing to risk losing. I don't dare to think of the shock it must have been to her to find that he was alive.'

'Gaston was to help her hide Paul?'

'I doubt if he could refuse. He was already too far involved.'

'But she couldn't have hidden him indefinitely in that cave.'

'She was probably far too shocked to have any definite plan.'

I said shakenly, 'All those things that happened to us – to Nikki and Francis and me – Bigorne carried out on her instructions.' I pitched my unsmoked cigarette out of the window. 'How do you know so much?'

'Late yesterday evening when Paul came to see his mother, I was in the library looking for a book your father wanted. I heard them talking. At first I couldn't believe that it was Paul. But there was no mistaking his voice. I meant to walk in on them, but I made too much noise. Paul heard. He panicked and escaped by the terrace. I had two choices – to go after him or to confront the Comtesse. I did the first. Even so, Paul moved so quickly that I probably would never have been able to track him down if it hadn't been for the Comtesse's saluki. It followed him, barking. He managed to silence it but by that time I had found Paul and followed him to the caves.'

'You spoke to him?'

'No. I needed to be more cautious. I called on Bigorne and scared him into telling me quite a lot. The price Monique d'Arachenne paid for his services was handsome. When I'd finished with him, and incidentally put the fear of God into him, I went to see Artois. He lives about fifty miles from here. He wasn't in when I called, but I left a message that I had to contact him urgently.'

'You were going to tell him that Paul was in Issandre?'

'I was going to ask him who died at Maladieu.'

'And you did that?'

'No. I didn't see him. I think he must have come here this afternoon and found out the truth from the Comtesse. I know he, too, chased Paul to Maladieu and got there just before we did. That's why he was already in the caves when we arrived.'

'Artois guessed that you knew?'

Max said dryly, 'I've no idea. I suppose he must have, but I didn't give him a chance to tell me!'

'He would never have harmed you.'

'When the reputation of a great banking house is at stake, a man who can kill once to save it won't hesitate to kill a second time.'

'That night at Maladieu, what must Artois have felt like when he saw me?'

'Shock would be putting it mildly. There he was, staging an accident, changing a dead man's clothes for Paul's, hustling him away. And along comes a girl. But he coped. He sent you off to get help and disappeared with the man before you returned. A closer look at the man's face might have shown you that it wasn't Paul, although I made a guess he saw to it that it was almost unrecognizable.'

I nearly said, 'But how could a civilized man do such a thing?' As if I didn't know that in desperate circumstances men became savages. I said, 'When you were in the caves, what did you and Artois say to one another?'

'Do you imagine we had time to say anything? We were there for the same reason, to get Paul. So far as Artois was concerned, I could be dealt with later. I wonder what he had in store for me since I knew so much?'

There was no answer. I sat, my hands gripped in my lap, and looked ahead of me. Ironically, the countryside was full of peace and swift twilight. Beyond the olive groves was Sonnengarde.

Max was saying, 'Do you realize that the night of the fête was one of the most important in all this?'

'When you dragged me away from that car – Artois's car?'

'From under the wheels of another. And while you were pounding me with your fists, you talked about a silver unicorn on the car. I recognized it from your description – I knew Artois d'Arachenne's car only too well. But why had he been there – at Maladieu, I mean? That's the puzzle that started me wondering if the whole affair was as clear-cut as I'd been trying to make it. Then Lucia – '

Of course, we had to come to her in our conversation. 'Lucia,' I said. 'What about her?' And for the first time since we'd begun to talk, I turned and watched his face.

His expression gave nothing away. 'I'd better take you home. You've had about as much as anyone can stand for one evening.' He switched on the engine on the car.

'Max – '

'What?'

His remote face crushed all impulse out of me. There was nothing to say; nothing to cling to. The lovely moment in the cave, then, had been prompted by nothing more than compassion, reassurance. Max's way, even, of saying, 'Forgive me.' As we drove towards home I knew that it was of Lucia he was thinking.

As we stopped outside the Villa Daphnis, the car's headlamps lit up a splash of bright blue moving among the olive trees. I knew the colour, I knew the dress. Lucia wore it, waiting, I felt sure, for Max.

I felt him touch my arm. 'Things go full circle, Rachel. The bad part is over and there's most of your life left.' He smiled at me.

Without a word I opened the car door and got out. I paused with my hand on the gate, giving him a chance to join me.

The moment I saw him turn away from me, I pushed open the gate and walked through. I knew he was crossing the road towards the grove of olives. He was going to Lucia. Whatever she had done – and who was I to criticize what might be the outcome of early environment and inherited characteristics? – Max loved her.

I had no doubt that his anger with her at the Château had been an impulsive thing, probably caused largely by jealousy that she had once been loved by Paul. Men had always forgiven Lucia.

I walked briskly up the path. Nothing would induce me to look back and watch their meeting. I had no intention of voluntarily hurting myself more than I'd already been hurt.

Another few steps and I would reach the veranda and then the safety of my room. I paused. My head moved, turned, looked over my shoulder. I couldn't help myself.

They were dim shapes among the trees, but by the car's headlamps I saw them too clearly. Max held out both hands to Lucia and she went forward to him.

I swung round and began to run, my sandals clattering up the steps and along the veranda to my room. I plunged inside, listening for the splintering of glass as I crashed the french windows together behind me. I thought for a moment that I had broken them.

I sat on the bed and pressed my fingers to my temples. I was free. I could now tell my father that nothing had been just in my imagination; I was not suffering from a persecution mania. I had nothing more to fear. The black interlude was over and I could be happy again. Yet, deep inside me, the ache wouldn't go. What had Max said? 'There's most of your life left.' Life, yes. But without Max whom I loved and who had left me to go to Lucia.

The room was dark. I got up and switched on the light. Outside I heard the slap-slap of Peppina's too-large espadrilles on the marble floor of the hall.

'Rachel, are you there?'

The door opened.

Before she could say anything, I asked, 'Where is my father?'

'In his studio, I think. You want him, yes?'

'Yes.'

I opened the french windows and took a deep breath of warm air. Behind me, Peppina said, 'You will tell your father that he will have dinner in half an hour.'

Someone stood at the veranda rail, his head merged with the vine leaves. He was too tall for Francis; too slim for my father.

'Max . . .'

He said, 'I must go to the Château. I shall be needed there. But I just had to come to you. I'm sorry I left you so abruptly, but I had to go to Lucia. I knew I must tell her about Paul. I hope I did it kindly.'

I joined him at the veranda rail and leaned over, looking down into the starry, unfolding faces of the tobacco plants. I was quivering with Max's nearness.

'She has lost so much,' he said. 'At least, so much according to her values.'

'First Paul – '

'It wasn't Paul first and foremost,' Max said. 'It was Sonnengarde.'

The pepper-pot towers were painted out by night. I wondered if Lucia were still among the olive trees, weeping for what she had lost. Or had Max really touched her tough little heart? I stood, tense and silent by his side, afraid of any question which might give me the answer I dreaded; determined to say nothing.

It was no use. I wasn't strong enough to resist the urge. I had to know just how much they meant to each other. I had to thrust the knife in deep, turn it, and feel the full impact. The truth would have to be known, so it might as well be now. 'You . . . and Lucia . . .'

'Lucia will recover. She has too much ambition not to get what she wants in the end.' He paused. I felt his hand touch my arm, tighten, draw me closer. 'So far as I'm concerned, do *I* get what *I* want?' The thick vine shielded his face from the light streaming from my room. 'Do I?'

'What – do you want?'

'My happiness.'

'How – should I – know about that?'

'Well, you're the only one to tell me. Or perhaps now isn't the time for talking. We have all our lives together for that. . . . We have, haven't we?'

I couldn't speak. My body was very still, but inside my blood was racing.

'Or am I jumping to conclusions? Perhaps vanity is another of my faults and I'm hugging an illusion.'

'No.'

It was then that he kissed me for the third time. And it was not in the least like the other two.

# Catherine Gaskin

'Catherine Gaskin is one of the few big talents now engaged in writing historical romance.' *Daily Express*

'A born story-teller.' *Sunday Mirror*

**The Property of a Gentleman**

**All Else is Folly**

**Blake's Reach**

**Corporation Wife**

**Daughter of the House**

**Edge of Glass**

**A Falcon for a Queen**

**The File on Devlin**

**Fiona**

**I Know My Love**

**Sara Dane**

**The Tilsit Inheritance**

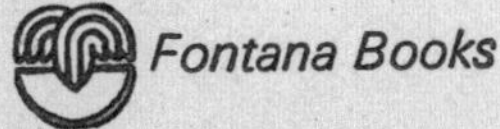

# Howard Spring

In 1938 his most famous book, *My Son, My Son*, was published; it was a world-wide success. Since then all his books, without exception, have been best-sellers and have earned Howard Spring a high reputation as an author of universal appeal.

'Howard Spring is a novelist of solid and considerable talent, whose ability to tell a story, sense of character, craftsmanship and industry should put hollower and more pretentious novelists to shame.' *Spectator*

'He is not afraid of stark drama, and he writes with real feeling.' *Sunday Times*

**I Met a Lady**

**A Sunset Touch**

**Winds of the Day**

**These Lovers Fled Away**

**My Son, My Son**

**There is No Armour**

# Winston Graham

'One of the best half-dozen novelists in this country.' *Books and Bookmen*. 'Winston Graham excels in making his characters come vividly alive.' *Daily Mirror*. 'A born novelist.' *Sunday Times*

His immensely popular suspense novels include:

**Take My Life**
**The Sleeping Partner**
**Fortune is a Woman**
**Marnie**
**Greek Fire**
**The Little Walls**
**Night Without Stars**
**The Tumbled House**
**Night Journey**

Winston Graham has also written The Poldark Saga, his famous story of eighteenth-century Cornwall:

**Ross Poldark**
**Demelza**
**Jeremy Poldark**
**Warleggan**
**The Black Moon**

And historical novels including:

**The Grove of Eagles**

Fontana Books